DEATH
of a
STARLING

DEATH
of a
STARLING

A Cabin by the Lake Mystery

Linda Norlander

LEVEL
BEST BOOKS

AUTHOR PHOTO CREDIT: Jerry Mathiason

First edition

ISBN: 978-1-953789-73-0

Cover art by Level Best Designs

This book was professionally typeset on Reedsy.
Find out more at reedsy.com

To Bree, Ted, Dustin and Billie

Praise for A CABIN BY THE LAKE Mysteries

. . . .An entertaining series. Jamie is tough but prudent and she loves her dog. Norlander can take Jamie in all kinds of directions. . .. — Mary Ann Grossman, St. Paul Pioneer Press

Chapter One

Winston Starling

All afternoon before I drove to Cascade to meet Winston Starling, I had a tingle in the back of my neck—a feeling like a bug edging up my spine. It was a new sensation I associated with moving from New York City to the North Woods of Minnesota. I'd first noticed it last summer, my first summer in my cabin by Lake Larissa.

Driving through the array of pines and aspens, I willed the feeling away. In this light, airy fall day the maples and aspens were turning reds and yellows. With my window down, taking in the crisp scents of the season turning from summer to fall, I left the tingle behind. At least, I left it behind until I arrived in Cascade, the small Northern Minnesota town where, two years ago, a student had killed a teacher and two students in yet another school shooting.

I planned to write a story on the teacher who died for *The New Yorker*. Winston Starling had been the new school counselor at the time of the shooting. So far, even two years later, he was the only person from Cascade High School willing to be interviewed.

He sat across from me at the Cascade Bar and Grill. The restaurant was a throwback from better times. The tables were worn and unsteady on the warped wooden floor. It even had a defunct jukebox sitting in the corner with a vase of dusty plastic flowers next to it.

The restaurant was crowded with diners wearing threadbare jeans and worn expressions. Behind Winston, a woman in her mid-fifties ate French fries and laughed loudly. Her mascara was so thick, I was surprised her eyelids didn't stick together when she blinked. The man she ate with talked in a low growl, like a snarling dog.

Winston was in his mid-twenties, slightly overweight with sandy hair and freckles. He hardly looked like my vision of a high school guidance counselor. He wore a red long-sleeved T-shirt imprinted with the words, "The Truth is Out There."

"Thank you for meeting with me, Mr. Starling." I resisted the urge to scratch the back of my neck, to brush away the imaginary itch. Opening my notebook, I held my pen ready to take notes.

"Call me Winnie," he said.

"And you can call me Jamie."

I smiled, thinking how much he resembled Winnie the Pooh. He even had a gap between his two front teeth.

"Nice weather," he commented as the server handed us the menus. He gazed at me with a knowing expression, "Enjoy it while you can. Winter is coming."

"That's what people tell me." I'd found in my months of living in Minnesota people inevitably talked about the weather. In my home city of New York, we were more likely to talk about traffic and the vagaries of the subway system.

I set the menu aside and picked up my pen. "As you know, I'm writing an article about the school shooting in Cascade two years ago. I want to profile the teacher, Tony Vincent, who was killed. What can you tell me about him?"

Something about this town with its empty storefronts and its rundown restaurant made me want to hurry through the interview, jump in my car and speed back to my cabin. I took a deep breath and concentrated on relaxing my shoulders.

Winnie looked up from studying the menu. His expression didn't seem right. Maybe it was the way he wrinkled his brow when I mentioned the teacher. Maybe it was the tight way he pressed his lips together.

Instead of answering my question, he said, "The cheeseburgers here are the best. You should order one."

Cheeseburgers never appealed to me, but to be polite I nodded. "Thanks for the suggestion."

"You won't be sorry."

Neither will my dog when I bring most of it home to him. When the server came, I ordered the same thing as Winnie and asked her to put all of it on my bill. Winnie grinned. "Not often I get treated around here."

I smiled at him and started the interview again. "Tony Vincent was one of the few full-blooded Native Americans teaching in this part of the state. He was shot along with several other Natives. Do you think he was targeted?"

Winnie hesitated. "It looked that way, didn't it?"

"Is that what everyone thought? This was a hate crime?"

"Maybe."

I felt like I was trying to wring a confession out of a grade school kid. We were interrupted by the server bringing our drinks. Winnie ordered a Diet Coke and I had iced tea. Once she left, Winnie apologized. "I'm sorry. I'm not trying to be evasive. It's just that the town is very touchy about the shooting. We've been told to keep things low-key."

Sitting in this shabby restaurant on a chilly September evening, I wondered what the hell I was trying to accomplish. I wasn't a journalist even though I'd written for the *New York Times Magazine*. I was an unpublished poet trying to eke out a living in Northern Minnesota by freelance editing bad romance novels. The only reason I was here was because someone I cared about had been wounded in the shooting, and I wanted to tell the story. And, to be completely honest, I hoped to make enough money on the article to afford to live in my cabin by the lake for the next several months.

Working to extract a little more information out of him, I tried a different tact. "Tell me more about why people don't want to talk about the shooting."

Winnie sat up a little straighter. "I'm not quite sure except some people want to downplay the reputation of the town as a dying redneck backwater."

"Really?" My cursory Google search of the town hadn't uncovered much. Contrary to its name, there were no cascading falls nearby, pristine lakes or

3

awe-inspiring overlooks. Instead, like many of the small towns in this part of the state, it was in economic decline especially since the closing of the iron mines.

I must have appeared puzzled because he started to laugh. "You aren't from around here, are you?"

"Did my accent give me away?"

"Uh huh. New York?"

"Born and bred until I moved here last spring."

He nodded. "Cascade...well Cascade has some rough edges."

"Hard economic times?" I tried to steer him back to the shooting. "Were the Native Americans blamed for any of this? Claiming rights to their lands and waters?" I wanted to find out if the community had strong feelings about the Ojibwe living in the area.

Winnie hesitated long enough that I wondered if I had hit on something. "I don't think it was the Indians as much as the perception that the environmentalists had forced the mines to close and were keeping them from reopening. You know—outside agitators."

"But the shooting could have been considered a hate crime. All those killed and injured were Indians." A group of Native American students had gathered in the high school cafeteria with their teacher to work on a diversity project when they were shot by a white student, Neil Kavanaugh.

The cheeseburgers arrived with mounds of French fries. Winnie was like a hungry kid who had missed his lunch and was making up for it. He ate with gusto. Ketchup dribbled off the burger and landed in splotches on his plate. He concentrated on the burger, his muddy blue eyes alive as he savored every bite.

I waited until he took a break from eating. "What do you know about the shooter? I understand he was a senior at the high school."

He put down his burger and squeezed ketchup on his fries. "I heard Neil got along well with all the kids including the ones he shot."

"Really? That hardly fits the profile of a school shooter. Do you know more about him?" The information I had on Neil was sketchy—high school senior, committed suicide after the shooting. No obituary in the local paper

4

and no further mention of him in a short follow-up article on the funerals of the people killed.

Winnie dipped a fry in the pool of ketchup. "I was new to the school. I'd only been here a couple of weeks. Hardly knew the kids yet."

I sensed something evasive in his tone and wondered how the shooting affected him as a new counselor. I was about to ask him when I heard the saloon doors of the backroom bar open behind me. He glanced over my shoulder, and it seemed like the color drained from his ruddy cheeks. I turned to see what he was looking at and was surprised to see a tall, slender woman with sleek dark hair pulled into a tight chignon. She had the poise of a model and was definitely out of place with the local crowd. More surprising, she carried a Hermes Birkin handbag.

Who in rural Minnesota carried $15,000 handbags? I decided it must be a knock-off.

She stood beside an older man with a grizzled face, wearing a red baseball cap. For a moment, he appeared to stare at me with the coldest eyes I'd ever seen. Without thinking, I rubbed the back of my neck, trying to tamp down the invisible spider. This town was getting to me.

A look of uncertainty crossed Winnie's face. I sensed he was trying to make a decision as he stared at the woman with the purse and the man with the red cap. He set the cheeseburger down in its basket and cleared his throat. With a deliberate glance at his watch, he said, "Um, I'm sorry. I forgot an appointment. I have to go."

"Wait. Maybe we can finish before you go?" I touched my empty notebook. "I have more questions. We can be quick."

He looked at me with a worried expression. Fumbling for his jacket, he stuttered. "Uh, well, we...we can talk some other time."

I dug through my bag for a business card and handed it to him. "Will you give me a call, so we can meet again?"

He grabbed it and stuffed it into his jacket pocket. "Sure, no problem."

When he stood up to put his jacket on, something slipped to the floor near my feet. I reached down and picked up a black ski mask. Holding it out to him, I smiled. "You really do believe winter is coming."

He didn't respond to my attempt at humor. He took the mask without looking at me and mumbled. "Must have been in my pocket from last year."

Unsettled by his abruptness, I watched him hurry out the door. The guy sitting across from the mascara woman turned as Winnie left. He mumbled something and went back to eating.

When the server came by with the check, she asked, "Is Winnie done?"

"Short date, I guess."

At first, she wasn't sure whether to take me seriously. I laughed. "He said he forgot an appointment."

"Oh."

I thought about the striking woman with her expensive handbag. "Do you know who the woman was who left a few minutes ago? She carried a pink handbag. Looked pretty ritzy?"

The server frowned. "Charity Whitacre. Her family owns a piece of the bank, and she has an online business. Sells bags like that, I guess. Too pricey for me. Plus, she's a stingy tipper."

As I gathered my things to leave, the phone from the man behind me played "Dixie." He stood up grunting into the phone, "Yeah? What the...?"

I didn't hear the rest as he lumbered out the door. He was soon followed by the mascara woman. She teetered on high heels that hardly fit with her squat frame. Certainly an odd couple.

After I settled up the bill, I walked to my car parked in the dirt lot next to the restaurant. The air was chilly and damp, which fit the dreariness of the town. I reached into my jacket pocket to put on my gloves and discovered one was missing. The gloves had been one of the last presents my father had given me before he had his stroke. They were red and made of a soft leather. "Damn!"

I went back to the restaurant and asked the server if she had seen it. She checked with a couple of other staff while I waited at the cash register. The glove was gone.

In the dimly lit parking lot, I noticed a group of men wearing red baseball caps smoking near the side door of the restaurant. One of them pointed in my direction and several of them laughed the kind of macho bar laugh that caused a shudder of disgust to run down my back. Lost interview, lost glove, redneck town—perhaps it was time to drop this project and hope something else would come along to keep me financially upright for the winter.

On the drive home, with the heater going full blast to warm the chill that had settled in me, I reflected on the evening. Winnie hadn't given me much except to say the shooter wasn't a loner who'd been bullied. I wondered about the town, though. What did Winnie mean about the town's reputation? What about those men gathered in the dim light of the parking lot all wearing the same red baseball cap. Although the tingle was gone, I sensed something dark and ugly about Cascade.

The woman with the pink handbag stuck with me, too. Like she was a cosmopolitan who had lost her way into the hinterlands of northern Minnesota. I knew a little about Hermes bags because of an article I'd fact-checked back in my days in New York. The article outlined how to tell a real bag from a knockoff. It talked about the traffic in knockoffs and how the fraudsters had gotten pretty sophisticated in creating fake merchandise using cheap Asian labor. When I talked with the author of the article to verify a few items she'd explained why the originals were so expensive. I remembered her words.

"Each bag is custom made with specific leather from specific parts of France. You won't find a knockoff handbag with such creamy texture or such exquisite stitching."

I wondered if Charity's bag had the craftmanship the author had described.

My thoughts moved from $15,000 handbags to my leather gloves. Not only were they sentimental, but also great driving gloves, despite the fact that Bronte, my part-lab, part-mutt had chewed one of the fingers.

By the time I reached my cabin, the tingle, and the subsequent headache were gone. I stepped out of the car and took in the crisp night air. Down the incline from the cabin, Lake Larissa lapped gently against the shore.

Bronte greeted me like she hadn't seen me in a week. How nice to be shown such unconditional love. If only the other person in my life, Jim Monroe, could do the same.

I set my non-Hermes bag with my notebook down on the kitchen table to give Bronte her full attention. The bag spilled over, and the receipt for the meal slipped out, wafting onto the floor as if it had a life of its own. When I picked it up, I saw something written in black ballpoint on the back in large cursive.

"Drop your snooping."

Staring at it, I had two thoughts racing through my brain. The first said, listen to the warning. The second said, wow there really must be a story here.

Chapter Two

Cascade Sheriff

When I woke up the next morning, I felt exhausted from a never-ending dream in which I was trying to pull Winnie out of the lake. He kept slipping under and when I called for help, I had no voice.

I drank my coffee and told Bronte about the dream. "I wonder why I thought I needed to rescue him. He left so quickly last night he didn't even finish his cheeseburger."

Bronte wagged her tail and leaned against my leg. She didn't care that my trip to Cascade turned out to be a waste of time. She was more concerned about getting her breakfast on time.

The empty notebook sat on the table in front of me. I pointed to it. "In fact, he didn't even thank me for treating him. Everyone in this state is usually so polite. That appointment must have been pretty important."

After I fed Bronte, I jotted down a few questions, mainly about Tony the teacher who'd been shot. Maybe Winnie could give me some insight on what the students and other teachers thought about him.

I called Winnie's cell phone knowing it was a school day and I'd probably have to leave a message. After a number of rings, I finally reached his voicemail. "Winnie, it's Jamie. Sorry we couldn't talk more last night. Can we set up another time to meet?" As I pressed the end button on the phone, a cloud covered the morning sun, throwing a shadow into the kitchen.

Bronte whined and asked to be let out. It was time to work on my other project, the one that was guaranteed to pay.

Florice Annabelle LeMay wrote historical romances, and I helped her with the storyline and the copy editing. Her last novel had finally sold after I suggested she cut it down from 100,000 words to 80,000. Though I knew it pained her, she cut out several chapters of repetitive not-quite-steamy lovemaking scenes.

The title page of this newest romance stared back at me—*Plucking a Rose*.

Bronte, back from her morning outdoor excursion, stood beside me. "What do you think, girl? I know you can pluck a chicken and an eyebrow, but can you pluck a rose?" Bronte's only comment was to saunter over to her water dish and take a drink.

Feeling a touch cranky, I picked up the first page of the manuscript. By the second paragraph, Rose, the dairymaid, had her cheek against "the earthy warmth of Ariel, the cow, as she squeezed and pulled causing the pearly white milk to spurt into a bucket."

"Oh, dear." Bronte pricked up her ears at my exclamation.

Out the window, the golden leaves of the aspens and birches in my woods swirled against the cabin. Whitecaps dotted Lake Larissa as I watched a gull swooping and soaring in the air currents. For a moment, I wished I could fly somewhere else, somewhere that didn't have a 300-page manuscript filled with cows and milkmaids.

The coffee maker on the counter hissed with the second pot of the morning, and the cabin filled with the aroma of fresh ground French Roast. Though I had to count every penny, I splurged on good coffee. Pouring a mug of the steaming brew, I grabbed my cell phone and walked into the living room. Bronte stood up and yawned before she settled at my feet. Even though she was still considered a puppy, she'd slowed down since being shot last summer by a local sheriff's deputy who mistook her friendly growl for an attack.

I needed to talk to Joe Pelletier about yesterday's conversation with Winnie. Joe was a newfound friend who had been one of the victims of the Cascade High School shooting. He survived, but his twin brother had not. The trauma had left him deeply scarred, both physically and emotionally.

He answered after four rings. "Clarence Engstrom law office."

"Hey, Joe. It's Jamie. How are you?"

Joe, a full-blood Ojibwe, was a man of few words. "Okay."

Phone conversations with him were filled with gaps, and I usually tried to meet with him in person. He was the one who had inspired me to try for an article in *The New Yorker.*

"Can I talk to you about Winston Starling?"

Another gap before he said, "Uh, sure."

"It was a strange meeting." Silence on the other end, so I continued. "He didn't have much to say, and he left rather abruptly."

Joe cleared his throat. "I thought if anyone would talk with you, it would be him. He was new to the school when it happened, so he wasn't part of the teacher clique."

"Teacher clique?"

"They, uh, stuck together."

Interesting. I wanted to dive into that a little more, but first I had a big question for him. "Winnie said Neil Kavanaugh struck him as a good kid. He wasn't someone you'd expect to bring a gun to school."

Joe had shared with me how difficult it was to be Native American at Cascade High School. He and his brother put up with petty harassment and bullying because they liked the football coach and thought they'd have a better chance for an athletic scholarship if they graduated from Cascade rather than the reservation school.

I recounted my conversation with Winnie to Joe. Bronte sat up and rested her head on my lap. "He seemed nervous about talking with me. Do you know why?"

Joe sounded vague. "Cascade is—well it's like a bad place."

"What do you mean?"

"Uh, I'm not sure. My cousins, you know, from up by the reservation stay away from there."

I asked him a few more questions and received a few more sketchy answers before I closed out the call. "Why don't we get together for lunch this week.

You can fill me in on your new job as Clarence's assistant, and I can run some ideas for this article by you."

It was Tuesday. We made a date for Friday at the Loonfeather Cafe in Killdeer, the town closest to my cabin.

After I set the phone down, I patted Bronte on her head. "I don't get it. Even Joe doesn't want to talk about Cascade. What's going on?"

Bronte's response was to trot to the door and ask to be let out. I decided to join her. Slipping on my bright orange jacket, I grabbed the coffee and headed outside. It was time to do some rock-sitting. My place of comfort and contemplation was a large smooth rock on the edge of the lake. With the rhythm of the lake as the waves pulsed against the shoreline, I did some of my best thinking.

Bronte found a stick and laid it at my feet. I picked it up and tossed it into the woods. The September wind off the lake was brisk but felt good against my cheeks. This would be my first fall and winter in the cabin. Already people had warned me of the capricious weather.

My Killdeer friend Rob had said, "You can get rain, sleet, snow, and sunshine on the same day. The temperature can drop below freezing and two days later be eighty degrees. That's why someone once called Minnesota 'The Theater of Seasons.'"

Across the lake, on Bear Island, the trees shimmered in shades of yellow and orange, while the sumac turned a striking red. Manhattan, my childhood home, never looked this colorful, even in the fall.

I wanted to think more about the Cascade project. If people didn't want to talk to me, was it worth the effort? The shooting had gotten very little press. When I checked the date of the shooting against the state and national news, I found two big items. First, a hurricane was bearing down on the East Coast. Second, a major corruption scandal had just broken involving state legislators receiving under-the-table money from an international mining company to allow copper and nickel mining on protected lands. Added to that, all the victims of the shooting were Indians, and compared to some of the other school shootings, this had relatively few victims.

"Sad that we have become so immune to the gun violence."

Bronte, ignoring my voice, dropped the stick at my feet and wagged her tail in anticipation. I tossed it behind me and listened as she leapt through the fallen leaves to retrieve it.

If this was a hate crime, the heroic part of me wanted to bring this to light. "Well, Jamie," I said out loud to the rolling waves, "Good for you, but someone still has to pay the electric bill. Your bank account is in dismal condition."

Bronte returned with the stick. This time, I threw it up the hill and noted she ran with a little more vigor. It was good to know she was healing from last summer's gunshot wound.

The phone in my pocket rang. The vibration seemed to shoot up my spine giving me the annoying tingle. Perhaps it was Winnie calling back. Instead, the caller was listed as Cascade County.

"Hello, this is Jamie Forest."

"Ms. Forest?"

"Yes."

"This is Jay Bolton from the Cascade County Sheriff's Department. I'd like to ask you a few questions."

"Yes?" A gust of chill wind rose off the lake as Bronte returned with her stick.

"Were you with Winston Starling last night?" His voice had a tone that told me this wasn't really a question. He already knew the answer.

Uh oh. I'd had bad experiences with law enforcement in the past. The advice of a drunken woman I'd once met in jail flashed through my head. "Don't tell 'em nothin', honey."

"Could I ask why you want to know?" I scratched the nape of my neck.

"Uh, we found your card in his jacket."

I knew before he said anything more, that something very bad had happened to Winnie, but I asked anyway, "Is he all right?"

Bronte must have sensed my distress because she dropped the stick and sat quietly beside me.

"Ms. Forest, Winston crashed his car last night." He paused for emphasis. "He didn't make it."

"Oh my god." I sat stunned.

"We need to talk with you about it." He had an edge to his voice.

Here in the peace of my cabin, I felt like history was repeating itself. One thing I would not do is let him come here. Last summer a stupid and rogue sheriff's deputy had threatened me in my own home. "I don't know how I can help you. I only met him last night, and our talk was very brief."

Jay cleared his throat. "Uh, we really need you to explain some things."

I gripped the phone but said nothing.

"Could we stop by?" By the tone of his voice, this was not a question, merely a statement.

He tried to soften his tone, but the tension was obvious. My reply was quick and sharp. "No." Bronte looked up at me with a worried expression. I took a deep breath and added, "I can come to you, if that would work."

If Jay Bolton really thought I had something to do with Winnie's accident, he wouldn't have asked permission to visit. He would have shown up with lights flashing.

We set up a time to meet in the afternoon in Cascade. I ended the call. Overhead, the clear autumn sky had grayed out, and a cold rain began to fall. In that moment, it felt like winter was coming.

Chapter Three

Clarence Engstrom

I paced back and forth in the cabin as the rain pelted the roof. I didn't want to take the 40- mile drive to Cascade; I didn't want to talk with Jay Bolton; and I didn't want to think about Winnie in a wrecked car. Bronte followed me around with a worried expression until I plopped down on the couch. She tried to crawl up onto my lap.

"No, girl. You know that's not allowed." She ignored me and settled her 90-pound self comfortably beside me.

I took out my phone and hit speed dial. A voicemail answered. "Hello. You've reached James Monroe, no relation to the president. Can't take your call. Leave a message."

Did I want to leave a message? I ended the call. Jim Monroe, State Trooper and occupier of my bed since last August hadn't communicated with me in several days. He, too, added to my anxiety. Last week, he'd patrolled the night shift. Usually he'd slip into my bed after work and rise later in the morning. Except, he didn't come home. Instead, I woke to an empty bed and a text message.

Sorry. Family issues. See you soon.

After two days of trying to reach him by phone and text, I'd given up. It had now been five days and no messages. Bronte had taken the opportunity to join me on his side of the bed. She snored contentedly beside me at night. I preferred the scent of Jim's aftershave to the scent of dog fur.

I called his number again. This time I left a message. "It's Jamie. Something is going on with the Cascade Sheriff's Department. Please call me back." What I really wanted to say was, "What the hell? Where are you?!"

My time in Minnesota had clearly tempered me. People here were so restrained. Jim had explained to me, "Too many of Scandinavian heritage. People don't fight around here, they purse their lips."

Right now, I was pursing my lips so hard they hurt. I nearly jumped when the phone rang. It wasn't Jim, though, it was Clarence Engstrom, the octogenarian Killdeer lawyer.

"Jamie, it's Clarence. I have a little job for you."

Clarence thought I had great investigative powers because I could navigate social media. He had hired me on an hourly basis last summer when he was defending Joe Pelletier against a murder charge. What I discovered with simple Facebook searches, helped solve the case. Because of that, Clarence considered me his private investigator. Of course, since he was supposedly retired, I didn't have much to investigate.

With Jim's absence, the mysterious call from the Cascade sheriff, and the death of Winston Starling, I was not in the mood for the old lawyer. "Yes? What is it?"

"You sound a little testy my dear."

I was a little testy. "Uh, sorry. What can I do for you?"

He explained that he just picked up a client who thought he might have been scammed out of a lot of money. "Old Pete Peterson, the idiot, got himself involved with some woman. Said she was a good cook. Next thing you know she needs money to send to her mother for cataract surgery. Then she needs more. Now she's disappeared. You know the story."

I shoved Bronte off my lap and stood up, stretching. "You know, Clarence, my area of expertise is actually nineteenth-century women poets. I'm guessing he wasn't scammed by Emily Dickinson."

Clarence laughed. It was a hearty, deep laugh, and suddenly I felt better.

"No, I don't think Emily was the culprit. But I'm wondering if you can use that magic computer of yours to see if you can find Pete's lady."

"I charge by the hour, you know. Besides, Pete's lady is probably long gone."

He laughed again. "Old Pete is willing to pay. He's damn mad that he let himself get snookered."

The rain let up as I talked with Clarence. I hoped it would be a dry drive to Cascade. As I thought about it, I had an idea. "Clarence, are you up for a ride?"

"It's raining."

"I need to talk with the sheriff in Cascade this afternoon. It would be nice to have some companionship."

"You in trouble with the law again?" His voice turned serious.

"I don't know. It's all weird." I sighed. "He wants to talk with me about a man I met yesterday who died in a car crash last night."

Thank goodness Clarence refrained from asking me more questions. Instead, he said, "Well, you know I haven't been out of Killdeer much since the wife died."

I sensed his reluctance. Shame on me for pushing an old man to go with me. Still, I hated the idea of being interviewed alone. "They have great cheeseburgers at the Cascade Bar. I'll treat."

The reluctance dropped immediately from his voice. "With greasy fries?"

"Of course. Mounds of them."

"Well, in that case, I'll dig out my umbrella."

I arranged to pick him up in Killdeer on my way north to Cascade. Later, when I put on my jacket to leave, I patted the pocket and pulled out the single red leather glove. Sighing, I left it on the kitchen table.

The sun came out in its autumn brilliance as I bumped down my rutted drive. I needed to get the road graded and graveled, but I didn't have the funds. Maybe between Florice's milkmaid and Pete Peterson's scamming lady, I could cobble together enough money to get it fixed before the snow fell.

"Dream on," I muttered, splashing through the biggest pothole.

Larissa Lodge stood at the end of my road. A few cars were parked in the lot in front of the main building. The Lodge's ownership was currently in dispute, and business had dropped significantly. I prayed they would stay solvent because they provided my internet hot spot. Without it, I wasn't sure what I'd do.

"It's a worry for another day." I signaled and pulled out onto the highway.

When I parked in front of Clarence's house in Killdeer, he was standing on the porch waiting for me. He had the dapper old man look with a gray woolen suit coat, vest, and tie. He was dressed far more formally than my ex had dressed for our wedding.

The sun glinted off the wet leaves in his yard. The hanging baskets of impatiens and begonias along the porch still radiated their brilliant reds and pinks. I took it as a good omen and hoped the interview with the sheriff would be brief.

Joe accompanied Clarence to the car, holding onto his elbow as Clarence shuffled with his cane. Since his arrest and exoneration in August, Joe had been living with Clarence, working as his assistant. He looked good. His hair was stylishly cut, and he had put on some weight. His eyes no longer appeared so dark and haunted.

He helped Clarence into the car and walked around to my side. "I heard from my cousin about Mr. Starling crashing his car." He shook his head and for a moment the haunted look came back.

I touched his arm. "He seemed like a nice guy."

Joe said nothing as he turned back to the house.

On the way out of town, Clarence pointed out a large house nestled back from the road. "That's Pete's place. He was in lumber. Made a helluva lot of money. But he was also a conservationist. Cut a tree, plant a tree. Can't understand how he got taken by that woman."

I only half-listened as I thought about Winnie. When I was in New York working as a contract fact-checker, I was once assigned an article on automobile accidents and how all the safety measures had cut down significantly on fatalities. The author had gone into far too much detail about the damage to the body when it's thrown through the windshield. I hoped that whatever happened to Winnie it had been quick and painless.

Clarence prattled on, pointing out various landmarks. "Used to be a recreation building over there by the playing fields built in the thirties as a

WPA project. Beautiful stonework but when the county stopped keeping it up, vandals destroyed it. A lot of those great old buildings are gone."

"Hmmm." Clouds covered the sun, and a little spray of rain fell gently on the windshield.

We were halfway to Cascade when Clarence turned to me. "Tell me why you wanted me to come?" His thinning white hair was neatly trimmed, and his eyes, behind the wire-rimmed glasses, sparked with intelligence. People often took him for a doddering old man. I knew differently.

I told him about meeting Winnie last night and about the phone call from Jay Bolton of the sheriff's office this morning. "You know that my experience with law enforcement has been less than optimal."

He nodded. He knew my story of being falsely arrested in New York on drug trafficking charges. He also knew my experience with the Jackpine County sheriff's deputy who'd shot Bronte. "You do have your adventures."

I thought of them less as adventures and more as traumatic experiences. "Well, the sheriff who called from Cascade sounded cagey. Like he had something more to talk about than my business card they found in Winnie's pocket. I want someone to be with me when I meet him. Something about this isn't right."

As if to emphasize my feelings, the skies opened up and poured rain down on the car. I had to pull over onto the shoulder for a few minutes because I couldn't see. While we sat there, several semis roared by. I wondered how they could stay on the road.

By the time we pulled into the parking lot of the Cascade County courthouse, I was a half-hour late for the meeting with Sheriff Bolton. The rain had stopped, but the town was veiled in a cold gray mist. I hoped, as I helped Clarence out of the car, he wouldn't catch a chill.

The courthouse, a three-story, yellow-brick structure, had seen better days. The shingles on the roof were a mismatch of patching, and one of the eaves had broken loose and was hanging down.

Clarence pointed to it. "The public infrastructure is a victim of a dwindling tax base. All the money is going to the very few rich oligarchs. I think we need a revolution here in the hinterlands."

Revolution? Nothing about Clarence surprised me. I would have commented but I was preoccupied with how to approach the meeting with the sheriff.

The clerk in the sheriff's office pointed us to a couple of orange plastic chairs. "I'll tell Jay you are here." It was hot and stuffy in the small waiting area. When I took off my jacket, I wondered if I would see steam rolling off my body. Next to me, Clarence appeared perfectly comfortable in his three-piece suit. His eyes were closed, and it looked like he was about to take a little nap.

The sheriff came out of the inner office and beckoned me in. He wore a pressed white, short-sleeved shirt with a sheriff's patch and dark pants. He was tall and thin with short brown hair and a receding chin. His manner was surprisingly abrupt. No greeting, no handshake, simply a nod, and a gesture to follow him.

I roused Clarence.

The sheriff squinted at him with a quizzical expression. "He can wait here."

"No." My voice was firm. "I want him to come."

Clarence opened his eyes and studied him. "You're John Bolton's boy, aren't you? We didn't always agree, but he kept a firm hand on this county."

I looked at Clarence in surprise. "You know people from Cascade?"

Clarence grunted as he stood up. "When you are one of the only lawyers around, you end up with a pretty big territory." He held out his hand. "Clarence Engstrom, nice to meet you."

The sheriff hesitated before taking his hand. "Uh, Jay Bolton." He seemed at a loss to say anything else.

Clarence shook the sheriff's limp hand. "How is your dad anyway?"

"Dead. Died two years ago."

I stepped in, holding my hand out. "Jamie Forest. Nice to meet you."

Jay nodded but didn't shake my hand. He wasn't being very Minnesota polite. Already I knew this interview was not going to go well. Outside, the rain started again.

Chapter Four

The Glove

Without any prelude, Jay pointed to two wooden chairs in front of his desk. A plaque on the desk read, *Jay Bolton, Sheriff*. Framed on the wall behind the desk was a diploma from an associate degree program in criminal justice studies.

He sat with the desk between us and picked up a file folder. He wrinkled his brow. "Now tell me, Ms. Forest, what was your relationship with Winston Starling."

I didn't like his tone, and I tensed up. Clarence must have sensed it because he placed a warning hand on my arm. I fought to keep my voice calm. "I don't, uh, didn't have a relationship with Winnie. I met him once, last night. He ate a cheeseburger and dashed out the door."

Jay didn't make eye contact. "Were you dating him?"

"What?" I wanted to say, look at me, I'm in my thirties, Winnie was in his twenties. Come on. What I did say was, "No. I was interviewing him for an article I plan to write."

Jay set the file down and leaned toward me. "What article? What are you writing?"

My hands curled into tight fists on my lap. I really did not like this man. I'm not sure if it was his attitude or the way he pinched his lips together when he talked, but I wanted to yell at him and tell him it was none of his goddam business. The practical voice in my head said, *calm down*. My cheeks reddened. "I am writing about the school shooting."

Jay's eyes narrowed. "That was two years ago. Why bring it up now and hurt people all over again?" He worked his mouth as if he wanted to say more.

I winced at his vehemence. Was he hiding something?

Clarence saved the day using a very polite but firm tone. "Young man, could we get to the point here? I'm old, I'm cranky, I have to use the bathroom, and I'm hungry. Just what is it you need to know from my friend, here?"

Jay sat up a little straighter as if he had been reprimanded by the teacher. "Ah, there are some irregularities in this death."

He opened a drawer, took out a plastic evidence bag, and held it up. "Do you recognize this?"

For a moment, I froze. Inside the bag was a red leather glove with a hole chewed in the thumb. Why was it in a plastic evidence bag in the sheriff's office?

"That looks like mine. Why do you have it?"

Jay leaned forward. "Why don't you tell me?"

I grew more uncomfortable with the sheriff's stare. "I lost it last night. I remember taking it off in the restaurant, but when I got into my car, it wasn't in my coat pocket."

"Oh?"

"Yes. I went back in and had the server check to see if I'd dropped it. She couldn't find it."

Clarence pointed his finger at the sheriff. "And what does this glove have to do with the poor man who died?"

Jay's eyes positively glinted in the yellow overhead light of his office. "We found it on the floor of the car."

I blinked. "Oh my god. How did it get there?"

Jay dropped the evidence bag on the folder and leaned back. "You tell me."

Clarence rescued me from sputtering. "I believe the young lady has told you she lost it. Unless you have more questions, I don't think we have anything more to say here." He touched my arm. "Let us find a bathroom

22

and then proceed to that cheeseburger you promised me."

He stood up, took his cane, and walked to the door. I followed him, still stunned.

I held my breath until we stepped outside. The town of Cascade was still sheathed in a cold, damp fog. As we walked to the car, I gazed down the main street and noted how deserted and empty it was.

"This place seems like a ghost town." I pointed to an empty storefront across the street from the courthouse.

Clarence nodded. "It's been in decline since the mines closed. Unlike Killdeer, it doesn't have a beautiful lake to attract tourists. Just swampland, scrub trees, and lots of places to hide." He slid into the passenger seat. "Now onto the place with good cheeseburgers. I need to rinse the bad taste in my mouth out with a little bourbon."

I started the car thinking about his housekeeper. She kept close tabs on his diet. "Good thing Lorraine isn't here. She'd make you drink milk."

He laughed, and the day brightened.

Once we settled into a booth at the Cascade Bar and Grill, I let out a deep, trembling sigh. "Wow. How do I get into these things? I don't know anything about the glove except that it was missing."

Clarence drummed his fingers on the table while we waited for the server. "Something is definitely not right here."

The server looked to be a little older than high school age. She had dark hair braided down her back and a rounded face. I guessed her to be at least part Native American. She smiled as she took our order.

"You aren't from around here, are you?" She commented after I ordered a tuna sandwich.

My accent stood out as usual. "I grew up in New York City."

"You kinda sound like those guys on *The Sopranos*. We've been watching it on Netflix."

"I left all my mob connections behind."

Her eyes got big. "Really?"

Don't make those kind of jokes, Jamie. "Just kidding. I've never met a mobster that I know of."

23

"Oh." She turned and walked away.

Clarence's eyes sparkled. "Are you sure you don't know any mobsters."

"Not unless the sheriff is one."

He grimaced in response. "Not a topic of conversation in a public place."

Before the order came, Clarence stood up and excused himself. "I should be back by suppertime. The old plumbing isn't what it used to be." He shuffled off to the men's room.

The Cascade Bar and Grill was located on the opposite end of the main street from the courthouse. I watched as a few cars rolled down the road. The two busiest places on the block appeared to be the liquor store and the bank. I noted the man with the red cap and cold eyes from last night stepping out of the bank. Charity, the woman with the Hermes bag walked out behind him. They made a strange pair.

The server brought our order, setting the tuna sandwich in front of me with some hesitation. "Really," I said. "I don't know any mobsters."

She studied me for a moment, glanced around to see if anyone was watching, then leaned close. In a whisper, she said, "I heard you were writing about the shooting. Be careful. People around here are touchy about it."

Before I could ask her more, the front door opened and several men in their forties walked in. Two of them had large bellies spilling over their jeans and walked with an exaggerated swagger. They all wore red baseball caps like the men outside the bar last night. The server, whose name tag said *Madelyn* quickly moved away. The men stood in the doorway watching me before they walked into the back room with the pool tables. The shortest man in the group who had dark sideburns turned for a second, and I was sure he cocked his thumb and forefinger at me. I felt the tingle on my neck except it was more like a jolt.

When Clarence came back, he groaned as he sat on the chair. "Boy are my bones stiff these days."

I leaned forward and said in a low voice, "I think one of the men who just walked into the pool room threatened me."

Clarence put up his hand. "Best if we talked in the car about it." Clarence's sense of caution made me even more uneasy.

The tuna salad sandwich turned out to be thick and tasty on a homemade Kaiser roll. I ate the dill pickle slices and watched as Clarence savored his cheeseburger. It reminded me of Winnie last night. As laughter rose in the pool room, I felt saddened that he would no longer have his cheeseburgers. Did he suspect that one minute he was enjoying a meal and the next he would be rolling his car? Yet, he'd seemed almost scared when he left the bar last night. I wondered what the "irregularities" Bolton had spoken of were. Something didn't add up.

On our way out of town, Clarence pointed to a shabby motel. A peeling wooden sign announcing "Cascade Inn Under New Management" tipped to one side. All the windows were boarded over, and browning weeds grew through cracks in the pavement in front of the one-story building. A chain-link fence surrounded the building. It looked abandoned except for a dented SUV and a new pickup truck parked outside the fence.

"That was the second jail for John Bolton's law operation. He had too many inmates to fit in the county jail, so he put them in the motel. Of course, he owned the motel."

"Sounds kind of corrupt."

Clarence chuckled. "Oh, that man was corrupt in many different ways. For amusement, he used to pick on the Indians who came into town. Arrested them for drunk and disorderly, vagrancy, and even jaywalking. Cascade had a reputation for being a place to avoid if your skin was darker than white."

"Really, he got away with it?"

"He did for a long time. Don't think that all the white supremacists are in the South. I worked with the prosecuting attorney on the case that finally broke him. Endured a few death threats. Some in the community really liked old John. In their minds, he was a law and order guy who kept America great."

"Prosecuting attorney. Really? I thought you specialized in wills and divorces."

Clarence gazed out the window. "Life would have been easier if that's all I did. Had to carry a gun for a while after that."

I waited for the rest of the story but when I looked over, Clarence's eyes

25

were closed, and his chin tipped to his chest. The trip had worn him out.

As I drove toward the county line, I noticed a pickup truck following me, about three car lengths behind. Just before the sign that welcomed us into Jackpine County, it sped up and careened past. The driver, who wore a red baseball cap, looked over at me with a menacing grin and pointed at me with his thumb up and his forefinger. I blinked in surprise. It was the same guy with the sideburns who'd made the threatening gesture in the bar.

I thought about Sheriff Jay Bolton and wondered, as my father used to say, if the apple hadn't fallen too far from the tree. I would have asked Clarence, but he snored softly in the seat next to me. As we crossed into Jackpine County, the pickup passed me going the other direction. I stared straight ahead. If the driver made another gesture, I did not see it.

A voice in my head said, *Jamie, there's danger here. Drop the article and let it go.* I thought about Winnie and the joy n his face as he ate the cheeseburger. "Sorry, self. I need to tell the story—whatever it is."

Beside me, my phone rang. I glanced down at it to see that the call was from Jim Monroe. I let it ring.

Chapter Five

Jim's Story

My phone pinged twice with texts before I dropped Clarence off. I accompanied him to the door, noting he shuffled more as he moved his feet.

"The legs aren't in marathon shape, I guess," he said, climbing the steps to his porch. "But the brain is still working." He took my hand. "Messing in Cascade County can be dangerous business. I'm not usually one to retreat from a fight, but you might want to reconsider writing that article about the shooting."

Gently, I let go of his hand. "Hey, I'm the biggest coward I know. But Winnie seemed like a nice guy who wouldn't run his car off the road. I feel it in my heart that his death is connected somehow to the school shooting." I didn't tell him about Madelyn's warning or the written warning last night on my dinner receipt. "I'll have a serious talk with Joe and then decide whether to let it go."

Clarence nodded. "I was afraid you'd say that. I'll help you in any way I can. I do not like Bolton and whatever is happening in his county."

On the way to the cabin, my phone pinged two more times. I ignored it. Once home, Bronte greeted me with her usual zeal. God, it was nice to be so loved. I let her out and watched as she trotted to her favorite spot in the woods on the edge of the lawn. It struck me how rich the colors were here and how washed out they'd seemed in Cascade.

While Bronte explored her territory outside, I took out my phone and checked the messages. Four texts from Jim with the same message, **In town. We need to talk**.

No kidding. I texted him back. **I'm home. Talk away**.

Thirty minutes later as I stared at my laptop, wondering what to do about Cascade article, I heard Jim's pickup rattle down the road. I steeled myself, the same bad taste rising in my mouth as I'd had several years ago with Andrew, my ex-husband. I squashed the urge to stomp to the door and greet him with folded arms and raging eyes.

Outside, Bronte yipped with excitement while Jim talked softly to her. Bronte was generally a good judge of character, but she didn't understand that people weren't supposed to disappear for days and then show up as if everything was okay.

I concentrated on creating an outline for the Cascade story so when he walked in the door, I wouldn't look either too eager or too angry.

"Hey," he called from the door. "Okay if I let this happy beast in?"

Bronte rushed in, her toenails scrabbling against the wooden floor. She exuded joy. To her, all was right with the world. Easy for her, I thought.

I stayed mute as Jim walked in, pulled out a chair, and sat down. The first thing I noticed was how tired he looked. He had dark smudges under his eyes and a weary expression. For a moment, he simply sat staring at his hands on the table. In a quiet voice, he said, "I guess I owe you an explanation."

The New York City girl in me readied itself for an angry outburst, but the look on his face stopped me. His eyes, those beautiful brown eyes that offset a crooked nose and a light brown complexion, were filled with distress.

"Something is wrong, isn't it?" I resisted the urge to reach over and touch him. Despite how much he appeared to be suffering, I couldn't erase the last five days of worry and waiting.

He rubbed his face and rested his arms on the table. "I don't know how to say this."

Was he breaking up with me? Just like that? I thought we were getting along fine.

I once read an article about giving bad news. The author advised to simply

28

say it and let the other person respond. "Jim, just tell me."

He took a deep breath. "I have a son, a little boy named Jacob. We call him Jake. He's four years old."

My cheeks felt suddenly hot even though I suppressed a shiver. He'd never told me about a son or a wife or a girlfriend. On the other hand, I'd never asked, mainly because I was afraid of what he would say.

"He's been diagnosed with leukemia. They have him at Children's Hospital in Minneapolis." Jim finally made eye contact with me. "I need to be there."

Of course, he needed to be with his son. But damn it, why didn't he tell me? I tensed my toes so hard inside my shoes that I got a sudden cramp. "Ouch!" I stood up and stamped my foot.

While I limped around the table trying to uncurl my cramped toes, he watched me with a perplexed expression.

Finally, he laughed. The good Jim kind of laugh from deep in his chest. "Well, that's not exactly the reaction I expected."

"Me either." I walked over and put a hand on his shoulder. He reached up and took it.

For the next fifteen minutes, he filled me in on the story of Jacob. The child was the result of a brief, but intense relationship, five years ago. Jim didn't know about him until just before Jacob was born. By then, the mother had another boyfriend and was moving from Killdeer to Minneapolis.

"Honest, I didn't know she was pregnant when we split. I've paid child support over the years and tried to spend time with him." He reached down and patted Bronte on the head. "But Marie, the mother, is flighty. Different men in her life. Last year she told me she was getting married and hoped that her husband would adopt Jacob. She wanted me to sign papers."

I sat down next to him and pressed my shoulder into his. The warmth of his arm against mine calmed the shivering inside me. "Did you sign the papers?"

"No. Something held me back. Even though I hadn't seen Jacob in over a year, I couldn't give him up. We were scheduled to meet with a counselor last summer to try to figure it all out, and Marie cancelled several times." He leaned closer to me but continued to look straight ahead. "I guess she broke up with the fiancé. But she never told me."

Jim had a son and he hadn't told me. I felt betrayed. "Oh."

He leaned on the table rubbing his temples. "I'm taking a temporary transfer to the Twin Cities, so I can be with him through the treatment."

I wanted to be sympathetic. I wanted to show that I cared. But the little demon in my head whispered, *do you think he's telling the truth?*

He must have sensed my thoughts because he pulled back, reached into his pocket, and took out his phone. "Here he is."

The photo was of a smiling little boy with dark hair and dark brown eyes. He looked too much like Jim to not be his son. As I viewed the photo, it hit me that this little boy might be dying. My eyes filled with tears. "He looks like you."

Jim put the phone away. "They'll do chemotherapy. The doctor says he's got a good chance."

"I'm sorry you're going through this." What else could I say?

He stood up. Today he seemed shorter than his six foot three-inch frame as if the burden had weighed him down. "They are going to start the treatments this week. I've rented a little apartment near the hospital." He didn't look at me when he spoke. "You can always come and visit, if you want."

I felt a tightness in my throat but said nothing.

While he gathered the things he had left in the cabin, I sat on the couch with Bronte resting her head on my lap. My brain was filled with dissonance. Anger that he hadn't told me about his little boy simmered just beneath the surface, yet I knew he was in pain.

"Bronte," I whispered. "What would Emily Dickinson do?"

Bronte offered no opinion, but I guessed that Emily would sit down at her desk and write a poem.

My phone pinged with a text from Joe. **Need to talk about Cascade.** Joe never initiated communication with me. He was one of the most inscrutable young men I'd ever met. I must have really stirred things up.

Jim emerged with his athletic bag and set it by the door. He came over and sat next to me. Bronte settled at his feet. "It's a three-month transfer. We should know by then if they've gotten the leukemia into remission. I'll be back, you know."

We talked a little more, kissed with little enthusiasm, and finally agreed it was time for him to go.

"Will you keep out of trouble while I'm gone?"

I told him I had another Florice LeMay romance to edit and that I planned to write an article on the Cascade shooting. Thinking about my visit to Cascade and the sheriff, I asked. "Have you ever had to deal with things in that county?"

"Wasn't part of my territory, but I've heard rumors. The old sheriff was a crook, actually went to prison. His son is there now, but I don't know anything specific. You might not want to ruffle feathers. Cascade has a reputation."

I told him about Winnie and how they found my glove in his wrecked car. "The sheriff, Jay Bolton, is creepy—like there's something wrong with him."

Jim frowned. "Do you have to write this now? Can you wait until I get back?"

One thing I did not want was to feel like I needed him to protect me. I stiffened, hoping my toes wouldn't cramp again and make me look ridiculous. "I can't imagine writing a story about the gunman and his victims could cause such an uproar."

Jim laughed. His eyes sparkled as he reached over and took me in his arms. "Oh, you Eastern tree-hugger. You have no idea what ruffles feathers in a small town." He looked at me straight on. "I'm serious. Tread softly with those people."

"I'll add you to the list of people who have told me that."

Bronte and I walked him to his pickup. The sun was setting in a radiant red against the darkening sky. I wondered, as his truck disappeared into the shadows of the driveway, whether I'd see him again.

Chapter Six

Joe and Cascade

The next morning, I checked my online bank statement. I had just enough funds to pay the bills and fill up the propane tank in back of the cabin. The beautiful stone fireplace in the cabin was esthetically nice but wouldn't keep the place warm as the temperatures steadily dropped below freezing. Unfortunately, a tankful of propane to fuel my furnace was not cheap.

When I let Bronte out, the sun shone at an angle through the trees, and the air had a crispness to it that reminded me of fall in New York City. Andrew, my ex-husband, had proposed to me in the fall with the leaves turning shades of orange and yellow. He'd actually gotten down on one knee in Central Park and proposed in a Shakespearian actor's voice that projected deep into the park. A crowd gathered, and when I blushed and said "Yes," the audience clapped. That should have been a clue that Andrew adored the show more than the content. Maybe that's why I liked Jim so much.

I felt such a mix of emotions as I watched Bronte chase a fat gray squirrel up a tree while its partner chittered at her. Oh, to have a life where someone fed me, kept me warm, and only asked that I not pee on the floor.

I left Bronte to her squirrels and pulled *Pluck the Rose* out of its box. It was time for me to correct the grammar and punctuation and figure out if Florice's plot made any sense. I needed the money, and I needed the break from thinking about Jim and from picturing Winnie crumpled in a wrecked car.

"So, Rose of the flaming red hair. Who will be the prince to rescue you from milking cows in the barnyard?"

Instead of getting my answer, the phone rang with the caller ID, "Cascade High School."

For a second the thought ran through my head, oh, it's Winnie getting back to me. My finger shook when I tapped the answer button. "Hello?"

"Jamie Forest? This is Matt Whitacre from Cascade High School. You've been trying to reach me?"

At least this was not a call from the dead. Matt Whitacre was the principal. I'd left him several messages over the past week to set up a time to talk with him. I was taken aback by the heartiness of his voice because I'd dug up a newscast from the time of the shooting and in it, he'd stumbled in a monotone through a couple of worn-out platitudes including the phrase, "thoughts and prayers."

"Thanks, Mr. Whitacre for calling me back."

He cleared his throat. "I understand that you've heard about poor Winnie."

"Um, yes. I met him the night before he…died. He seemed nice." My voice trailed off. I wasn't sure what to say.

"Your message said you wanted to ask some questions about the shooting. I'm not sure there's much to say, but I'd be happy to talk with you."

We set up a time to meet in his office at the end of the school day on Friday. When I hung up the phone, I had the strangest taste in my mouth. It was like I'd bitten the inside of my lip but instead of blood, I tasted a combination of honey and vinegar.

"Jamie, you are getting weirder by the minute." I picked up a blue pencil and started reading *Pluck the Rose*.

My editing process had three stages. Stage one was a read-through to get a sense of the story and pick up places where it lagged or got lost in the weeds. Stage two was to add the comments about areas that needed to be looked at, and stage three was the actual copyediting. I was on chapter three of stage one, where Rose has an encounter with one of the marauding Vikings who is after her maidenhood. She fends him off with a broom handle. "Her arms were strong from milking the cows, yet shapely and smooth as cream."

I made a note. "Shapely arms?"

The phone rescued me from the rest of the chapter. "Jamie, it's Joe."

I'd forgotten to reply to his text. "Oh, Joe. I'm sorry. I forgot about your text."

"Can we talk today?" Joe normally spoke in a subdued and measured way of talking. I caught a note of stress.

"Sounds important. I'm in the middle of a project. Can you come here?"

We agreed on mid-afternoon, which gave me time to get through a few more chapters. Maybe I'd find that Rose not only had shapely arms but also shapely, creamy knees.

Joe arrived at the same time clouds rolled in and the wind picked up. I watched the whitecaps on the lake and worried the wind would blow down all the leaves. I loved the colors and didn't want to lose them quite yet.

Bronte greeted Joe like an old friend, even though she'd never met him. How she decided whether she liked someone was a mystery to me. She had a track record of being both right about people and wrong.

We settled at the kitchen table. Joe had lost the gauntness of last August when he had been jailed for a crime he did not commit. His eyes held more life, and he actually smiled at me. These were big changes for a boy who had been shot and who had watched his twin brother die in front of him.

"How are you and Clarence getting on?"

"He keeps me busy." Joe looked amused. "I'm trying to move him into the twenty-first century."

I laughed. "That's a challenge."

Bronte slurped at her water dish. When she was done, she walked over to Joe and settled at his feet. I noticed how Joe casually massaged his arm before he reached down to pet Bronte. He'd been wounded in the shoulder in the shooting and had lost some use of it. I pointed to his shoulder, "Is it any better?"

Joe shrugged. "I'm getting some physical therapy. I think it helps." He paused. "They said I should have gotten it two years ago after the shooting."

"Why didn't you?"

34

"I'm Native. Everyone was in dispute about who should pay—the school, the tribe? My family didn't have insurance, and I guess I just gave up trying to get help."

God, I thought. He was only eighteen, had just lost his brother and no one stepped forward to help. What kind of a community was Cascade that didn't rally around the victims?

As if Joe read my thoughts he said, "A lot of people in Cascade think all the Native Americans should either move to Minneapolis or go back on the reservation. The only reason they tolerated me and my brother was because we were good at football."

"That's a sad indictment."

He shrugged. We sat in silence for a few moments. I'd learned since moving from New York that people around here tolerated silence better than my New York friends. It was hard for me not to jump in and talk, but I knew Joe had asked to meet with me, and he would eventually tell me about it.

He shifted in his chair, looking beyond me and out the window. "I think you need to know something was going on in Cascade before the shooting. It was something no one talked about but some of the kids whose dads weren't working much suddenly had new phones and computers and stuff. Maybe Neil Kavanaugh was part of it."

"Really? Do you know what it was all about?" I jotted down a note to ask Matt Whitacre if he was aware of it.

Joe shook his head. "Frank, my brother, and I didn't hang around the kids who might have been part of it. Us rez kids kept to ourselves."

"Do you think this had anything to do with the shooting? Winnie said Neil was a good kid, not the usual loner you read about in these school shootings."

Joe wrinkled his brow as if he didn't want to think about it. "I don't know. He was decent to us, that's for sure."

"What do you mean, 'us'?"

"The other kids from the reservation. He was one of the kids who was friendly. Like, he offered to help my brother with his pre-calculus." The sorrow in Joe's quiet voice when he talked of his brother filled the room. "No one else ever stepped forward like that."

From reading various articles about the typical school shooter, I pictured an angry, depressed white kid who didn't get along in school. I said this to Joe. "He doesn't sound like the other shooters I've read about."

"Neil was a good student, always raising his hand in class. He was also a computer whiz. Any time something went wrong with the computers at school, they called Neil. But he wasn't like some hacker who spent all his time in his parent's basement. He was a nice, friendly kind of guy. I think the teachers really liked him until that fall when he changed, I guess."

"What do you mean?"

"Suddenly he got real quiet, kept his head down, and stopped talking. Mr. Vincent even tried to reach out to him, but it was like something was really bothering him."

"Do you know what it was?"

Joe shook his head and slumped a little in the chair with a barely perceptible shudder. Bronte sensed Joe's sorrow and put her head in his lap. He stroked the top of her head. At that moment, I saw how healing a pet could be.

We sat in silence for a time. "Joe? What can you tell me about Mr. Vincent? It sounds like Neil was deliberate in targeting him when he shot at the group."

Joe continued to stroke Bronte. "I don't know. I really don't understand it."

It was time to get to the point. "Why did you want to talk with me so urgently?"

Joe looked at me and then away. "I like you, and I don't want you to get hurt. My cousin says that she's heard some talk about a foreigner from out East trying to dig up dirt on the town."

"Me? They think I'm a foreigner?"

Joe's mouth twitched a little like he was trying to hold back a smile. "We don't get out much."

I grimaced. "Clarence and Jim both warned me about Cascade." I paused, noting how Joe nodded. "To me, it's a story that should be told—especially if Neil Kavanaugh is not the kid he was portrayed to be." Studying his eyes, I asked. "What do you think?"

Outside the wind whipped up the dead leaves. They swirled against the cabin as if they were looking for shelter.

Finally, Joe spoke. "I think you should do the story. Mr. Vincent, my brother, and Jenny Trueblood who died in the massacre deserve to be heard." His voice dropped to a whisper. "They deserve to be more than someone's 'thoughts and prayers.'" Pausing, he gazed beyond me. "But you should be careful. Bad things happen in Cascade."

After Joe left, I made a pot of tea and sat on the couch. How should I be careful? The waves of Lake Larissa broke against the shore, and the wind blew in gusts. The cabin darkened as the rain clouds rolled in. Bronte settled on her cushion by my feet and closed her eyes. Lulled by the rhythm of the lake and the aroma of mint from the tea, I drifted off.

Winnie came to me in my dream. Except he was a little boy with ketchup on his chin. He wore a ski mask. Beckoning to me, he pointed to a map. But I couldn't read the map and when I turned to Winnie, he had a telephone in his hand. The map faded and the only thing left in a darkened room was my red leather glove. Winnie's phone rang, but I couldn't find it in the dark. I called out, "Wait, I'm coming."

I woke up with a start just as the light went off on my phone. I stared at the phone trying to shake off the dream. It faded so quickly all I could remember was Winnie in a mask, the map, and my glove. My phone chirped to let me know I had a message.

"Hello, Ms. Forest, this is Sheriff Bolton. I have more questions for you. Please call me back."

The last thing I wanted to do right now was talk with Jay Bolton.

Chapter Seven

Matt Whitacre

I gritted my teeth and walked away from the phone. If Bolton wanted to talk to me, he could call back. I had more important things to do like eat supper and tackle the next chapter of Florice's book.

While I ate a vegetable stir fry, though, my attention moved back to the message. What did the sheriff want? I had nothing more to add to what I'd already said, and yet, I'd detected a threatening tone in his message. I played it again and decided I was imagining things. Halfway through the stir fry, I gave up eating and called him.

When he answered I identified myself even though I was sure with caller ID he already knew. "I understand you wanted to talk with me."

I heard the sound of several men in the background. "Now is not a good time." His tone was sharp and abrupt.

"Well, I have an appointment to talk with Matt Whitacre on Friday. Maybe we could meet at the school." I did not want to go back to the sheriff's office with its orange plastic chairs. I also wanted to have a little control over the conversation.

"Why are you talking with Matt?" He demanded.

I didn't answer. It really was none of his business. After some silence with only the rumble of the men in the background, he agreed to stop over at the school on Friday.

On Thursday, I worked my way through *Pluck the Rose.* I was surprised and pleased that Florice had done her homework on the era of the Viking invasions in Ireland. Thorgest, the noble Viking who fell for Rose was an actual historical character. I smiled as I researched him. He supposedly died by drowning. Florice generally liked her heroine to ride off with her man into the setting sun. She wrote HEAs—happily ever afters. In this case, he plucked Rose from the wretched farm, and they rode off to the sea. Florice left it open to the reader whether they drowned or not. As an author, Florice was definitely improving, although she still couldn't figure out where to put the commas, and she still relied on her stable of overused phrases like "I felt his throbbing member." I pictured a thumb after someone had pounded it with a hammer.

* * *

Friday dawned with a cloudless sky. As the earth warmed, I brought my coffee to the rock by the lake to decide what I wanted to ask Matt Whitacre. I'd already talked with a couple of the surviving victims and had the taped interviews the late editor of the *Killdeer Times* had done last spring. After breakfast, I planned to read through the transcripts before heading to Cascade.

The leaves rustled in the breeze as I thought about the shooting in Cascade two years ago. It had happened a year before I moved from New York to Lake Larissa, and I might not have known anything about it except it was a project Nancy Bywater, the local newspaper editor, had worked on before she died. Her family had given me permission to use the materials she had gathered.

Joe let me borrow the yearbook from his junior year at Cascade High with photos of the students and the teacher who had died. Joe's twin, Frank, was identical to him except he had longer hair and a little scar on his forehead. The math teacher, Tony Vincent, was full-blooded Lakota from a tribe in South Dakota. In the photo, his hair was pulled back into a braid. He had a large smile exposing a crooked front tooth. He looked too young to be a teacher. The third victim, Jenny Trueblood, had a round face and serious eyes. Joe told me she was quiet and very smart. "Definitely heading for college."

I flipped to the photo of the shooter, Neil Kavanaugh, and studied it as if it would tell me why he gunned down his classmates. He had thick light-brown hair that curled down his forehead and an enigmatic, almost Mona Lisa smile. Nothing in his light blue eyes revealed the dark thoughts that must have been hidden behind the smile.

"What a sad waste, Bronte." I picked up a stick and threw it for her. She trotted through the leaf-strewn lawn after it, her tail wagging. I surveyed my yard and wondered if I should rake it. As a city girl, I'd never had to rake or mow or even take out the garbage. This lake living had its drawbacks and its charms. I wasn't sure if raking was the former or the latter. On a day like today with the temperatures rising into the 70s, I could see spending the whole day piling up the leaves and jumping in them.

When Bronte came back with the stick, I proposed it to her. "How about if we play tomorrow?" Bronte was happy with any suggestion I made to her.

The sun stayed bright and fresh as I drove to Cascade. I remembered the other day with Clarence, how it had been cloudy and drab and rainy. Maybe this was a good omen. My light mood changed abruptly when a deer leapt out from the woods. Thank god my Subaru had good brakes, or I would have hit the poor creature. I skidded and nearly ended up in the ditch. As I straightened out the car, I thought about the different dangers we face in life. In New York City one of the biggest hazards involved people glued to their smartphones walking out into traffic. Here, it was wildlife.

Cascade High School was a newer one-story brick building on the outskirts of town. A sign in front said, "Welcome to Cascade High School, Home of the Mighty Cougars. Visitors Please Register at the Desk." I arrived just as the last classes let out for the day. Students streamed out the front door. Most of them were fresh-faced white kids. Jim had explained to me that in this part of Minnesota diversity meant that you had a combination of Lutherans, Methodists, and Catholics. "You might think because we're so close to the reservation, we'd see more integration—but we don't."

I sat in the car for a few minutes to let the last student stragglers exit the building. When I approached the front door, a man standing just inside peered at me. He was in his mid-fifties with muscled arms and a burly build. He wore a name tag saying "Bill" on a maroon polo shirt. I recognized him right away as the man in the restaurant eating with the mascara woman.

When I tried the door, it was locked. The man continued to stare at me from inside but made no effort to open the door.

I smiled at him, but he didn't move. Knocking again, I called, "Hello? I have an appointment to see Mr. Whitacre."

Bill blinked at me, as if I was a ghost, but again didn't move. I looked around for someone to help me, and when I looked back, Bill was walking down the hall with his back to me.

I called the number I had for Matt Whitacre. After four rings it went to voice mail. "Hello, Mr. Whitacre. This is Jamie Forest. I'm at the front door, but it's locked."

Behind me, I heard someone approach. When I turned, a high school girl, who appeared to be about sixteen, gave me a questioning look. I pointed to the door. "I'm trying to get in to see Mr. Whitacre but the door is locked."

She nodded, her blonde hair blowing in the breeze. "This security thing is crap. That Bill won't let anybody in after 3:30."

"So how do I get in?"

She continued to study me. "You're not a shooter are you?"

"Hardly. I'm doing a story on the, uh, shooting." I smiled trying to look as non-threatening as possible. "I'm here to talk with Mr. Whitacre about it."

"Oh, sure. I heard about you. My mom said something. You sound like those guys on *The Sopranos*."

I shrugged. "I get that a lot. I grew up in New York City." And, no, I didn't have a Jersey mob boss accent. To people in Minnesota, we Easterners all sounded the same.

She hesitated for a moment. "Listen, I know a different way to get in. Come with me."

The backpack she carried bounced as I followed her around the building to a door leading into the gymnasium. "Sometimes us kids prop it open, so we don't have to deal with Bill." She led me through the empty gymnasium

DEATH OF A STARLING

and pointed to a hallway lined with lockers. "Mr. Whitacre's office is at the end of that hall."

I thanked her and was about to walk to the hallway when it occurred to me to find out a little more about how the students felt about the shooting. "Would you be willing to answer a few questions for me before I see Mr. Whitacre?"

The girl hesitated, a look of pain in her eyes. "Um, we're not supposed to talk about it."

"Really? Who told you that?"

She shrugged. "Mostly the teachers."

Why would the teachers want to silence the students? That didn't make sense to me. "Hey. I don't want to get you into trouble, but if you decide to talk to me, here's my number." I handed her one of my cards. "By the way, what is your name? In case you call?"

She took the card and quickly stuffed it into her backpack. "Tess. Tess Bolton."

I saw the resemblance almost immediately. "You must be related to the sheriff."

"He's my uncle."

Someone was walking down the hallway. Tess quickly turned and said, "I gotta go. I'm not supposed to be here, but you should know Neil isn't… wasn't a bad person. If you see Mr. Whitacre, you won't tell him I helped you, will you?"

"No, I won't."

Tess raced to the locker room.

Before I got all the way to the hallway, a man met me. I recognized him from the yearbook. Matt Whitacre was medium height and thin to the point of being skinny. He walked with a straight military posture that didn't fit his scrawniness. He wore crisply ironed khakis and a maroon polo shirt like Bill's. A whistle dangled around his neck. I didn't realize he was a coach.

"Mr. Whitacre? I'm sorry I'm late. I couldn't get in." I held out my hand to shake his. The grip was lukewarm as he smiled at me with nearly perfect teeth.

"You can call me Matt. I was just going to the front to check. I'm guessing Bill wouldn't let you in."

I told him I had called him when I couldn't get in and then decided to try another door. "The side door to the gym was open. I hope it didn't look like I was trying to sneak in."

"Most people want out of school, not in." He spoke with a slight tic on the right side of his face.

We walked down the darkened hallway to his office. "On Fridays, everyone including the teachers and the janitor clear out as soon as they can. They'll be back this evening, though, for the football game."

My school in Manhattan didn't have a big sports program. All the athletic kids played soccer. I tried it one year, sprained my ankle during the first practice, and spent every game on the bench. High school sports were not my area of expertise. Here in Minnesota, high school football was big in small communities. I couldn't imagine mothers sending their kids off to be smashed in the head—but what did I know?

Matt's office was small with room for a bookshelf, a filing cabinet, a desk, and a couple of chairs. He sat down behind his desk and motioned for me to take the chair meant for misbehaving students. He watched me looking around the room.

"It's small, I know. I could have had an office in the administrative wing that was larger, but I wanted to be out here where the kids are."

"Sounds like you care about them," I murmured.

He pointed to a framed diploma that indicated his Master of Education. "I took a few detours before I got here. Went from high school into the Marines. After that, I got a degree in accounting and worked for a couple of big firms. Bored me silly. I like to be in the middle of things, not squirreled away with spreadsheets." Again, the tic.

I could picture him with spreadsheets and a calculator. It was harder to see him as a marine or a high school principal. He had the look of a scarecrow. I imagined him in "The Wizard of Oz" and had to fight back a smile.

Settling into the chair, I shook the image out of my brain. "I was so sorry to hear about Winston Starling."

Matt wrinkled his brow. "Tragedy." He peered at me. "I understand you met him before he died. Did he...uh...talk about the shooting?"

The abruptness of his question caused me to sit up straighter. Where were the accolades, the "thoughts and prayers" for the family, or the "he was a good counselor and we'll miss him"? Matt might have been good at accounting and education, but he definitely lacked some social skills.

"No," I lied. "We didn't have time." I took out my notebook and pen, not looking at him. It felt like the temperature in the room had dropped ten degrees and I wasn't sure why.

Searching for a way to restart the conversation I pointed to a photograph in an ornate frame sat on the bookshelf behind him. I recognized the woman in it right away. She was the one who carried the Hermes bag.

"Is that your wife? She's beautiful."

"That she is."

For a few moments, we had the uncomfortable Minnesota silence. I opened my notebook. "I don't want to take up too much of your time—especially if you have a football game to catch."

He nodded.

Before I could ask any questions, footsteps approached. Matt quickly stood up. "Excuse me."

Outside his door, I heard him speak in a low voice. "It's fine. No change in plans."

The other person mumbled something and walked away.

Back in the office, Matt sat down. "Just one of the teachers worried about the game tonight."

I pointed to the whistle around his neck. "Are you coaching?"

He fingered the whistle and said, "No. Coaching is not one of my duties."

Once again footsteps approached. Matt had a pained expression when he said, "Excuse me again."

While he was out in the hallway talking, I stood up and walked over to the photo with his wife. Charity and Matt appeared to be a mismatched pair. She was slightly taller than him and had a Slavic beauty with high cheekbones and a wide smile. She definitely fit with the Hermes crowd.

Another photo stood behind it. I bent over to look at it, just as Matt walked back in. He cleared his throat in an abrupt way. The fleeting tingle crawled up my spine as I turned away from the photo. In it were several people including Matt and Charity in hunting camo holding rifles. Charity's expression was one of complete comfort wielding a weapon. One of the other men wore a red baseball cap. I was sure he was the man with the ice-cold eyes talking to Charity at the restaurant.

Chapter Eight

Tess

He sat back down and folded his hands on his desk. "Sorry. Student issue."

I pointed to the photo. "Looks like a hunting trip. Who is that man in the red cap? I think I've seen him before."

Instead of answering, he cleared his throat. "Now, where were we?"

I sensed irritation in his tone as I poised my pen to write. "Can you tell me what you know about the shooting?"

Sighing, he said, "I wish people would stop asking. The community needs to heal."

Same words I'd heard from Sheriff Bolton. Interesting. I waited for him to say more.

When he spoke, it was almost as if he'd memorized the speech. "Kavanaugh came in with an assault rifle and shot those kids and the teacher. And then he ran out the cafeteria exit. No one else was in the room except the cooks who were back in the kitchen."

"So, he specifically went for that group?"

Matt shrugged. "Looks that way."

"What happened to the shooter? The only thing I've read about him is that he was found dead later. Was it suicide?" Nothing in the news reports indicated where or how.

"We don't talk much about him around here. Best not to make him some sort of anti-hero, you know?" Matt leaned back, folding his arms. His expression darkened. "I hope you aren't going for some kind of smear of the community. Cascade is proud of its diversity and proud of the students we have from the reservation."

His canned speech irritated me. I fought to keep a neutral tone. "Actually, I'm particularly interested in Tony Vincent. There aren't a lot of Native American teachers in this part of the state unless they work in reservation schools. How did he get along with the students and the other teachers?"

Matt appeared to be a little taken aback by the question. Hadn't anyone ever asked him about the teacher? His voice had an uncertainty to it. "Uh, well, Tony was a good teacher."

"But he wasn't well-liked?"

He leaned forward, his jaw tensed. For such a wimpy-looking man, he maintained an air of authority. "Why would you say that? Have you talked with someone else?"

It was my turn to be taken aback by the vehemence in his voice, but I decided to be honest with him. "Uh, no. It's just the fact that no one wants to talk about him."

I waited for him to say more. It was as if he hadn't rehearsed this part of the interview.

"Tony was a good teacher. My wife was working with him on the diversity day. He was doing good things." He looked at his watch. "Listen, I have to help get things set up for the game tonight. You are welcome to stay and watch it if you like." He cleared his throat. "But if you do, I would ask you not to ask about the shooting. People in the community are still recovering."

"I see." But I didn't. Why, when I brought up Tony, did he suddenly clam up? "Maybe I could talk with your wife?"

Matt pushed his chair back to stand up. I noticed his forehead was shiny with perspiration. "Best to let it go."

"One more thing." I held my pen up.

Matt let out a sigh. "Yes?"

"I heard talk that some of the kids had new phones and electronic equipment even though their parents weren't working. Was Neil one of them?"

Matt scowled. "Who told you that?"

I shrugged. "Just a rumor, I guess."

His lips tightened. "We don't pass on rumors around here."

He stepped out from behind his desk and moved to the door. I followed, again noting how he carried himself ramrod straight.

At the door, I handed him my card. "If you think of anything else, please feel free to contact me."

He took it as if I'd handed him a dead mouse. After a pause, he said, "Oh, one other thing, if you're interested. I still have a box of Tony's things. The, uh, family never picked it up. Would you be able to get it to them?" Without waiting for a reply, he walked to a small storage closet and pulled down a lidded box. "It's just a few things from his desk."

I took the box, surprised he was so willing to give it to me. I wondered if they were trying to erase all evidence that Tony Vincent was part of the school in a misguided attempt to heal.

Matt escorted me to the front door and let me out. The sun was fading behind a stand of pine trees, and the air had a damp cool to it. I slipped the box into the backseat of the car as Jay pulled up in his official SUV.

In all the confusion of getting into the school and the strangeness of the conversation with Matt, I had totally forgotten about him. Clearly, he hadn't forgotten about me.

He walked over to me, pressing his hand into his lower back as if in pain. Even in the waning light, it was obvious that he was angry.

He moved in close enough to me that I smelled the leather of the jacket he wore over his white shirt. He was shorter than I remembered from the other day. I guessed him to be about 180 pounds. At five-three and 110 pounds, I was no physical match for him.

"You said you'd call me when you were done talking with Matt," he growled.

I tried to look as sheepish as possible. "I'm sorry." In my experience, the less I said to law enforcement, the better.

"Why don't you come down to the courthouse and we can talk?"

I stood with my feet planted. The last place I wanted to be with him was the courthouse after-hours. "Better yet," I suggested, "let's go to the Cascade Bar and Grill. I missed lunch, and my stomach is making terrible noises."

"You think I'm not serious?" He moved in a little closer. This man knew how to violate personal space. If he was trying to intimidate me, it worked. Still, I stood my ground.

"I think I need to eat."

I don't know what he would have done next if Tess hadn't approached from behind us. "Uncle Jay. I see you've met my friend."

Jay backed off immediately. "You know her?"

Tess grinned at me. "Sure."

"Has she been asking you questions? You know what we've said about talking to reporters?" He glowered at me as he talked with his niece.

Tess shrugged. "No. We talked about football."

Really? I kept my mouth shut.

"She lives near Killdeer and they're playing our Cougars tonight." She smiled at me. "Right?"

I was saved from answering when his cell phone rang. The ringtone, a bird chirp, surprised me. Macho lawmen didn't use chirping birds, did they?

"Excuse me." He walked back to his car.

"He's really a nice guy underneath," Tess whispered to me. "Don't let him scare you."

"He has a funny way of showing it."

We waited while he talked. I noticed Tess had transformed from the plain, clean-faced look, to heavy makeup, skinny jeans, and Doc Martens. I pointed to the boots, "Bet your mom doesn't like you wearing those."

She giggled, "You won't tell, will you?" She had an impish excited air about her. I wondered what she was up to.

I smiled at her. "I did the same thing when I was your age." My dad was unhappy about my goth stage when I was in high school. He had the sense, though, to keep quiet about it. I think he figured I'd grow out of it, and I did.

A car with a missing muffler roared toward the school. Tess watched it with anticipation.

"Your ride?" I asked.

When it was near enough to see the sheriff's vehicle, it did a sudden U-turn.

"Cowards. Uncle Jay's bark is worse than his bite." Her eyes sparkled and she shifted nervously on her feet.

He glanced up as the car disappeared down the road but continued talking on the phone.

"He and my mom are having some kind of an argument," Tess confided. "Since my dad is gone most of the time, he thinks he's in charge."

I nodded. "I suppose he figures it's part of the job."

Tess made circles in the gravel with her boot as we waited.

Maybe I could get a little more information from her. "Can I ask you a question?"

Tess shrugged. "Sure."

"I'm wondering why all the adults around here say you shouldn't talk about the shooting. I would think that talking about it was a good thing. What do you think?"

Tess continued to make the circular pattern beneath her boot. "Well, I was only in ninth grade when it happened, and I didn't see anything. But I still have nightmares."

She peered at the ground. I noticed how her shoulders trembled as if she was cold. She kept her voice to a whisper. "All the people who died or were hurt were Indians. Yet, the school didn't even have a memorial service. Nobody said anything about Neil either. Like his name had become a curse word. But he was nice." She looked up at me, her voice rising. "Something is wrong with this town. Now nobody's talking about Mr. Starling either. Like he did something wrong by dying. I can't wait to graduate and get out."

"You said Neil was a nice guy."

She gazed beyond me. "We kinda went together for a while."

"Wow, all of that must have been hard."

In the twilight, I saw tears in her eyes. She wiped them with the back of her hand and whispered, "Thank you."

Jay interrupted us. "What are you talking about?"

Tess blinked at him. "Nothing. Just school and stuff."

I moved between the two of them. "Listen, Sheriff. I have to get back to Killdeer. Could we talk some other time, or is this an emergency?"

His phone chirped again.

"Busy man," I said as he walked away again.

Tess had her backpack off and was digging through it. When she found what she was looking for, she slipped a piece of paper to me. "Here. Don't let Uncle Jay know I gave this to you."

"What is it?" I quickly stuffed it in my bag.

"It's my phone number. If you text me, maybe we can talk. This place has a lot of secrets."

Jay walked back to us frowning as he rubbed his back.

"I've got a situation in town. We'll have to talk next week." He added, "In my office."

It sounded like a threat to me. If I talked with him again, I'd be sure to have Clarence, my octogenarian bodyguard, with me.

As soon as he drove away, I turned to Tess. "Can I drop you off somewhere?"

She shook her head. "No. My friends will be back. I'll wait here."

"Okay. Stay safe. I'll text you later to set up a time to talk."

She waved as I drove away. She looked so alone in the empty parking lot. Despite what she said about her ride, I wondered if I should wait around until her friends came. I decided I needed to get back to my cabin and my dog and the fiery romance between Rose and Thorgest. The longer I stayed in Cascade, the more I longed for home.

Chapter Nine

Road Rage

It was dark when I reached the city limits of Cascade. Two orange school busses from Killdeer passed me going toward the school. In my rearview mirror, I saw a glow of lights from the football field. I wondered if Tess and her friends planned to watch the game. "Dressed like that?" I shook my head. Whatever she was up to, it probably had nothing to do with football.

With the fading light and the quiet of the two-lane highway, I felt secure as I sat cocooned in my car. I hadn't realized how tense I'd been in Cascade until I relaxed in the driver's seat and an ache melted from my shoulders. What had Tess said? The town had its secrets. Was she simply being an imaginative teenager, or was she on to something?

Now that I was away from the school, the encounter with both Matt and Jay seemed even stranger. I could tell Whitacre had a script and stuck with it. His reticence when I asked him about Tony Vincent told me he was holding something back.

What about the nonsense of the town needing to heal? Nothing was said about the families of the victims or the survivors. Didn't they need to heal as well? At this point, I might have considered dropping the article, except Joe's words reverberated with me, "They need to be heard."

My thoughts were interrupted a couple of miles outside of Cascade, when a car behind me approached with its bright lights. I adjusted the rearview mirror to avoid the glare and checked my speedometer. I was going seventy in a sixty-five mile an hour zone. Jim, as a state trooper, had advised me to never go beyond seven miles per hour above the speed limit if I wanted to avoid a ticket.

The car kept on my tail.

"Pass me, you jerk. I'm not speeding up." I slowed down, and the car behind me slowed down. He was close enough to my tailgate that if I had to suddenly brake, he would rear-end me. An electric chill raced down my back as the car continued to tail me. I sensed the driver toying with me. My cell phone was tucked in the bag on the floor of the passenger seat. I couldn't reach it if I needed to call for help.

"Steady, Jamie. Could just be a stupid driver." The tingle said something different.

As if to answer me, the car pulled out into the opposite lane. I expected him to pass, so I slowed down to sixty. Instead, he drew alongside of me. I glanced over to see he had a passenger who wore a red cap like the guys who had come into the bar when I was with Clarence. The passenger grinned and gave me the finger as he yelled something at me. This was clearly not a friendly encounter.

The car was a light-colored, dented-up SUV. The driver blared his horn but stayed next to me. Instinctively, I sped up.

Get away from them.

The SUV stayed with me as I pushed the old Subaru past eighty. A highway sign indicated a curve ahead. Would that idiot stay with me on the curve?

I was not an experienced driver. Growing up in New York City, I didn't get my license until I was twenty and, for years, only used it as an identification. The Subaru I bought last spring was my first car. I knew I would not be able to handle the car going into the curve at eighty, but I also knew that the guy beside me, yelling and waving his fist, meant to scare me or worse.

Is that what happened to Winnie?

The back of the Subaru skidded as I entered the curve. The madman beside me didn't slow down. My front tire hit the shoulder, spewing gravel, and the steering wheel shook as I fought to keep from going into the ditch.

Posts with reflectors lining the curve whizzed by. My hands gripped the steering wheel so hard my knuckle joints ached. The passenger pitched an empty liquor bottle at my car. It hit the back door and disappeared on the pavement.

Ahead, I saw oncoming lights and thought, "Oh my god! We're going to crash!" Should I stay on the road or try for the ditch? If I went for the ditch and the approaching car did the same, we'd have a head-on collision.

This was one of those moments when people talk about your life flashing before your eyes. Mine didn't. Instead, for that irrational millisecond, I remembered I was supposed to be helping a client of Clarence's find a woman who had defrauded him. I would die, and the woman would be free to scam someone else.

Then as I was about to turn the wheel and head for the ditch, the SUV beside me suddenly braked, skidded, and did a half-circle. I watched in the mirror as it slid into the ditch on the other side of the road, just before the oncoming car met me.

I could have been a Good Samaritan and turned around to make sure the mad men hadn't rolled over and were hurt. Instead, I kept driving until I passed the sign announcing, "Jackpine County." I was out of Cascade County, and for the first time since the SUV had approached me, I felt safe. I pulled over and sat, taking deep breaths, willing my hands to stop shaking.

With my eyes glued on the rearview mirror, I waited for the SUV to come back. Instead, the road was quiet. After a few minutes, headlights peeked around the curve. I grabbed my phone, ready to call 911, when a pickup truck passed by me. Not the crazy driver and his passenger with the red cap. Setting the phone down on my lap, I pulled back onto the highway. Overhead, the stars sparkled in the clear sky.

The rest of the drive was quiet until I turned onto the gravel road to my cabin. Just before I reached home, I saw lights in my rearview mirror.

"Not again." No one would be on this road after dark, since I was the only one who lived on it. I fingered my phone, ready to make a call. My heart beat faster. This was not turning into a very good day.

Before I parked in my usual spot, near the back door of the cabin, I checked to make sure my car doors were locked. Behind me, I heard the squeak of the vehicle suspension as it bounced over the potholes in the driveway. Inside the door of the cabin, Bronte barked her greeting. If only she knew how to open the door so I could dash in.

"Oh hell," I muttered. If someone was after me, they'd get me outside or inside. It was time to move. I opened the car door, ready to dash to the cabin, when a pickup truck pulled in behind me.

My knees felt weak when I stepped out of the car and into Jim's warm embrace. "Am I ever glad to see you," I whispered.

Chapter Ten

Jim

I nestled in the crook of his arm, the sheets tangled around us. "That was nice."

Jim caressed my shoulder. "Definitely worth the five-hour drive back here."

Outside, the leaves rustled in a gentle breeze. Inside the air was infused with the sweet smell of scented candles. For a moment, my world was at peace. That moment of serenity was interrupted when Bronte whined at the bedroom door.

"I'd better let her in, or her tender heart will be crushed." I kissed Jim on the cheek and dashed naked to the door. In the flicker of the two candles glowing on the bedside table, I felt his gaze on me. My body had grown strong and lean over the summer and the fall, despite spending too much time at the computer or the kitchen table editing manuscripts. Living in a cabin, I'd learned, involved mowing and raking, and hauling wood. On top of that, I'd been swimming more.

Bronte, delighted to be welcomed into the bedroom, nearly tripped me as I ran back over the cold wooden floor to the bed. So much for looking naked and graceful as I stumbled back under the covers. Bronte stopped before jumping up and gave Jim a questioning look with her soft brown eyes.

Jim reached out and patted her head. "Sorry. Beds are for people, not canines."

At the sound of his voice, she settled on her rug on the floor.

"How come she listens to you and not to me?"

"I'm Indian. It's natural."

"Bullshit. I'm part Ojibwe, and she ignores me."

"That's because you sound like a mobster from New York."

That night, with him beside me, I had a deep and dreamless sleep. When I woke up, the cabin already smelled of dark roast coffee. He brought me a mug and sat on the bed beside me. How had I stumbled onto this man? My ex-husband never made coffee and on the rare occasions that he brought it home from the coffee shop on the corner by our Queens apartment, he always got me what he wanted so he could finish it when I didn't like it.

Life was good. Or would be good if I only knew he was staying.

Over breakfast, I recounted my trip to Cascade and the banged-up SUV that tried to intimidate me. "I don't know if they wanted to push me off the road or simply scare me."

"It doesn't matter. They were playing a dangerous game. People have died doing that." He leaned over and took my hand. "Why don't you drop the Cascade thing. If it's about the money, maybe I can spare a little to keep you going."

I drew my hand away. "I'd rather have you than your money." I tried not to sound offended, but I didn't want him to think he had to take care of me.

"Well, at least promise me you won't go back to Cascade alone."

I stood up and walked around the table to him. Reaching around, I hugged him and rested my chin on the top of his head. His hair smelled of my strawberry-scented shampoo. "I'll be careful."

The day warmed up as the sun shone through clear skies. Jim and I sat, side by side, on the rock by the lake listening to the waves scrape against the rocks and sand. He told me Jacob had finished his first week of chemotherapy.

"He's a plucky little guy. He was so calm when they put a port in his chest for the chemo. Now he's losing his hair but happy he can wear his Minnesota Twins baseball cap all the time." He gazed out across the lake to Bear Island. "Someday, when he's better, I'm going to bring him camping to the island."

I squeezed his hand. "I'll bet he'd love that." I didn't tell Jim that I had done a pretty deep search on the internet about the kind of leukemia Jacob had. His chances weren't more than 50/50, and after I read about it, I was sorry I'd researched it.

We spent part of the day raking leaves, and when we had a big enough pile, we took turns jumping in them. It was a new experience for me to have dry leaves stuck under my shirt and in my hair. Bronte thought it was great fun and skidded into the piles with me. At one point, I picked up an armful of leaves and threw them at Jim. When I ran, he tackled me, swooped me up, and carried me to the bedroom. What was the old saying, "Make hay while the sun shines?"

Florice couldn't have written a better romance scene than our Indian summer afternoon. I smiled thinking about her overused phrase "the heat of his lips." For the first time in my life, I understood what she was talking about.

Later, after a shower, I sat on the edge of the bed toweling my hair and watching Jim put a few clothes into a duffle bag. While he still had the body of a bicycler with muscular thighs and toned arms, he'd put on stress weight around the middle. Too much sitting, too much coffee, and too little sleep.

He picked up a baseball cap and stuffed it in the bag. It reminded me of the red cap on the passenger in the SUV. "I saw several men in Cascade wearing red caps, you know like the MAGA caps but with a logo that looked like a confederate flag."

Jim stopped putting a few of his clothes in his duffle. "Did you say red caps? Like baseball caps?"

"You've seen them?"

He zipped up his bag with a wrinkled brow. "I'm going to check with some of my fellow troopers. I seem to recall something about an extremist group in Minnesota who called themselves the 'Red Cap Militia.'"

"You're kidding. You mean like the Ku Klux Klan?"

"More like an anti-government, anti-tax pro-gun group."

"Really? I'm happy to pay my taxes, by the way."

He laughed. "You're just one of those Eastern snowflake liberals. You probably eat all that funny food and drink those ten-dollar lattes."

I pictured the greasy cheeseburgers at the bar in Cascade and gave him the finger.

Before he left, he hugged me. "I don't know when I'll be able to come back. But if you have any problems, text me. I have lots of friends around here."

"Good to know." I doubted I would need his help, especially if I stayed away from Sheriff Bolton.

I watched his pickup disappear down the road and into the dark. The stars twinkling overhead couldn't wipe out the feeling of melancholy as I walked back into the cabin. Jim had kept a good front, but I knew underneath, he was in turmoil about his son and about his future. What if, through all of this, he ended up going back to Jacob's mother?

"Stop it," I said out loud. Bronte bowed her head like she'd done something wrong. "Not you, girl. Me."

Chapter Eleven

Tony's Box

With all the fresh air and other activity, I fell into bed exhausted. The pillow next to me smelled of Jim and of emptiness. While I tossed and turned, awake with my thoughts, Bronte slowly crept from the foot of the bed to her spot beside me.

"You are an opportunist," I whispered as she nuzzled her chin into the pillow.

In the dark, I was overwhelmed with sadness. When I finally fell into a light sleep, images of Winnie morphed into the photo I had of Tony. In my subconscious, they were the same.

I woke with a start when a blast of rain blew against the bedroom window. Outside, the calm starry night had changed to a wet, blustery storm. It matched the storm that was sweeping through my brain. Somehow, Winnie's fate was tied to Tony's.

"Not yours to figure out," I said out loud.

Bronte raised her head, licked my shoulder, and settled back to sleep. If only I could be like her and not spend the night cogitating about the things I had no control over.

I slipped out of bed and to the bathroom for some ibuprofen. The day's activities had left me stiff and sore. Once I snapped on the light over the sink, I was wide awake. As I studied my face in the mirror, I saw the dark circles under my eyes. They emphasized the brown in my eyes, the most noticeable feature of my Ojibwe ancestry.

My grandmother was a full-blood, my mother half. After Mother graduated from high school, she'd fled the Northwoods of Minnesota for college on the East Coast and met my father—a genuine Yankee. I came into this world knowing very little about her side of the family. Here, on Lake Larissa, I was slowly learning about my Native American background. It might have sounded ridiculous to my New York friends, but I felt somehow connected to the earth here. If I tried to return to the big city, I knew I'd be called back by the lake and the pines and the loons in the water.

"Enough," I said to the mirror. "Either go back to bed and sleep or do something useful."

By now, I knew I couldn't go back to sleep. I took two ibuprofens, threw on my thick robe and fuzzy slippers, and walked out to the kitchen to make a cup of tea.

While I waited for the water to boil, I noticed the box that Whitacre had given me of Tony's things sitting on the floor by the back door. I picked it up and put it on the kitchen table.

The aroma of mint from the tea filled the kitchen as I sorted through the box. It looked like someone from the school had simply taken everything from Tony's desktop and thrown it into the box. To me, it felt either careless or hostile, like he'd committed a crime by getting murdered.

A photo of Tony with his older brother was facedown, the glass of the frame cracked. I studied it. Tony had a classic Native American look with a broad face and high cheekbones. His eyes sparkled and he had a half-smile. His brother was lighter-skinned but had the same classic look. They stood on the shore of a lake with full Duluth packs at their feet. I guessed they were heading out for a canoe trip.

I'd never met Tony's brother, but I'd talked with him on the phone when I was putting together the proposal for the article in *The New Yorker*. He was a software engineer in Minneapolis who told me Tony had always wanted to be a teacher.

"I told him, man, you can make better money in the tech world. He didn't listen. He wanted to be in the classroom. He was really happy the first year in Cascade, and then something seemed to go wrong." His voice dropped off.

"Do you know what that was all about?" In the back of my mind, I wondered if he was getting harassed for being Native.

Tony's brother sighed. "He wasn't much for talking, but I suspected it had something to do with a girl."

We'd talked for a little more, but he didn't have anything else to share. Now, as I studied Tony's photo, I wondered about it. I made a mental note to ask Joe if he knew anything.

The rest of the box had the kind of things you might find on a desk. A coffee mug with *Cascade Cougars* printed on it had dried coffee on the bottom of it. Whoever packed the box hadn't bothered to rinse it out. I found pens and pencils and a solar calculator. At the very bottom was a day planner. It was crinkled, probably from the spilled coffee from the mug.

The planner started at the beginning of the school year. Paging through it, I saw notations for events and assignment due dates. Nothing seemed out of the ordinary until I came to the week before the shooting. Tony had marked in red and circled the name Marla and made a note "dirty laundry?" No other names were in the planner.

"Who is Marla and what does she have to do with laundry?" I flipped through the pages and found no further mention of her. A little voice in the back of my head told me, *put it back. This is none of your business.* Tomorrow I'd email Tony's brother to find out what he wanted me to do with it.

Outside, the wind continued to howl. I finished my tea and was about to put everything back in the box when I noticed a piece of paper half stuck under the bottom flap of the box. When I pulled it out, it appeared to be a crudely drawn map. It showed a lake, labeled NL with an island on it. On the southern side of the island was a small circle in red labeled "landing." On the eastern tip was an X. A line from the landing point to the X snaked through the middle of the island.

Dad had kept old topographical maps in the magazine rack for vacationers when they rented the cabin. I rummaged through them until I found one of Cascade County. Nearbow Lake appeared in the northern part of the county with little access other than one "unimproved" road to a boat launch. The lake had one large and several small islands. The large one was called Gravediggers Island.

Interesting name for an island. Did this map have anything to do with Tony's death or was it simply a map to a good camping spot?

I turned the drawing over and found something penciled in at the bottom. *Mt me on sat. I'll explain.*

I stared at it. It looked like an invitation to something on Gravediggers Island. Was it from Tony and never got delivered? Or was it to Tony? The note had no date.

I stared at it for a long time as if the answer would miraculously appear. Remembering the photo of Tony and his brother, I decided it must have had something to do with camping. I set the map back in the box. Relaxed by the tea, I returned to bed where Bronte raised her head with a look that said, "About time."

I slept late the next morning and woke to the constant patter of rain on the roof. This would be an indoor workday.

By midafternoon, I'd finished my first read-through of *Pluck the Rose* and was on my second. Florice had actually done a pretty good job of describing the landscape and building the plot. Her weakness, other than the overuse of words like "hardness," "throbbing" and "ruby red lips" was her tendency to forget how she described her characters. Thorgest went through several changes from long blond hair and a red beard to long red hair and no beard. Meanwhile, Rose sometimes had raven hair that fell fetchingly around her creamy shoulders, and sometimes it, too, turned red. At least Florice was consistent that Rose didn't have a beard.

"Maybe I'll restrict my editing to short stories from now on." I set my blue pencil down to rest my cramped fingers. "Or better yet, maybe I will insist that Florice send Word documents so I can track changes and replace all."

Partway through the second read of the manuscript, I decided to call it a day. My head ached and the cabin felt empty. It was time to do something else. I spent the rest of the day rereading some of my nineteenth-century poets. "What do you think of Sophie Jewett?" I asked Bronte. "Listen to this: 'That hour when birds leave song and children pray. Keep the old tryst, sweetheart and thou shalt know. If spirits walk.'"

For a moment the writing on the back of the map flashed through my head. Maybe it was an old tryst.

That night, I dreamed of a spirit floating just above me.

My phone rang on Monday morning as I tackled Rose and Thorgest once again. The caller ID was blocked, and I was tempted to let it go to voice mail. I answered because I hoped it might be an inquiry from someone looking for an editor. "This is Jamie Forest. Can I help you?"

"Uh, Jay Bolton calling."

The box with Tony's things sat on one of my kitchen chairs. I looked at it and felt a sudden pang of anxiety. "Yes?"

"I need to talk to you." His tone was clipped.

"Can we do this over the phone? I'd prefer not to drive back to Cascade." Or run into any more men in red caps.

"Uh, this isn't about Winston Starling. I got that figured out. Someone said he picked up your glove in the parking lot of the bar. That's why he had it."

My next question sounded petty as soon as it came out of my mouth. "Will I get it back?"

The momentary silence on the line was deafening, and I felt heat rise in my cheeks. Poor Winnie had died, and I was worried about a glove with a hole in it. When Jay spoke, his tone was hesitant. "Friday night before the football game you were talking with my niece. Tess?"

"Yes?"

"She hasn't come home and I'm wondering if she told you something."

I pictured watching her in the rearview mirror as I drove away from the school. "How long has she been gone?" I looked at the calendar hanging on the wall by the back door. It was Monday. One thing about living alone on the lake without a regular job, I easily lost track of the days.

"No, Tess didn't say anything to me. I assumed she was waiting for friends." I thought about how she was dressed in her thick makeup and her Doc Martens. Had she been up to more than hanging out with the other kids?

The officiousness had drained out of his voice. "Her friends say they were going to someone's house for a party. But she asked them to drop her off near home. No one knows what she did after that."

"I'm truly sorry that I can't help you. She seems like a nice kid."

Jay's voice was thoughtful. "I think she got in with the wrong crowd. Older kids."

I remembered I had given her my card. "She has my business card. If she calls for some reason, I'll let you know."

Jay's response was immediate and accusatory. "Why does she have your card?"

I sighed. Cascade people were so suspicious. "I asked her about the shooting and if she remembered anything unusual to give me a call."

"That shooting is old business. Leave it alone." Abruptly, he hung up.

I stared out the kitchen window at the steady rain. I'd given my card to two people and one was dead and the other missing. Was this a coincidence?

Chapter Twelve

Red Cap Militia

An hour later, my phone rang again. This time it was Clarence. As soon as I saw the caller ID, I was flooded with guilt. I'd forgotten to follow up on his assignment to find the woman who defrauded old Pete Peterson.

"Is this Jamie, my detective?"

"Hi, Clarence. This is Jamie, your derelict detective." I confessed I had gotten so involved in *Pluck the Rose* that I'd forgotten about Pete.

"I'm calling to say that it's no problem. Pete let me know this morning that he and Sunny are back together. He wants to cancel the investigation."

"Please don't tell me the woman's name is Sunny Day."

Clarence chuckled. "Almost. He said her name is Sunny Morne spelled M-o-r-n-e and not to laugh because it's an old family name."

"I'd like to see her birth certificate." I remembered reading about the Hogg family in Texas that named their daughter Ima. Still, this sounded more like a name in one of Florice's romances.

"Well, Pete's a long-time friend of mine, and I'd like to comply with his wishes. However, if you happen to have a few minutes here and there, perhaps you could check her out."

"I'll do a quick search. Meanwhile, here's what I've been up to." I filled him in on my latest trip to Cascade and the SUV that escorted me out of town. "Have you ever heard of the 'Red Cap Militia'?"

Clarence paused before speaking. "Not in a long time. Bad lot. Maybe fifteen of them up in Cascade County mostly related to each other. They claimed they were an independent nation, like the tribe, and didn't have to abide by our rules."

"What happened to them?"

"They got dispersed by the feds after the big murder trial."

"Murder trial?"

"That's the trial I assisted the prosecutor with back then. The leader of the militia, Stone Kavanaugh, was the defendant. Shot a local banker and claimed self-defense, except the banker wasn't armed."

"Is Stone any relation to Neil Kavanaugh, the kid who did the shooting?"

"It's possible. There's a whole slew of Kavanaughs up there."

I told him about seeing several men walk into the pool room at the Cascade bar wearing red caps with a confederate logo.

"Back before they broke them up, those militia boys had a deal going with stolen merchandise. It would come in by floatplane to an island up there. Some folks in town weren't very happy when the feds came. It was their only source of income. Sheriff was in on it, too, I suspect."

I pictured the crude map in Tony's things. "Was it by any chance an island on Nearbow Lake?"

Clarence paused. "Now how would you know that?"

"Matt gave me a box of things from Tony's desk. I found a handwritten map of Gravediggers Island at the bottom of the box. It had a note about meeting someone there." I pictured the note. "Coincidence maybe?"

"Curious. To say the least. I doubt the militia is doing anything now. Too much surveillance these days because we're so close to the border with Canada. A regular floatplane to an isolated lake? Not likely."

Outside, the sun peeked through the gray curtain of clouds for just a moment, lighting up the darkened cabin. I looked out the window to see a quickly fading rainbow. Not many rainbows in New York City. Another reason I loved living by the lake.

"Well," Clarence continued. "Make sure you keep track of your time when you look into Sunny. I have a feeling I'm going to hear from Pete again as soon as she gets a little more cash out of him. As for the Red Caps, stay away from them. If they're like any other white supremacist group, they are armed, stupid, and dangerous."

I assured him I had no intention of going back to Cascade anytime soon. *The New Yorker* would have to wait for a profile on the teacher who got shot.

The clouds dispersed and the sun stayed out. I made my way over the soggy lawn to my rock by the lake. Setting a towel over the wet stone, I sat and watched the waves wash in. I imagined the lake like a giant, benign creature breathing in and out, keeping its secrets.

Tess had mentioned that Cascade had secrets. Was she referring to the militia? Or something dark behind the shooting. Were the militia connected to the school massacre? It would make sense if it was a hate crime except Neil Kavanaugh didn't fit the profile.

"What do you think, Bronte? Was the shooting a hate crime committed by a deranged, deluded eighteen-year-old, or was it something else?" The more I thought about it, the more I was bewildered by what little I knew. Something ominous overshadowed the community of Cascade. Definitely, time to put that project on hold, and hope Florice had a writer friend or two who could use my expertise with punctuation before I ran out of money.

Bronte placed a stick by my foot and looked at me with expectation. I picked it up and threw it into the water. She happily splashed into the lake to retrieve the stick. When she came out, she stopped in front of me and shook the water off her fur.

As the sprinkles of water cooled the bare skin of my arm, I shivered. "Boy am I stupid. Now I have a wet dog to contend with." I threw the stick back in the water.

With the sun still sparkling off the lake, I walked barefoot through the grass back to the cabin. My phone vibrated and rang on the kitchen table. By the time I reached it, the ringing had stopped. I didn't recognize the number, and the caller left no message.

"If they really want to talk to me, they'll call back."

The cabin cooled as the day faded into evening. I hauled in logs from the woodpile and built a fire in the fireplace. The flames snapped and crackled casting undulating shadows on the walls of the living room. I sat on a rug in front of the fireplace absorbing the warmth and wishing Jim was here to absorb it with me.

Bronte lay with her head in my lap as if she sensed my loneliness. I stroked the soft fur. It came off in handfuls. Bronte was shedding fur readying her body for winter. I wondered how my first winter in the cabin would go. I didn't like to be cold, and I had been reassured that I'd never experienced cold like I would here.

Something bothered me, but I couldn't quite bring it to the surface. It wasn't until I'd poked at the logs in the fireplace that it came to me. I'd decided out on the rock that I had to let Cascade go, yet now, in the warmth and comfort of my cabin, I knew I couldn't. Joe's words came back to me again.

"Someone has to speak for them. But why am I the appointed one?" Bronte licked my hand in reply.

As if the universe had picked up my thoughts, my phone rang. Again, no caller ID.

"Hello?"

A female voice replied, "Is this Jamie Forest?"

"Yes?"

"I...I don't know if you remember me? Betsy Latelle? You talked to me last summer about Joe Pelletier and the shooting at school?"

Betsy had been one of the students who was wounded. "Oh, sure. I remember you. You were very helpful."

"I need to tell you something." Her voice had quieted to almost a whisper. "I heard you were asking questions about Mr. Vincent."

Word certainly gets around in a small town. "I was hoping to do a story about him—not so much about how he died, but more about what he'd accomplished as a teacher before he was killed."

"Um, well, me and my friends have some information. Do you think we could talk with you? Things are getting real weird around here."

"What do you mean?"

Now she did talk in a whisper. "I can't say over the phone. Could we meet?

69

There's a little gas station north of Cascade called Eyeman's Corner—it's like a general store but they have coffee and stuff."

I remembered a rundown gas station with one pump from the time I'd taken Bronte for a ride last summer to explore the area. It was the last indication of civilization before the road wound into thick forest land. "You mean the place just before you enter the state forest near Nearbow Lake?

"That's it. Can you come tomorrow in the morning—like ten o'clock?"

"Sure. Can you fill me in a little before I come?"

"I'd rather not say anything on the phone." The line clicked dead. I stared at it like it might light up again, but it remained dark. I waited for her to call back, but the phone remained quiet.

"Is this something I really want to do?" I asked Bronte. She was too busy licking her paws to reply.

After supper and a glass of wine, I opened my laptop and decided to see if my investigative skill could help me find Sunny Morne. The first place I tried was a Facebook search. No one was listed under her name. I tried a couple of variations on the spelling but still came up with nothing usable.

Back in the days when I was a contract fact-checker my first step was to go to the source. Since I couldn't call Sunny and ask her if she was scamming an old man, I did the second-best thing. I called my Killdeer friend Jilly—the accounts and office manager for the *Killdeer Times*. She knew the community so well, I once joked with her that she knew about an emergency before it happened. In response, she'd claimed she'd spent years cultivating the "good ole girl network," at LuAnne's Cut & Curl hair salon.

Jilly answered on the third ring. "Hey, Jamie Forest, what do you want?"

I explained to her about Pete Peterson, wondering as I talked if I was breaking some kind of confidentiality. Of course, I lived in a small community where nothing was confidential.

"Hmmm." I heard Jilly's fingers tap on the table as she thought. "I heard something about her. Showed up about six months ago to work as a dealer at the casino. Fiftyish and kind of dumpy."

"Hmm. I pictured a bleached blonde floozie sort."

Bronte stood up, shook herself, and trotted to the door. It was nearing her bedtime and she had her business to take care of first. "Just a minute," I whispered.

"What?"

"Sorry, talking to the dog."

Jilly laughed, a deep chuckle. "Please tell me the dog doesn't talk back."

"Not often."

We chatted for a little bit about the newspaper. The newest editor was a young woman who just graduated from journalism school.

Jilly said, "She's green, but she's a quick learner. Not much of a personality. I give her a year before she goes on to bigger and better things."

Bronte wiggled her butt at the door. Time to end the call. "Listen, Jilly, if you hear anything about Ms. Sunny, let me know."

After we hung up, I let Bronte out, smelling the damp evening air. It had a slight odor of skunk, reminding me to keep an eye on Bronte.

With the days growing shorter, I found I was going to bed earlier. In fact, I had to make a rule that I wouldn't retire before nine, but it was getting harder and harder. I stared at the kitchen clock until the hour hand was on nine. "God, I'm turning into an old lady." If Jim had been here, we would have fooled around in front of the fire until at least midnight.

"Bedtime, girl."

Tomorrow I would head back to Cascade. I wasn't sure it was the smartest thing to do, but I was committed.

Chapter Thirteen

Eyeman's Corner

The next morning dawned sunny but chilly. The lake was still and glasslike with a rising mist. I watched out the window as a loon paddled through the quiet waters calling to its mate, the water rippling behind her.

Perhaps dogs have a sixth sense or perhaps I was projecting my anxiety because Bronte followed me around the kitchen like she was afraid I'd disappear. "It's okay, girl. I'll be fine."

The thought of being back on that highway and being pursued by the banged-up SUV finally gave me pause. I picked up the phone and called Joe. Perhaps he could go with me. The phone went immediately to voicemail. Next, I called Clarence to see if he knew where to find Joe.

"Engstrom." Clarence was never good at polite greetings.

"Clarence, it's Jamie. I'm looking for Joe."

"He went to Duluth to get more of that computer paraphernalia."

I laughed. "He really is introducing you to the twenty-first century."

Clarence harrumphed. "Guess if I'm going to build my law practice, I need it."

I thought about asking Clarence if he wanted to go with me, but I felt silly. I didn't need an escort every time I drove to Cascade. "Tell Joe to give me a call when he gets back. I have more questions for him about the shooting."

The mist cleared into a cloudless light blue as I drove toward Cascade.

When I reached town, I scanned the main street for a dented SUV, but the place appeared to be deserted with a few cars and several pickups parked at the bar and grill. Otherwise, it could have been a set for an old Hollywood ghost town. The only thing missing was the tumbleweed rolling down the middle of the street.

Once through town and heading north, I didn't see a single vehicle. I'd read that a highway in Arizona was named the loneliest highway in America. I decided this one would rival it. Five miles out of town, just as the road rose out of the lowlands, I saw the sign for the gas station. I wondered what the story was behind Eyeman's Corner. It must have been a general store at one time.

The building hadn't been painted in my lifetime, and the sign for the store and gas station swayed with a rusty sound in the morning breeze. An old gas pump sat in front of the building. The only thing that appeared to be new and cared for was a red Coca-Cola dispenser by the door. I pulled up to the side of the building and looked for signs of life. One rusted-out pickup truck was parked on the other side of the building. Otherwise, the place appeared to be deserted. With rue, I remembered my reassuring words to Bronte, "It's a public place."

I saw no signs of the public.

"What have I gotten into?" I looked at my phone to see if I had any messages or texts and realized that I was in a place with a spotty signal. I took a deep breath and opened the car door.

The temperature was warming but still chilly as I walked to the door of the station. A handprinted cardboard sign said, "Closed for Season."

"You've got to be kidding? I just drove fifty miles to find this place closed?" Where was Betsy Latelle? I surveyed the area around the gas station. An unpaved road went perpendicular to the highway and disappeared into a forest, thick with second-growth pine and aspen. A dilapidated metal utility shed stood behind the gas station, and next to it, were the remains of a concrete foundation that could have been a house at one time. I saw no houses or other buildings near the corner.

I should have been more apprehensive. What if I'd been lured out here?

The only person who would know about it was Jim because I'd texted him last night. But Jim was in Minneapolis. Why hadn't I told Clarence? Or left a message for Joe? Or simply stayed home?

"Jamie," I said through gritted teeth. "For a street-smart city girl, you sure are dumb."

Unsure what to do next, I debated going back to the car and sitting in it with the doors locked. My phone said it was 10:10. Betsy was late. My thoughts were interrupted by a gruff voice calling from inside the store. "If you're coming in, then do it."

If this was an ambush, then it was a strange one.

I pushed open the store screen door to find a dimly lit room with shelves for food and supplies. Most of the shelves were empty except for a few canned goods. The air inside smelled of old cigarette smoke, and the wooden floor creaked under my footsteps. Squinting into the room, I saw a shadowy person bent over an old-fashioned beer cooler. He did not turn to acknowledge me as he reached inside.

"Excuse me?" I heard the sound of cans being moved around.

"Wait."

I stood in the doorway, holding the door handle. If I had to, I hoped I could make a quick dash to my car.

When he turned around, I saw a large man with gray-white hair to his shoulders. He carried two cans. One he held up to me. "Coke?"

As my eyes adjusted to the dim light filtering through the dirty, smeared front windows of the store, I saw that he was Native American. He looked to be in his early sixties, with a lined and weathered face. His dark-rimmed glasses were taped at the nose piece and he wore a checked flannel shirt and faded jeans. A sheathed knife was attached to his belt.

I let go of the door handle and took the Coke. The can was icy in my hand. "I'm waiting for Betsy Latelle."

"Not coming."

The man was medium height but squarely built. If he decided to attack, I was no match. Strangely, I didn't sense any danger. I had no spidery feeling on the back of my neck.

"You're that writer lady." It was more a statement than a question.

"Yes," I nodded. "I'm trying to do a story on the shooting." I paused. "Actually, less the shooting and more about the teacher who died."

He turned away from me and walked to a back room. "Come." He led me to a little room that had a wooden table and several chairs. Easing himself into a chair he pointed to one. "Sit and have your Coke."

I slid carefully onto the chair as if it might be wired.

"George Big Horse. Most people call me George. I own this place."

"Nice to meet you. I'm Jamie Forest. Most people call me Jamie."

In the light that filtered through the window, I saw a hint of amusement in his eyes.

"Do you know why Betsy isn't coming?" The Coke was fizzy and too sweet inside my mouth.

"I told her not to. She's my niece, and I don't want to put her in danger."

I took a deep breath. "Wow. This gets weirder and weirder. No one wants to talk to me, and I sense that a lot of people are scared." I leaned forward. "Why? The shooting seemed pretty simple. Deranged kid with a gun targets a group at school."

George peered at me as if he was trying to see inside my head. "Hard to know who to trust. Why are you writing this?"

I had to think for a moment. Why was I writing this? When I answered, I felt I finally understood my need to pursue the story. "Because everything I read about these horrible school shootings focuses on the shooter and not on the people who were killed. I don't really care to say anything about Neil Kavanaugh. I want to look at Tony Vincent and the work he did. Except that no one will talk about him or the shooting. It feels like a conspiracy of silence." The words tumbled out.

George continued to study me. The quietness of the room and his scrutiny made me uncomfortable. I gazed around trying to ignore the way his eyes focused on me. A dark-green, three-drawer filing cabinet sat in the corner. On top was a dead potted plant and behind it a red cap. I caught my breath. It had a confederate logo on it.

Setting the Coke down, I tensed, ready to stand up and leave. "Uh, I guess

I should go then if Betsy isn't coming."

George held out his hand in a stop gesture. "Wait." He followed my gaze to the cap. "That cap's not mine. I keep it as a reminder that bad people still do bad things."

I saw a flash of anger on his lined face. He slowly shook his head as if he was pushing the anger away. "Betsy wanted me to tell you some things."

My shoulders relaxed, but I silently vowed to leave as soon as possible. "What did Betsy want me to know?"

George shifted in his chair and let out a quiet sigh. "She's a good kid, and she wants to do the right thing."

"Okay."

"And you say you want to write about the teacher—the Vincent guy?"

I nodded, wondering where this was going.

"He was the only one who saw the shooter, you know."

This was news to me. The description of the scene had been sketchy. The tapes I'd heard of interviews with the survivors mainly talked about the blood and the chaos and the cries of the wounded students. None mentioned Neil Kavanaugh or how he looked. One of the wounded girls said that she saw Neil run by her with a gun as he fled out an emergency exit in the cafeteria.

"I don't understand what you're getting at."

"Betsy doesn't think that Kavanaugh was the real shooter."

I stared at him. None of the accounts I'd read equivocated on who did the shooting. "Why?"

"Betsy's had a hard time since the shooting. Got into trouble with drugs and alcohol. She's in a program now with some good counselors. She says bits and pieces of memory are coming back to her. The thing is, all the students were at a table facing Vincent. They had their backs to the door where Kavanaugh came in. She remembered at the sound of the gun, she turned around and someone was behind him. Kavanaugh didn't have his gun raised, the other person did."

"Oh my god. That's a whole different story."

"She also thought she heard Kavanaugh yell something like, 'It's a drill.'

76

But she's not sure.

George set the Coke can down hard. It made a thunking noise on the wooden table. "You see. That's why she's scared. If she remembered it right, then the real murderer is still out there."

I was at a loss for words. Is this what Tess meant when she said that Cascade had secrets? "Will she tell the sheriff what she knows?"

"Bolton is no friend of ours." His tone was flat and angry.

Reaching in my bag, I pulled out my phone. "Could I record this?"

George was emphatic in his "No. Too dangerous. In fact, that's what she wanted you to know. If you try to get more information, you could be in big danger."

I thought about the SUV and the red caps and all the warnings. There were so many different threads here—the shooting, the silence about Tony Vincent, the red caps, and maybe even the death of Winston Starling. On top of that, I didn't know how much I could trust George.

We sat in silence as an old wall clock ticked away. The Coke tasted sickly sweet. I set the can down and asked, "Is the death of Winston Starling related to this somehow?"

George glanced over at the red cap and shrugged. "I don't know."

He did know or at least suspected. I could tell by the way he wouldn't look me straight on when he'd answered my question.

George pushed his chair back. "That's it. That's what Betsy wanted you to know. For her sake, I hope you stop your investigating." He stood up. "Best if you don't come around again."

"If Kavanaugh didn't do it, don't you want to know who did?"

"Would it bring back those who died?"

I stood up. "No. But it might prevent it from happening again."

A slight smile twitched at George's lips. "You aren't from around here, are you?"

With that, he walked me to the door. I stepped outside into the sunshine and the sound of crows lined up on the electric wire cawing at me. I felt like my presence in Cascade had scratched the scab off a wound that festered beneath the surface. A truck with a missing muffler roared down the highway moving north. It slowed just enough as it passed the gas station for me to see that the driver wore a red cap.

"Time for me to get the hell out of Dodge."

Chapter Fourteen

Highway Emergency

As I drove the lonely highway through the boggy lowlands, I kept my eye on the rearview mirror for signs of the truck without a muffler. Behind me, I saw only empty road. Traffic picked up when I approached Cascade. I thought about Jay Bolton's call to me about Tess and wondered if I should stop in and find out if she'd turned up.

"Are you kidding? Not my problem." But in some way, it was my problem. I felt like I now had information about the shooting that should go to the sheriff. While I engaged in an internal debate about it, I slowed through downtown Cascade. It wasn't quite as deserted, but still had the air of a dying place. I resolved my dilemma about the sheriff by deciding I'd confer with Clarence first.

Once outside the city limits, I pushed the gas pedal up to highway speed. Relief flooded me. This afternoon I would email my editor friend at *The New Yorker* and tell him I was struggling with getting a good hold on this project. Hopefully, I could pursue it later when...well, I wasn't sure when later would be. Fortunately, I hadn't entered into a contract or received an advance. I would be free to give Florice and her milkmaid my full attention.

My elation at having made this decision lasted about two miles. When I looked into my rearview mirror, flashing red lights approached.

"Please, pass me by on your way somewhere else." The palms of my hands prickled with sweat as I gripped the steering wheel. The patrol car grew closer. I slowed to pull over and he slowed with me. "Damn. Now what?"

I stopped on the gravel shoulder and waited for the sheriff's car. Jim had coached me on the proper etiquette when being stopped. "Wait in the car with your hands on the steering wheel. That way, the trooper won't worry that you have a weapon." As I watched Jay Bolton get out of his car, I wondered what excuse he had for pulling me over. I wasn't speeding, my turn signals worked, and I wasn't on my phone.

When he approached, I noted once again he was walking as if his back bothered him. In fact, it appeared that he was in significant pain as he swayed toward my car. Rolling down my window, I waited, feeling very alone on this stretch of highway.

He leaned in to the window with an expression I couldn't read. "I saw that you were weaving on the highway. Texting while driving?"

Did I detect a slur in his speech? At least I knew his excuse for stopping me. "Hello, Sheriff. No, I wasn't texting. My phone is in my bag on the floor." I pointed to the passenger seat.

"You could have stuck it there right now."

The word stuck came out "shtuck." A slight breeze wafted in the open window and I was sure I smelled something strong like alcohol on his breath. "Are you okay?"

"Get out of the car."

My first temptation was to start the car and drive like crazy until I reached my cabin by the lake. Common sense prevailed, but I wasn't able to erase the fear that caused me to grip hard on the steering wheel. I used the calmest voice I could muster. "I'd prefer not to."

"Come on. Get out." He bumped his hip against the car door trying to maintain his balance.

He was drunk. Of all things, I'd been stopped by a drunken sheriff. What was the protocol for this?

"Sheriff. I don't think you are all right. I think I'll stay in the car." I leaned over to reach for my cell phone. If I called 911, would they radio him?

"Out!" He tapped at his gun, holstered on his belt.

I grabbed my phone and held the phone up so he could see. "I'm calling for help. You aren't okay."

He fell heavily against the door, one hand holding on to the door to steady himself while the other tried to pull out the gun. I quickly hit the emergency call on the phone.

Nothing happened. No bars, no reception.

"Gee out tha car!" His eyes had a wild look to them. If his flailing hand could grip the gun and pull it out of the holster, I would be dead.

"Listen." My voice trembled. "See, I'm getting out. You need to stop leaning against the door so I can open it."

Leaves and dirt eddied against the pavement as the wind gusted through the scrubland that bordered the highway. I looked around to see if I could escape through the passenger side of the car and make a run for the brambles of wild blackberries. I felt like I'd once felt trapped in a holding cell in Queens for a crime I did not commit. No way out. No one to come to the rescue.

Jay backed off, nearly stumbling then righting himself. Maybe I could leap out the door, knock him down, and grab his gun. Maybe, if I was a Hollywood stunt person on a controlled set, I could do that. Here in the middle of nowhere, I needed to play a careful role of the compliant driver.

"Should I get my license and registration before I get out?"

Jay blinked at me as if he was having a hard time focusing. "Wha?" It appeared that he had forgotten about drawing a weapon and concentrated instead on staying on his feet.

Slowly, I opened the car door while I scanned the highway for any cars. Perhaps I could flag one down. The roadway was empty as if someone had blocked traffic going both directions. The only sound was the scrape of the leaves washing across the road and the distant cawing of crows.

Once out of the car, I pressed myself against the door. Jay blinked at me, opened his mouth as if to say something, and lurched at me. He tripped as he approached and slammed into my body.

Where were the cars? The trucks? Anyone to witness this scene. I was pinned against the car door while Jay panted and tried to push himself upright. His face was directly in mine and I could see not lust or anger, but extreme confusion as he slowly slipped to the ground.

"Jay. Talk to me."

He slumped to his side, falling on his gun.

With my heart racing, I stooped down to check on him. Nothing in my experience told me what to do in this situation. "Jay, can you talk to me?"

"Wha?" Sweat beaded on his forehead.

In desperation, I looked in both directions for someone. Right now, I'd even take the dented SUV filled with red caps. I reached in the car for my phone and for the bottle of water I kept in the cupholder.

I tried the emergency button again and again nothing happened. Twisting the cap off the water bottle, I brought some to his lips. "Can you drink this?"

Jay did not respond. Years ago, my father had sent me to a first responder class where they'd taught us CPR. One of the first things the instructor had said was "Don't start chest compressions unless you are sure the heart has stopped."

I checked for a carotid pulse. It thumped against my finger. Was he simply drunk and passed out?

Maybe if I could figure out how to use his radio, I could get help. He didn't have anything on him, but I could hear the scratchy sound of the radio in his car. As I stood up to run to his car, I heard the sound of an approaching truck.

Oh, please be someone who could help. If they saw the flashing lights of the sheriff's car, maybe they would slow, and I could flag them down. Instead, it was a logging truck filled with fresh-cut trees, and it was speeding. It whooshed by me kicking up dirt and gravel.

Blinking away tears from the dirt spray, I knelt down again by Jay and took his hand. It was cold and clammy. That's when I noticed that he wore a medical alert bracelet. Jay was diabetic. That's why his breath had smelled so sickly sweet, he wasn't drunk he was in a diabetic crisis.

My college roommate was diabetic. I knew from my experience with her that this was a health emergency. Jay probably needed insulin, and here I was without cell connection.

For a moment I was frozen. If I didn't do something, this man could die. I needed to figure out the radio in his car, or I needed to get him in my car to drive him to the hospital. Another vehicle approached coming from the opposite direction. I ran out onto the pavement waving my arms. "Please help!" I yelled knowing the driver couldn't hear me. The car slowed when it saw me and turned on its flashers. It was a maroon-colored Minnesota State Patrol vehicle. The trooper did a U-turn and pulled up behind the sheriff's car.

He got out of the car with his hand hovering by his gun. It occurred to me that he thought I'd done something to Jay. I didn't care as long as he didn't shoot first and ask questions later.

"Hurry," I yelled. "We need an ambulance!"

He ran to me, already talking on his radio. When he squatted down next to me. I pointed to the bracelet on Jay's wrist. "I think he's having a diabetic reaction. He was acting strange when he pulled me over and then he collapsed."

The trooper checked for a pulse, pulled off his jacket, and put it under Jay's head. He bent down and listened for breathing. "Should we try to get some sugar in him?"

"No," I shook my head emphatically. "He's got too much glucose in his system. I think he needs insulin."

"You a doctor?"

I almost said, no I'm a poet. "I had a friend who was diabetic. This happened to her once when we were walking back to our dorm from dinner. The paramedics gave her insulin."

It seemed like it took the ambulance an hour to come. In reality, it was probably no more than ten minutes. I told him how Jay had pulled me over and how he was wobbly on his feet and slurred his speech.

"I thought he was drunk until he collapsed. When I saw the medical alert, I remembered my roommate. His breath didn't smell of alcohol, it smelled fruity, just like hers had."

The ambulance arrived at the same time as a Cascade sheriff's deputy. The deputy ran to the scene. "Jesus god, it's Jay."

I filled the EMTs in on what little I knew including the medical alert bracelet. They loaded him onto a stretcher and sped away with lights flashing and the siren wailing.

The trooper and the deputy spoke quietly with each other while I stood on the shoulder not knowing what to do with myself. Did they need me to stay?

Meanwhile, the deputy went back to his car and headed in the direction of the ambulance. At least I didn't have to talk with him.

"Are you okay?" The trooper walked over to me.

My heart still thumped like I'd been in a race. It must have shown on my face. My hand shook as I took a drink of water. Was I okay? Probably not, but I wasn't about to tell him that. All I wanted was to get in my car and drive home to Bronte. "I'll be fine. Just a little rattled."

He cleared his throat. "Um, well, I hate to do this, but I need to see your license before I can let you go. I'll also need to get a report from you on what happened."

Dismay must have been written all over my face when I silently opened the car door and pulled out my bag with the driver's license.

He studied the license and looked at me with a puzzled expression. "You're the one who talked with Winnie before he died."

It was then that I noticed the resemblance. Although he was older, maybe in his mid-thirties, he had Winnie's face shape including the light skin and freckles. I couldn't see the color of his eyes because he wore dark glasses, but I guessed they were the same muddy blue.

His name tag said, Travis Booker. "Um, are you related to Winnie?"

"My cousin." In a grim voice, he added, "We need to talk."

How I wished Clarence had been with me. Would I end up behind bars?

Perhaps he noticed the expression on my face because his expression softened. "I mean, let's talk over lunch."

Curious, now, I allowed myself a brief smile. "Okay. As long as you aren't arresting me."

"Not yet, at least."

I wasn't sure if he was serious or not.

He pointed to his car. "Follow me into Cascade and I'll buy you coffee. We can debrief there."

CHAPTER FOURTEEN

Once again, I found myself at the Cascade Bar and Grill. Would I ever be rid of that town?

Chapter Fifteen

Travis

A s I parked in front of the Cascade Bar and Grill, the noon whistle blew. A siren telling the town it was noon was a new phenomenon for me. In Manhattan, we had all sorts of bells and beeps and horns but none of them signaled noontime. I was told it was a throwback from days when most people worked outside, and it was the signal to go in for lunch.

People in Cascade must have taken it seriously because the restaurant was full. We found the last booth in the back near the doorway to the pool room. People stared when Travis and I walked in. He greeted a few of them as he led the way to the empty booth.

Behind me, I heard a few whispers.

"That's the woman who's stirring things up."

"Why can't those people let it go."

I was tempted to turn to them and tell them that I had no plans to set foot in Cascade County again. My days of investigative journalism were over. Instead, I slipped silently into the booth feeling tension grip my shoulders.

Travis sat opposite me. Now that we were inside and away from the drama on the highway, I had a chance to study him. I was shocked to note how much he looked like an older, slimmer version of Winnie. They could have been brothers. He watched me with a serious expression.

"Sorry. I don't usually stare but you look so much like your cousin." I thought about how Winnie relished the cheeseburger just before he died and felt an ache in the back of my throat. "I only met him once, but he seemed like a nice guy."

"He was." Travis stared at the table.

I wanted to ask him what he knew about the accident, but it really was none of my business. We were locked into an uncomfortable silence until the waitress came. It was Madelyn, the one who had warned me the other day. She smiled at Travis as if they knew each other.

"Hi, Mads," he took the menu from her. "How are you doing?"

She turned her head slightly to indicate the pool room. "Glad someone else is serving them." Her voice was tight.

Travis nodded as if he understood what she was talking about.

I ordered coffee and a BLT. Travis ordered a cheeseburger. Madelyn grinned. "You want I should bring an extra ketchup for you?"

I was about to say something about ketchup and Winnie, but I caught myself. Might not be good to bring it up right now. Harsh laughter came from the pool room. It sounded almost like the barking of a dog. It was followed by a string of four-letter words.

Clearing my throat, I said, "Did you want to debrief?" I took my business card out of my bag and handed it to him. "In case you need to reach me again."

He held it up for a moment and a look of sorrow crossed his face. "They found your card in Winnie's pocket. Did anyone tell you?"

Remembering the accusing expression on Jay's face, the other day in the courthouse, I said, "Yes. The sheriff made sure to tell me about the card." I didn't tell Travis about the leather glove, but I guessed he already knew.

"Why did he have your card?" He didn't look at me.

I drew back at the tension in his tone. Did he think I had something to do with the death? "We had dinner together just before, um, before he had his accident. I gave him my card in case he had anything else to tell me about the teacher who died in the shooting. I was planning to do a story about him." I made little circles on the table to keep calm. "But I think I will put the project on hold."

Madelyn brought the coffee along with an extra bottle of ketchup. She lingered at the table for a moment, unconsciously pushing a tendril of hair away from her face. "Need anything else right now?"

Travis smiled at her in a distracted way. "We're fine, Mads."

In the back room, someone shouted, "You asshole!" It was followed by some bumps and thumps and more swearing. I wondered if Travis, as a lawman, would get up and intervene. He read my look. "Not my jurisdiction."

Considering that we had just sent the sheriff off in an ambulance, I wondered who would come if a fight broke out. I said nothing.

A short man in dirty jeans and a faded T-shirt that clung to his growing belly stomped out of the room. He wore the red baseball cap with the confederate logo. I cringed as Travis reached out and grabbed his arm. "Now Roger, don't get worked up. You don't want to violate your probation."

"Fuck you, Booker!" He ripped his arm away.

I pushed myself hard against the back of the booth trying to shrink into the fake leather upholstery. The man with the cap was the passenger in the dented SUV that tried to push me off the road. His unkempt sideburns were a dead giveaway.

As Roger stormed out, the restaurant became eerily quiet. The only sounds were guffaws coming from the pool room and the clanking of dishes from the kitchen. Travis watched until Roger was out of the building.

When he turned to me, he frowned at the expression on my face. "Are you all right? He's just a small-town redneck—my brother went to high school with him."

"I...I think he tried to run me off the road the other day."

I told him about the SUV and the passenger with the red cap. Travis grimaced. "You could file a report. I'd like to see him back in jail."

"No. I couldn't positively identify him. It was dark, and I was too scared to know for sure."

Travis mumbled something as he wiped a splotch of ketchup off the table. It amazed me how much he was like his cousin.

"Did you say something?"

He looked up. "Sorry. I was thinking about all the hell that Red Cap Militia raised around here. I hoped it wouldn't come back to haunt us now that Kavanaugh is out of prison."

"Stone Kavanaugh? I heard he murdered a banker. I wondered if he was related to the Kavanaugh who did the shooting."

Travis took a deep breath and gazed at the wall behind me. Outside, a car roared down the road. When I looked out the window, I saw it was a battered SUV. Boy, did I want to get out of town.

"Stone Kavanaugh is Neil's uncle. He was one of the main leaders twenty years ago when the militia was on the loose. He should have been sentenced to life without parole, but he got out several years ago."

"I heard he was big with the militia and that they were a white supremacist group."

"That's what Stone wanted the dumbasses in the group to think. Had all sorts of neo-Nazi literature and slogans. But I don't think Stone cared one way or another. He wanted money and simply didn't want to pay taxes and thought the government owed him for—well, I'm not sure what he thought he was owed. In his cold heart, he was nothing but an outlaw. The whole group got busted for selling stolen property."

Madelyn arrived with the food. She leaned in far enough to touch Travis's shoulder as she set down his plate. "Got everything you need?"

I wondered if I was reading something into her question. Travis responded with a smile. "Best cheeseburgers in the state."

"You got it."

After she walked away, I commented, "She seems nice."

"Uh huh."

Sometimes men are such dopes. I bit into my BLT and found that they'd cooked the bacon to perfection.

"Tell me more about Stone Kavanaugh."

Travis set down the cheeseburger while he squeezed more ketchup onto his fries. "He murdered my uncle. Winnie's dad."

I stared at him. "Wow."

"Yeah."

Between bites of food he told me that Winnie's dad, Sam Starling was the local banker. Stone Kavanaugh had property outside of Cascade. He was behind on his payments. Sam went out to talk with him and Kavanaugh shot him. Details of the shooting were sketchy but Kavanaugh claimed it was self-defense. He was convicted in a messy trial.

"Kavanaugh was popular with a fringe part of the population. I was fifteen at the time and remember things were pretty ugly around town for a while. The Starlings even got death threats. Like some of those idiots thought it was poor Aunt Alice's fault that Kavanaugh was on trial. Winnie was just five, and I don't know what he remembered of it. His mother moved the family to Duluth shortly after the trial."

"But he came back to Cascade?"

"After college. I never understood it. He was such a great kid. Why come back to a place where your father was murdered and your family threatened?"

Madelyn brought coffee refills. "I see you cleaned your plate."

Travis handed her the empty platter. "Yes, ma'am."

"Pie?"

Travis looked at me, and I shook my head. I was ready to leave Cascade permanently.

We were interrupted by Travis's phone. I dug in my bag for money to pay for my sandwich while he talked. He mainly listened and when he put the phone away, he said, "Dispatcher says Jay will be okay. They're keeping him overnight for a few tests and then they will let him go."

"That's a relief."

"Which reminds me, why was he pulling you over?"

I shrugged. "I don't know. I get the sense he doesn't like me much."

"Not a good reason to pull someone over. Now, his dad, John would have done that. He had the scruples of a cop on the take. But Jay, he isn't a bad guy."

Madelyn came back with the checks. "You can pay up front." She giggled. "And I didn't charge extra for all the ketchup."

I watched her walk away. It seemed her hips swayed a little more. Travis didn't notice.

"I need to get back." I slid out of the seat.

"I'm headed for Killdeer to check in on Jay. I'll follow you and make sure Roger doesn't harass you."

Escorted out of town. What a great way to finish this episode.

Chapter Sixteen

Call for Help

B y the time I got back to Killdeer, it was midafternoon. I thought about stopping to talk with Clarence about my meeting with George Big Horse but realized this was his naptime. Best to catch him in the morning. I wanted to hand it over to him and let him decide if something should be reported.

Behind me, Travis flicked his lights and turned left to the hospital. My escort was completed. Now home to Bronte and a life without Cascade. My big question was how I could afford not to do the article for *The New Yorker*.

"Worry about that later. Maybe you could head to the casino and make a fortune."

Last summer I'd been very lucky with a poker machine. The winnings would keep me afloat for another month. After that? Hopefully, Florice had a friend who needed some editing.

As luck would have it, a package sat between the screen and my backdoor. After giving Bronte her expected attention, I ripped it open. It was another manuscript with a check included.

"See," I pointed to it. "The stars are aligned."

Bronte waggled her tail with enthusiasm.

The manuscript was indeed from a writer friend of Florice. Letty DeVoss wanted the editing on paper and she, too, was willing to pay my price.

"Hurray."

My enthusiastic bubble burst when I read the title. *The Vladess of Transylvania: Nights of Blood and Roses.* I detested books that portrayed vampires as romantic.

Bram Stoker's *Dracula* had a significant impact on me when I read it as a teenager. In fact, the book scared the daylights out of me to the point where I wondered if I should convert to Catholicism so I could wear a crucifix around my neck.

"This is going to be a challenge," I told Bronte. "Four hundred pages of it. And what's the thing about roses these days. One you pluck and the other comes with blood?" Bronte ignored me.

Paging through it, I found the first grammatical error on page two. "Her lips yearned to taste the red blood that surged through his veins as she laid in bed."

"Will people ever figure out the correct way to use lie, lay, and laid?" Bronte trotted over to me with a sympathetic expression.

I set the manuscript aside and texted Jim. **Cascade project a mess. Need to talk. Give me a call.**

Jim called me five minutes after my text.

"Hey," I said. "How's it going?"

"Okay."

I'd learned in my short time in Minnesota that people around here tended to minimize problems. A reply of anything less than "fine," meant things were not going well.

"Something is wrong, isn't it?"

Jim's voice had a catch in it. "Jake's having a hard time of it." He filled me in on the details. Jake's blood counts were low, and he had developed a fever. "They're treating him for pneumonia, and he hates being in the hospital. He keeps asking when he can go home."

I pictured the bright-eyed little boy with Jim's face shape and found I had no words except trite phrases. Instead, I simply said, "I'm so sorry."

"Marie isn't handling it well. We've been taking turns at the hospital but…
"

I waited for him to continue.

"She's, uh, drinking. I have to keep an eye on her."

A pang of unreasonable anger welled up inside me. Why did he have to care for her as well as a son he didn't really know? I took a deep breath, let it out, and said, "That must be hard."

For a few moments, silence filled the airwaves. When Jim spoke again, he asked, "So how are things with you? I hope you are treading carefully with the Cascade thing."

My issues with Cascade seemed trivial at this point. I quickly filled him in on my trip, talking mostly about the medical incident with Jay Bolton.

"He collapsed after he pulled you over?"

"Once I saw his medical alert bracelet, I knew he was in trouble. Fortunately, one of your State Trooper buddies showed up." I told him about Travis Booker and how he followed me back to Killdeer.

"Booker. He's not a bad guy. I heard a rumor that he's considering running for sheriff in Cascade County."

"Really? Against Bolton?"

"Yup."

I told him about the manuscript that had just landed on my doorstep. "Seriously, she titled it *Nights of Blood and Roses.* Yuck."

Jim chuckled. "I guess I'm glad I'm not stuck in the cabin with you when you're editing it."

Even though he laughed, I felt it was forced. I wasn't sure what I could offer him, but I tried. "I can come to visit you if that would help."

The line was silent for too long. "I think it would be better if you didn't."

We talked for a few minutes in generalities about the weather and things I needed to do to get the cabin ready for winter. Before he hung up, he said, "I'll call you when I can. Take care."

As if she sensed my unease with the phone call, Bronte walked over to me where I sat at the kitchen table, and nuzzled my lap. I set the phone down and looked out the window at the lake. The water glittered in the afternoon waning sun. "It's not what he said, it's what he didn't say." I stroked the soft fur on her head. I knew what Jim really wanted to say. "Don't call me. I don't have time for you."

"Let's go outside and get some fresh air, girl."

Bronte responded by trotting to the door. Instead of walking down to the lake, I took the path behind the cabin into the woods. While I loved my thinking rock on the lakeshore, I also loved the whisper of wind through the trees and the rustle of the leaves on the forest floor.

As I stepped outside, a bald eagle soared high above me. I smiled at it, feeling the tension of the phone call melt a little. Perhaps it was the quarter Ojibwe blood in me, or perhaps it was simply my resolve to drop the Cascade story. The walk in the woods calmed me. Bronte bounded ahead, disappearing in the underbrush, while I stopped to admire the palette of colors from the greens of the pines to the reds of the sumac.

The peace was interrupted by my phone. I pulled it out of my pocket, wishing I'd left it on the kitchen table. I expected it to be Jim calling back to apologize. Instead, the caller ID was "unavailable." I should have let it go and continued my walk, but something told me this was important.

"This is Jamie Forest."

"Can you help me?" It was a female voice, high and tremulous.

"Who is this?" Immediately I wondered if this was a prank call.

"Tess. It's Tess from the school the other day." She spoke so fast I hardly understood her. The phone crackled with static.

I kept my voice slow and calm. "What is it, Tess?"

"I can't get home and they took my phone and all I had was your card in my pocket. I want to come home." Her voice faded.

"Tess, where are you? I can call your folks to come and get you." I shouted into the phone.

I heard a sob on the line. "No, can't tell them."

"What is going on? Are you in trouble?"

I heard voices in the background. Tess whispered, "They're coming. They said something about the island."

"What island? Where are you?"

"I can't..." Abruptly the call disconnected. I quickly tried redial but nothing happened.

Bronte came running back with a stick as I stared at my phone. "What was that all about?" Was Tess in trouble or was I being pranked? I pictured her standing alone in the school parking lot with her heavy makeup and Doc Martens and decided I needed to take the phone call seriously.

"This is turning into a no good, lousy day." I picked up the stick and threw it as hard as I could into the woods.

Chapter Seventeen

Uncle Jay

I stared at the darkened phone screen as if it would tell me what to do next. I could call the Cascade sheriff's office. I could simply call 911 and let them deal with this. Neither of those options felt like the right thing to do.

Jay, Tess's uncle, was in the hospital in Killdeer. He'd called me this week to ask about Tess. He was the person I needed to talk with. I hurried back to the cabin where I had better cell reception. Bronte chased after me, the newly retrieved stick in her mouth.

"Not now, girl."

Once inside, I took a moment to catch my breath before I called the hospital.

Killdeer Memorial was a small community hospital. Most of the calls went directly to the nurse's station. As the phone rang, I prayed that whoever answered would let me talk to Jay.

"Killdeer Memorial, this is Norma."

Thank god. I knew Norma because we both volunteered for the Lady Slipper Trail, a volunteer trail maintenance group. She was a workhorse, who happily pitched in digging out roots on the trail and laying down woodchips. She was also the head nurse for the hospital.

"Norma, it's Jamie Forest. I really need to speak with Jay Bolton. Is he still there?"

"You and about four hundred other people. I had to take away his cell phone so he could get some rest."

"Could I come by and see him?" It occurred to me that this conversation needed to be in person.

"I don't see any visitor restrictions on his chart. Just so you know, he's been itching to leave. Doc wants him overnight to try to get his insulin regulated. I've been instructed to tackle him if he tries to sneak out." She chuckled.

Norma was a square, muscular woman. I didn't think he had a chance against her.

The ten-mile drive to Killdeer from Lake Larissa felt like it took forever. Tess's voice rang in my head. She sounded so scared.

The sun was setting when I arrived in town. Main Street was nearly empty except for the Loonfeather Café. I guessed it was filled with locals, winding down from the day's work. Jim and I would go there on Sunday evenings when he wasn't working. They had an all-you-can-eat fish fry. The food wasn't particularly good, but the companionship was. This evening would be the "Taco Tuesday" special. Tacos at the Loonfeather were similar to the cheap frozen ones that you microwaved, but the customers didn't mind.

The hospital visitor's lot was nearly empty. As I pulled into a parking slot, a pickup truck pulled out. The driver wore a red baseball cap. It was too dark to see if it was one of the militia caps, but as he drove away, I found my palms had broken out in a sweat.

When I walked in, Norma was at the nurse's station talking on the phone. She glanced up at me and pointed to the room directly across from her.

Jay dozed, his face pale against the white pillowcase. An IV pump made rhythmic clicking noises next to the bed. The only light in the room came from the open door to the bathroom and a muted light above the bed.

Clearing my throat, I walked into the room, my shoes making a squeaking noise on the polished floor.

He opened his eyes and blinked at me in some confusion. "You?"

Already I regretted my decision to talk with him. I should have called 911 like a normal person.

CHAPTER SEVENTEEN

"How are you feeling?" I worked to keep the tension out of my voice.

He wrinkled his brow. "Why are you here?"

I couldn't read his expression in the shadowy light of the room. Was it accusing or simply bewildered? "I need to talk to you about Tess."

He fumbled with the control to lift the head of the bed. "What about Tess?"

Maybe he hadn't remembered that he'd called me about her. "You called me the other day looking for information on her. You said she hadn't been home."

He shook his head. "I don't think so."

That was not the answer I expected, but I decided this wasn't the time to argue. "She called me today. She sounded scared."

As I stood at the foot of his bed, what little color he had in his cheeks appeared to drain. What was he hiding?

He shook his head. "No. She's home, and she's fine."

The fear in her voice came back to me. "Are you sure? She called me less than an hour ago. She said they took her phone and something about an island. She sounded scared and she wanted to go home."

He stiffened, his hands gripping the thin blanket on the bed. "Prank. Just a prank."

I wanted to argue with him, but I had no basis other than an interrupted phone call. "Please check with her parents. Would you at least do that?"

When he looked at me, I was sure alarm registered in his eyes. When he spoke, his speech was slurred like a drunk. "Not your business. Leave it alone."

"Okay," I shrugged, determined to check with her parents myself. On my way out, I said, "I hope you are feeling better."

He didn't reply.

At the nurse's station, I stopped to talk with Norma. Gesturing to Jay's room, I whispered, "Something is not right with him."

Her nod was almost imperceptible. I knew she couldn't give me any information on his medical condition, and I didn't want to put her on the spot. However, I did ask if he'd had any visitors.

"That good-looking trooper stopped by this afternoon."

"Travis Booker?"

"You know him, huh? You certainly get around," she winked at me. "I hear he does, too."

I was about to retort when I changed my mind. People in this part of the country didn't talk back. I pursed my lips and tried to look offended. Judging by Norma's expression, I wasn't particularly successful.

The sound of a soft snore wafted from Jay's room.

Norma leaned close to me over the desk. In a low voice, she said, "You didn't hear this from me, but he had another visitor just before you came. Older guy with the meanest eyes I've ever seen. People don't usually spook me, but that man did."

I thought about the person with the red cap leaving the parking lot. "Did he wear a red baseball cap?"

"It had an ugly logo on it, like a confederate flag. I think he scared Jay. He was so agitated that I had to give him a sedative."

"He seemed kind of out of it."

"Remember, though, I didn't tell you that."

"Scout's honor."

We talked a little about progress on the Lady Slipper Trail and the grant we'd applied for to build a wooden walkway over a swampy part of the trail. I wanted to ask Norma more about the man with the mean eyes. To my shame, I also wanted to ask what she meant by saying that Travis Booker got around. I was saved when a light and a buzzer went off in a room down the hall.

Norma stood up and moved swiftly and quietly to the patient's room. For a large woman, she moved with a grace that I would never have.

I walked into the shadowed parking lot, checking my phone. Jim had texted while I was inside.

Sorry for being a jerk. Jake better this afternoon. Hope to see you this weekend.

I texted a thumbs up emoji, but still felt things were not right between the two of us.

A voice startled me as I stood in the empty lot concentrating on my phone.

100

"We meet again."

"Whoa," I gasped. "I didn't see you."

Travis was out of uniform and talked to me through the rolled-down window of his car. He drove a Ford Focus, not the car I expected from a lawman.

"What are you doing here?" He asked.

"I had to tell Jay Bolton something."

"Really?"

Frowning at him, I hoped he'd get the idea it was none of his business. I'm not sure he read my expression. Sometimes the best defense is a good offense. At least that's what Florice's milkmaid said in *Pluck the Rose*. I had crossed it out with a note to the author that I doubted they used those terms back in the days of the Vikings.

I tried it. "And what are you doing lurking in the parking lot?"

He chuckled but didn't answer the question. In a little swampy area behind the hospital, crickets chirped as the twilight turned to dark. The night air smelled of mist and fall decay.

"Interested in a drink?" he asked. "It's still happy hour at the Loonfeather and two tacos for two bucks."

Why not? After everything that had happened, I felt like I'd earned it. I opened my car door and said, "Meet you there."

A beer and a greasy taco sounded pretty good right now.

Chapter Eighteen

The KKK

We found a table by the window and ordered beers and tacos. Without his trooper's hat and uniform, Travis appeared both shorter and younger. Again, I noted the resemblance with Winnie.

"So," he said, drawing out the word. "Jay Bolton."

"We do seem to have him in common. I'm curious to know why you were in the parking lot."

He leaned back with a half-smile. "Wondering the same thing about you."

My father, who was an educator, had no time for beating around the bush. He'd tell me to get to the point. His voice echoed in my head.

I folded my arms on the table. "All right. I don't really know you, but I'm not sure who else I can talk with. So here goes." I told him about meeting Tess at the school, slipping her my card, and her phone call this afternoon. "She said, 'the island.' Do you know what she was talking about?"

Travis rubbed his cheeks before replying. "Gravediggers Island is the only one I can think of near Cascade."

I pictured the crude map from Tony's box. "You mean the one on Nearbow lake?"

"It's where Kavanaugh stored the stolen goods. The only way to get there is by floatplane, boat or snowmobile in the winter. The lake is not a recreational lake. Hardly anyone goes there."

"Maybe she was referring to something else? A hangout or something? Although I'm sure she said they took her phone. Who would 'they' be?"

Travis leaned forward wrinkling his brow. "I don't like the sound of this."

I told him about my brief conversation with Jay at the hospital. "He said Tess was home, and it was a family issue. The message was clear, 'butt out.'"

When the beer came, mine was more foam than liquid. I let it sit on the table. Travis drank his like he had just come off a desert trek.

He drained half the glass before he put it down. "Let me tell you a little about Jay and his family."

I bit into my taco wondering how they could make the hamburger filling taste so bland. Another thing I was learning about Minnesota, people weren't into spicy food.

Travis continued, "I grew up in Cascade. My mother was Winnie's aunt. After Winnie's father was murdered, my folks said, 'enough,' and we moved to the Cities. I remember them talking about Jay's dad, John, the sheriff. My dad, who never swore, called Bolton a 'damned godless jackass.'"

Outside a truck without a muffler roared by. It reminded me of the dented SUV, and I suppressed a shiver. "I'd heard John Bolton was corrupt."

"Criminal. Could have been the model for a fat white sheriff in Alabama. But the murder brought a lot of attention to Cascade and Bolton ended up being investigated. He eventually went to prison." Travis finished his beer and signaled the bartender for another. "We were all surprised when Jay ran for sheriff a couple of years ago. As far as I know, he had no law enforcement experience except for a certificate from a community college. My dad wondered if he would take up where his dad left off."

"Did he?" My beer tasked too yeasty. I set it down.

"No. I actually think that he has been trying to make amends. But he has the personality and authority of a toothless, snarling dog."

I pictured a toothless, snarling dog, and the description fit. "I sense he's scared of something."

Travis nodded as the bartender walked over and handed him another beer. "Cascade County has always had an element of lawlessness. The Red Caps aren't the first group like that. Believe it or not, they had a pretty active Ku

Klux Klan chapter back in the nineteen twenties."

"KKK in Minnesota?" I'd learned since moving here that the rural culture was one of restraint and politeness. "Don't people talk about 'Minnesota nice'?"

"What might come across on the outside as nice sometimes covers something darker. Yup, even here. The KKK was active and in some places, very open."

I thought about my Native American ancestors and wondered if they had been visited by men in white cloaks and pointed hats. More family history that had been lost when my mother died.

"Could the school shooting be part of this?"

Travis shrugged. "I've wondered." He paused to take a big bite of his taco. Sauce dribbled onto his shirt and he absently wiped it. He had nearly finished his second beer while I had barely touched mine. "But there are others in Cascade who believe it had to do with that teacher and Neil Kavanaugh's sister Marla."

"Really?" I leaned forward remembering that I'd heard a sentence or two about Tony and Marla on the interview tapes with the survivors and also a note in his appointment book. "What do you know?"

"Only that she worked at the school and there was a rumor that he was seeing her."

"Neil shot the teacher and the other kids because of a romance with his sister?" Somehow, it didn't make sense to me—especially after what George Big Horse had told me. I almost told Travis about the conversation this morning, but I wanted to consult with Clarence before involving anyone in law enforcement.

We talked a little more about the shooting. I told him I had become interested in it last summer when I met Joe. "I wanted to do a story on Tony Vincent because he was Native and because you read so little about those who have been killed in these school shootings."

"Another shameful chapter in the history of Cascade." Travis signaled to the bartender for another beer. I continued to nurse mine.

"Well, my project hasn't gone very well. No one wants to talk to me. It's like a lynching I read about in the South, where fifty years later people still won't talk about it."

A flush had risen on Travis's cheeks as he worked his way through the third beer. "It's a tight community."

"No kidding."

Travis finished his beer about the time I finished mine. His words were beginning to slur, and it was time for me to head back to the cabin. I made a point of looking at my watch. "Wow, it's later than I thought. I need to go."

"Sure you can't stay for another one?"

"No, my dog needs me."

"Your dog, huh?" Travis stood up as I eased out of my chair. "I'll walk you to your car."

"No need. It's right out front here." I pointed out the window hoping he'd leave it at that. Travis with three beers in him made me a little uneasy. Fortunately, as I put money on the table for my food and beer, a clerk I recognized from the grocery store walked in. She had dark hair cut in a Cleopatra style with straight bangs and dark make-up on her eyes. She waved.

"Hey, Trav, how are you?" While his attention was on her, I slipped out hoping he wouldn't notice.

The stars glittered overhead as I drove out of town. In Manhattan, I'd never paid much attention to the sky other than to watch the airplanes roar by. Here, nighttime, especially when the skies were clear, was magical. When I pulled onto the darkened highway, I saw a falling star. Was that a good omen or a bad omen? I wasn't sure.

Out on the deserted highway, I thought about my conversation with Travis. It occurred to me I never found out why he was sitting in the parking lot of the hospital.

Once home, I fed Bronte and fixed myself a cup of tea. I needed to wash the taste of bad taco filling and yeasty beer out of my mouth. The warmth of the tea felt good. In Northern Minnesota when the sun goes down in the fall, the chill rises quickly. The cabin had cooled off, and I didn't want to start the furnace because I was trying to conserve propane.

"Want a fire?" I looked at Bronte. She wagged her tail.

Rob, a friend who had done some of the remodeling work on the cabin last summer had taught me about building fires. As a city girl my only experience with them had been the one disastrous summer Dad had sent me to summer camp in Upstate New York. Instead of learning how to build a fire, we all got food poisoning from bad hamburger. The camp sent us home, and I spent the rest of the summer reading and hanging out with friends. The only wilderness survival skill I learned was to make sure not to leave raw hamburger out in hot weather.

I crumpled newspaper and built a nest of kindling on top of it before lighting the fire. Slowly, I fed it larger and larger pieces of wood until the fire was stable enough to add logs. Bronte sat next to me, mesmerized by the flames.

"Good enough, huh?"

After I built the fire, I settled on the rug in front of it with my laptop and checked my email. I had one query from a writer who had heard about me through Florice and wondered about my rates. I didn't think I could take on another romance quite yet, so I replied that I had a waiting list and if she wanted to be on it, I would require a deposit. In my near-broke state as an independent contractor, I'd gotten tougher about collecting money upfront.

My phone rang just as I hit send.

"It's Joe. You called?"

With the fire sending a warmth through me, I told him about George Big Horse and what he'd said about the shooting. When I was finished, Joe's first reaction was a simple, "Oh." I waited, knowing that he would eventually say something.

When he finally talked, his words were slow and hesitant. "Don't like thinking about it. I had my back to the door. Uh, but Frank, Jenny, and Mr. Vincent were facing the shooter, I guess."

Interesting. More than one person saw the shooter.

"Do you remember hearing anything?"

He hesitated. "Pretty much a blur. Gunshots and Frank fell to the floor, and I tried to reach him."

The fire crackled and hissed licking at the bark on a birch log. I watched it flair up as Joe struggled to talk. I realized how painful this was for him. "Listen, Joe, I don't want to put you through this. I know how awful it was. Let's leave it."

"No, I remember now. Just before the shots, Mr. Vincent looked at someone and frowned. Then the shooting happened. I thought he was frowning at Neil, but maybe not." He stopped for a moment. "It seems like when it happened, and people were screaming, I heard something else. Something like, 'It's only supposed to be a drill.' But I might have dreamed it up."

I mulled this over. "Do you think what George told me was possible?"

"Don't know."

I remembered one other thing from my conversation with Matt. "Mr. Whitacre said his wife Charity was helping with the diversity project. Do you remember her?"

The line was silent for a few moments. "No, I don't remember her helping. I remember she came to the school a few times. Nice looking and real sophisticated like."

Hermes bag and all.

The line crackled. "Joe? Are you still there?"

After more static on the phone, it went quiet. Cell phone reception on the shores of Lake Larissa could be iffy. I waited for him to call back, but the phone stayed silent. I checked and I had my usual three bars. Joe must have been out of range. No sense calling him back.

Flames around the birch log subsided into a yellow glow of embers. Bronte sighed next to me, snuggling close as I stared at the fire. It should have calmed me, yet I glanced at the silent phone, feeling a growing apprehension. My resolve to let the shooting story go melted as I watched the fire slowly die out. If I didn't do something, the truth would stay buried.

"Well, girl, I think I've really stepped in it."

She lifted her head, licked the back of my hand, and settled back down. I used the poker to jab some life back into the fire. What next?

Chapter Nineteen

The Furnace

As the fire died out, I felt cold creeping up my back. I needed to either turn on the furnace or build the fire up. With a sigh, I stood up. "Time to get more wood." Bronte wagged her tail. "No, you stay in. We might have a skunk in the woodpile."

The last thing I needed was to have her scare a skunk. Rob had warned me last summer that skunks carried rabies. "People worry about rabid bats, but they aren't as big a problem as skunks. Plus," he'd added. "You've never experienced something so nauseating as a direct spray from one of them. It takes weeks to get the smell out of your skin."

Last summer Bronte had been sprayed once. It took several baths in tomato juice before I could let her in the house. Poor girl, she didn't understand why she'd been banished.

Outside, my eyes adjusted to the dark. Mist rose from the lake and the air had a damp chill about it. We hadn't had a hard freeze yet, which people said was unusual. More evidence of the earth's temperature rising. Still, with the longer nights and shorter days, the big chill was just around the corner.

I took a deep breath of the fresh air before piling my canvas carrier with logs. Tomorrow, when it was light outside, I'd bring more in.

Once the fire was crackling again, I opened my laptop thinking about Tess and our brief conversation in the school parking lot. Something about the way she talked about Neil stuck with me. I decided to find out more about him. How did he commit suicide? Did he shoot himself after being apprehended? Nothing I'd read gave me an indication of how he died.

I started by simply googling his name. He was briefly mentioned in an article about the shooting, but nothing else appeared.

"Wouldn't there be a death notice somewhere?" I looked at Bronte. She was so comfortable in front of the fire she didn't bother to lift her head.

My next step was to look at vital statistics. Unfortunately, in order to find the record on him, I needed either his birth date or his social security number.

As the fire died down, I realized I was exhausted. It took some effort not to fall asleep in front of the fireplace. "Bedtime, girl." Bronte followed me into the bedroom and immediately jumped up on the bed and made herself comfortable in Jim's spot. Did I really need a man in my life when I could have her next to me? My eyelids drifted shut before answering the question.

I fell into such a deep sleep that I had a hard time understanding the annoying ringing sound near my face. I woke up batting at it until I realized it was my phone. I reached for it and knocked it between the bedside table and the bed. After one more ring, it stopped.

Groaning, I dug around on the floor to retrieve the phone. As soon as I had it in hand, it rang again. The caller ID said, "T. Booker." Why was Travis calling in the middle of the night? Except the phone said it was only eleven.

"Hullo?"

"Did I wake you?"

At this hour, half asleep, the Minnesota politeness I'd been cultivating since I moved here last spring escaped me. "Of course, you woke me up. What do you want?"

"Kinda testy, aren't you?"

"Seriously, why are you calling?"

The slur in Travis's voice was strong over the phone. "Just wanted to know you were okay."

"Please tell me you aren't driving."

"Home safe. Just checking on you."

"Thanks. I'm fine. I have a big nasty dog to protect me." Beside me, Bronte lifted her head and yawned.

"Cascade is a bad place. Need to be careful who you talk to."

"I'll keep that in mind." I ended the call and turned off the ringer on the phone.

The morning dawned overcast, the gray light muting the colors of the leaves. Even though the lake was calm, it looked cold outside. The temperature in the cabin hovered around fifty-five degrees, and the air smelled of burned-out wood from the fireplace. Shivering in my flannel pajamas I broke down and turned up the thermostat.

"It's just to take the chill off the place," I said to Bronte. The furnace came on with a rattle and a clunking sound. Rob had warned me the furnace was on its last legs. He thought it might make it through one more winter. When the fan finally came on, it squeaked, blowing tepid air.

After thirty minutes of blowing, the cabin had not warmed up.

"Damn it! I don't need another expense." After stomping around in frustration, I called Rob. "Can you come out and look at the furnace. I don't think it's doing what it's supposed to do."

"Not surprised. I'll be out later this morning. Best if you turn it off."

I built up the fire in the fireplace musing about how inefficient it was. People around here who heated with wood used wood stoves and furnaces, not fireplaces. Fireplaces were more for show or for the tourists who rented cabins.

Once the fire was going, I brewed a strong pot of coffee and settled in front of the crackling wood with the phone. My first call was to Clarence. The best time to talk with him, I'd learned, was morning when he was the freshest.

Clarence had a landline without voice mail. I hoped that Joe would talk him into at least getting an answering machine. He answered after a number of rings.

"Engstrom."

"Clarence, it's your lazy investigator."

"Who? I only have one investigator and she's usually right on top of things."

"That's right. Pour on the guilt. I haven't found anything on Sunny Morne

110

yet, but I sent out some feelers."

Bronte barked at the door to be let in. I opened it to a cold draft. Knowing what everyone had told me about Minnesota winters, the furnace needed fixing as soon as possible.

"You talked to Jilly." It was a statement, not a question.

No secrets in this town. I told him what little I'd gleaned from Jilly about Sunny and then filled him in on my visit to Eyeman's Corner. "Is it possible there was a second shooter? Should I report this to someone? If so, who?"

Clarence made a humming sound as he thought about what I had just said. "A conundrum, I would say. The investigation is closed, and I don't see Jay Bolton stepping forward to reopen it."

I remembered Travis's description of Jay as a snarling, toothless dog and had to agree.

"But, if there was someone else, then he or she was in on the murder and is running around free." I thought about Joe's words, *it's supposed to be a drill.*

"Hmmm. Let me ponder this. Your information is third hand. Doesn't carry a lot of weight when you say 'someone told me that someone said.' See what I mean? My advice right now is to say nothing and stay away from Cascade."

Everyone was giving me the same advice—drop it. Stay out of it. Except the victims deserved to be heard. I scratched Bronte behind her ears as I thought about all of this. "I won't say anything for now, but I think I have to go back to Cascade."

I told him about Tess. "I need to know she's all right. I also want to ask Matt Whitacre about Marla Kavanaugh. Maybe Neil was simply after Tony and the other kids were an accident."

"Young lady, you are poking at a hornet's nest. Are you sure you want to do that?"

The New Yorker paid fairly well, and I was looking at a major furnace expense. "Clarence, I need to write this article, or I'll freeze my tush off this winter."

He sighed. "You New Yorkers. You're so brash."

When had anyone called me brash? I agreed to give him a status update daily and to call him right away if I found anything more on Sunny Morne.

While I waited for Rob to come, I paged through *Days of Blood and Roses*. I was not surprised to find that Letty DeVoss was good at stringing together clichés. If I could get Florice's manuscript done by the end of the week and Letty's done by next week, maybe I could afford a furnace repair. Neither of them would pay for a new furnace, however.

Rob arrived just before noon. As a full-blooded Ojibwe, he had classic features including a strong face and deep brown eyes. He stood tall and hefty in my doorway, his salt-and-pepper hair in a single braid down his back. Rob made his living as a combination carpenter, handyman, and artist. He used to also help the Killdeer veterinarian. Most unique about him, though, was the community acceptance of his marriage to Brad, the owner of the local gift shop. He once said, "I guess they put up with us because Brad is so loveable."

Bronte greeted him with a combination bark and squeal. Rob had a calming way with animals and within moments she'd settled content to be by his side.

"So, the old bear of a furnace doesn't want to heat."

The furnace was in the back of the utility room with the water heater and laundry. Rob had explained to me that cabins like this were usually built without a basement because they sat on pretty solid rock. Not having a basement in Minnesota could be problematic especially in a frigid spell where the water pipes underneath could freeze and burst. He told me in the winter the cabin had to be kept at 55 degrees. Most people with places like this drained the pipes, added anti-freeze to the toilets, and closed up for the season.

He checked a few things out while Bronte watched him from the doorway. I paced in the living room waiting for the diagnosis. When he came out, his expression was inscrutable.

"How's the patient?" I had my fingers and my toes crossed.

"I'd say it's time to call the undertaker."

He recommended a local plumbing and heating guy. "Cal is as honest as they come. He won't try to sell you something you don't need."

"I hope he takes a credit card." I let out a long sigh. "Who knew living in the woods could be so expensive."

After he left, I sat in front of the dying fire and let the misery take over. The tears rolled down my cheeks. Bronte nuzzled me with a worried expression. "It's okay," I hiccupped. "Really I'm just mourning the death of the furnace."

Was it time to pack up and move back to New York? I knew I could piece together enough contract work there to keep me going until I found a regular job. Wouldn't it be nice to not have to rake leaves and carry wood and worry about some yahoo in a dented SUV running me off the road and a teenage girl calling for help?

As if to answer, my phone rang with more bad news.

Chapter Twenty

Madelyn

"Is this Jamie, the reporter person?" The female voice was familiar, but I couldn't quite place it.

"Yes? Who is this?"

"It's Madelyn. You know from the bar in Cascade?"

Madelyn the waitress who flirted with Travis. "Sure. I remember you."

Her voice sounded high and strained. "Those red cap boys. I was working the backroom yesterday and I heard them talking. They said they were going to get that 'New York bitch.' I think they were talking about you."

It struck me as ironic that I had just been sitting here crying over a dead furnace rather than crying over a dead me. "Wow. I don't know what to say."

"They think you know something—like about the school shooting."

Bronte stayed close to me as I gathered my thoughts. "Madelyn, how did you get my phone number?"

"Uh...a friend gave it to me?"

"Betsy Latelle?"

She paused long enough that I knew Betsy was her source.

"Okay. No problem. I'm checking because I wouldn't want those guys to have it."

"Oh no, I wouldn't never give those creeps your number."

Outside in the cold gray of the day, a crow complained, repeating his hoarse cawing.

114

"Did you hear anything else?"

"One of them saw me and they stopped talking. They're stupid mean. Like I know they could hurt you like they hurt..." Her voice dropped off.

"Who? Who did they hurt?" I thought about Winnie and the car accident. Had he been forced off the road? "Are you talking about Winnie?"

A motorcycle roared by. She must have been talking outside. "I should go." Her voice was little more than a whisper.

"Wait. Do you think Winnie knew something they didn't like?"

"I really have to go now."

In the background, someone yelled, "Mads, get back in here. Your order is up."

"Gotta go. Please be careful." She ended the call.

I sat so still with the phone in my hand that Bronte finally whined at me. "WTF, girl. What is going on?"

Before I could react further my phone rang again. A male voice identified himself as Cal, the furnace man. "I can get her looked at this afternoon. Best to do it now before the hard freeze."

We set up a time, and I gave him directions.

"Yeah, I know the place. Was just a teenager when I helped my dad put that furnace in. He wondered why anyone would install such a workhorse in a summer cabin. Your folks must have planned to live there year-round."

Growing up, this was always the summer cabin. I had no idea anyone planned to live in it year-round.

After I disconnected, I stood up and paced in front of the fire that was now more ash and smoke than warming embers. Too much on my mind. Bronte followed me with a tentative wag of her tail.

"Let's take a quick walk. I need to sort out some things."

I put on a heavy windbreaker, wrapped a knit scarf around my neck, and pulled on a woolen hat. Once outside, the wind whipped a few sprinkles of icy rain into my face. Bronte trotted ahead of me toward the lake, oblivious to the nasty weather. At the shoreline, I watched the water foam against the rocks and thought about everything that had happened in the last week.

"Winnie, Tess, and all the others. Oh, yes, and let's not forget the red cap

SUV guy. What is going on?"

Bronte thought my question was her cue to lay a stick at my feet. I picked it up and threw it away from the lake. The lawn Jim and I had raked was once again covered with leaves. With the rain, the vibrant colors had dulled, and they lay limp and soggy on the ground.

"I don't know what to do," I said to her when she returned with the stick. Sprinkles of rain grew steadier. Shivering, I threw the stick one more time and headed back to the cabin. Before I walked in, I looked at my home nestled so comfortably surrounded by the woods. I wondered about Cal's comment that it was built for year-round use.

My mother had inherited the cabin from her mother. I'd never met my grandmother or any of my relatives. Many of them, I knew, had scattered, escaping the poverty of the reservation. My grandmother had managed to hang on to this property even when land speculators were buying land cheap from the impoverished Indians. She must have been a strong woman.

Bronte galloped behind me still holding the stick. "Someday, I'll explore my roots. Meanwhile, I need a new furnace, and I need to pay for it."

Before Cal arrived, I wrote down some thoughts on the school shooting. My investigation into the story had been haphazard at best. I needed to focus it and tell a compelling story. My original thought was to profile the teacher, Tony Vincent, and keep the story about him. Now I wondered if I should take a different tack. Perhaps, instead of Tony, I should talk about the peripheral fall-out—a town that wanted to bury the killings, students like Tess who suspected a conspiracy to withhold the truth. Or maybe Winnie. Was he another casualty?

Cal showed up with his van midafternoon. After he examined the furnace, he gave me the same news as Rob. "Needs to be replaced. I got a good one that'll fit in with your ductwork. Save you some money."

He figured out the price and handed me the estimate. I tried not to look horrified. "Do you take a credit card?"

He shuffled his feet. "I think you should look at the energy assistance program they got going. You can get it through the bank. Part loan and part grant."

I sighed. We figured out a deal where I would make a down payment with my credit card and then apply for the loan. He could install it next Monday. "Weather is supposed to stay pretty warm. You should be okay until I come back. I disconnected the thermostat, so the furnace won't turn on." He cleared his throat. "Good thing you caught it now before something bad happened."

I almost asked him what he meant by "something bad" but decided I'd rather not know. Did furnaces explode?

After he left, I marched to the refrigerator and took out a beer. I almost wished I had a shot to go with it. Turning on the oven with the door wide open, I sat in the kitchen while it heated the room. As I glared at the estimate, I heard a car approach. For a moment I felt a lift in my mood. Maybe Jim had come back. But it didn't sound like his pickup and Bronte didn't react like she knew who it was.

I watched through the window as Travis eased out of his Ford Focus. He walked like he had a hangover. Before I opened the door to him, I stuck the half-drunk beer back in the refrigerator.

"Hey." I let him in. "You look a little worse for the wear."

Bronte stood silently by my side like she was sizing him up. Her tail remained still. He reached down and gave her a pat before taking off his jacket and sinking heavily into a kitchen chair. "I came to apologize. Guess I tied one on last night. Sorry for waking you up."

"Coffee?" I made a fresh pot, conscious of how quickly he'd made himself at home.

He pointed to the open oven door. "Not a very efficient way to heat."

"No kidding. Propane around here isn't cheap." I told him about the death of my furnace. "I guess when I moved here, I thought I could live on the fresh air and sunshine. No rent payments, no tips for the doormen. I was naïve."

Travis cupped the mug of coffee, while I set a slice of cornmeal bread in front of him. "Eating helps a hangover."

"And not drinking prevents one." He tsked.

Bronte sat a little distance away watching us. Unlike Joe, she wasn't sure of Travis. At least she wasn't growling at him.

I sat down across from him with my coffee. "Okay, why are you really here? And how did you find this place?"

He looked at me with an amused expression. "Everybody knows where you live. You're that mob lady at the end of the road."

"Does everyone around here watch reruns of *The Sopranos*? I'm trying to get rid of my New York accent, but I can't get the hang of that Scandinavian lilt you people have." I laughed. "To me, everyone sounds like the sheriff in the movie *Fargo*."

He took a bite of the cornbread. "Tasty." He stopped talking and concentrated on eating the rest of the slice.

"Enough stalling. Why are you here?"

Travis sat up straighter and took a deep breath. "When I saw you in the parking lot at the hospital?"

I nodded.

"I was waiting for someone."

Pricking up her ears, Bronte took a step toward Travis.

"And?" His hesitancy made me nervous.

He let the air out through pursed lips, making a whooshing kind of sound. "I was waiting to talk with Stone Kavanaugh."

The murderer who headed the militia twenty years ago. It was Kavanaugh I'd seen leaving the hospital.

"When I stopped in yesterday afternoon to make sure Jay was okay, he asked me to call Kavanaugh for him. He said he needed to talk with him, and the nurse had taken his cell phone."

Norma had told me she took his phone because he wasn't getting the rest he needed.

"I called the number Jay had and got a voice mail. I left a message. When my shift was over, I changed into civvies and went back to the hospital to see if I could catch him." Travis looked at me with a grim expression. "Jay is mixed up in something bad. I don't know what it is, but I think it's related to the militia."

"I saw someone with a red cap leaving in a pickup when I arrived. Norma told me Jay had a visitor with mean eyes."

Bronte continued to watch Travis from a distance. She looked like a sentry alert to unusual movement. Did she trust Travis? Did I?

I sifted through everything I'd learned in the past couple of days about Cascade, trying to decide what to tell Travis and what to keep to myself. I decided that he should know about Madelyn's call today.

"You know Madelyn, the waitress at the Cascade Bar?"

Travis smiled. "You mean the one who flirts with me?"

He wasn't so oblivious after all. I told him about the phone call and the warning. "She said something, though, that really stuck with me. She said they'd hurt someone else. When I asked if she was talking about Winnie, she got really quiet."

Travis looked up at the ceiling. "Oh my god. Did someone run him off the road?"

I glanced down at my scrawled notes on Cascade. "I have to go back there."

He frowned. "Maybe not such a good idea."

Earlier, when I was sorting through everything I knew, I'd come up with a plan that seemed safe to me. "I'm going to try to meet with Matt Whitacre again. He strikes me as being pretty harmless. I want to track down the rumor about Tony having something to do with Neil Kavanaugh's sister Marla."

"Like they were an item or something?"

I shrugged. "Tony's brother told me Tony had changed over the summer before he died. He'd gotten quieter and communicated less with his family. He thought it had something to do with a woman."

"Marla?"

"Maybe. Whitacre told me his wife Charity was helping Tony on the diversity project. She might know more, too, if she'll talk to me."

Travis raised his hand. "Whoa. You might be wandering into touchy territory. I'm told Whitacre is very protective of his wife. Quite the A-lister in the community. She runs some kind of online business and employs a bunch of people."

"Must make some good money. I doubt a Cascade High School principal

119

is rolling in the dollar bills." I told him about the Hermes bag. "The cheapest ones go for five figures. Even good knock-offs are expensive."

Travis looked amused. "New York girl knows her purses, huh?"

Time to change the subject. "Tell me what you know about Marla. I feel like the town has worked to erase her name, too. I can't find anything about what happened to her or where she is now."

I'd checked for a Facebook page or something on Instagram but found nothing.

Travis wiped crumbs off his lap before replying. "I don't know much. Madelyn might be a better source." He leaned toward me on the table. "Listen, you need to stay away from Cascade."

"I've been told—by a lot of people. You know, we New York Mafia types are hard to scare off."

He shook his head. "At least let me know when you're going to talk with Whitacre."

We talked a little more about Jay and Stone Kavanaugh while Travis finished his coffee. Before he left, he said, "Give my regards to Jim next time you see him."

The gray outside had deepened as the sun set. I watched the taillights of his car from the doorway. Bronte stood next to me, still alert.

"You know, girl, I'll bet Jim asked him to check on me."

I wasn't sure if I was flattered that he wanted to keep an eye on me or annoyed that he didn't think I could take care of myself. Tomorrow I would try again to break through to someone in Cascade. Tonight, I'd build a fire and finish my beer.

Chapter Twenty-One

Back to the High School

I checked the temperature in my bedroom before I slipped under the covers. Fifty degrees and time to plug in the old electric blanket that had been in the closet since I was a kid. When I pulled it out, it had the musty smell of fabric that has been through a lot of temperature and humidity changes. At least the moths hadn't gotten at it.

The blanket, despite its age, heated nicely. I fell asleep, cocooned in warmth and the smell of dusty fabric. My first chore in the morning would be to air it out on the clothesline in back.

The dream came in the middle of the night. It was the recurring one that went back to when I was ripped out of my bed by men in SWAT gear in Queens. They thought they were arresting Jamie Forester, drug dealer with multiple connections to the Mexican cartels. Instead, they got Jamie Forest, freelance fact-checker and new recipient of an MFA in poetry. I was again boxed into a small, dank holding cell with shadow people all around. When I looked down, my feet sank into a smoldering fire. The air filled with the smell of smoke as I tried to pull my feet out and run.

Bronte's bark woke me up to the odor of an electrical fire. "Oh god." The control on the blanket sparked and smoked. I grabbed the cord and yanked it out of the socket. The circuit breaker flipped, and when I tried to turn on the light, nothing happened.

My first irrational thought was to leave it all alone and go back to sleep.

Bronte jumped off the bed and barked at me just before the smoke detector in the kitchen started blatting. The blanket was smoldering. First the furnace, now this? What else could go wrong?

I pulled the blanket off the bed, dragged it to the door, and heaved it out. Holding the door open to the chill air, I shivered, waiting until the smoke cleared out enough to stop the smoke detector from rousing the dead. With my phone as a flashlight, I found the circuit breaker and flipped it back on. At least, when I'd updated the cabin last summer, I'd had all the wiring redone, draining my savings down to nothing. The rest of the night, I tossed and turned under several blankets. Even Bronte burrowed in with me.

When I awoke to a crisp morning, I resolved to drive into town and buy a little space heater. I hoped it wouldn't max out my credit card. Queens was looking good right now. My old apartment had ancient hot water registers that clanged all night and kept the rooms overheated. And, if something went wrong, the super was there to fix it.

I built a fire in the fireplace, brewed coffee, and sat in front of it with my laptop. Outside, Bronte romped in the frosty grass and leaves. The early morning sun shone wanly through the trees. As it rose, the frosty mist began to clear, and the air began to warm. I prayed for a long Indian summer. At least one that lasted until I got my new furnace.

As I worked out an outline for the Cascade story, pieces began to fall into place. I sorted through the various threads of the story and settled back on my original idea to focus on Tony Vincent. I would profile him and his work at Cascade using the interviews from the survivors. If I pushed a little, I hoped to find a couple of teachers who knew him and would talk about him. And Charity Whitacre might have an interesting perspective since she worked with him on the diversity project.

With a sense of purpose, I called Cascade High School and asked to speak with Matt. The secretary put me through to his voice mail, and I left a message saying I'd be in town this afternoon and would like to speak with him again.

It was one of those days when the lake barely rippled as it rolled gently into the shoreline. With the sun burning off the rime, I put on my orange jacket, grabbed my coffee, and went out to the rock. In my head, I made a list of things to do before driving to Cascade. Buy a little space heater, stop at the bank and see about a loan for the furnace, and text Travis to let him know about my plans to talk with Matt. It all seemed so normal. Except that nothing really was normal. All the warnings about Cascade rumbled in the back of my head.

"Stop it."

Bronte immediately sat down, like she'd just chewed up my favorite pair of socks.

"No, not you. Me."

Back in the cabin, I showered, grateful the water heater was new and worked fine. I dressed in what I called "work casual," black slacks, ankle-length boots, and a turtleneck sweater. In Manhattan, the attire would have been considered "work sloppy." Here, it was close to formal—another reason I liked Minnesota, despite the fact that people didn't emote well here.

In Killdeer, I was able to find a reasonably priced little electric heater at the hardware store. The clerk warned me, "Don't turn it on and leave. It gets pretty hot and I'd hate to see you burn down your place. It's happened, you know." I thanked her and stowed it in the back of the car.

At the bank, I filled out a number of forms including one that listed my monthly income. When I put the number down, I was appalled at how little I made. I needed *The New Yorker* article to come through. The loan officer tsked at my figures and told me I was definitely eligible for energy assistance. A wave of guilt washed through me as I thought about the people who were truly impoverished. On one hand, I shouldn't be taking their funds. On the other, I needed the furnace. I signed the forms before heading to Cascade.

Last night's frost had deepened the colors of the changing leaves. In the sunshine, I passed forests of green, gold, and red. It was a calendar photo day.

Funny how the beauty of the landscape changed the closer I got to Cascade. The trees thinned out into more scrubland. A few cleared fields held broken stocks of poorly harvested corn. This was not the rich farmland of southern Minnesota and Iowa. This was rocky, poor-quality soil that should never have been cleared to raise crops.

Cascade once again had the feel of emptiness to it even though cars were parked along the main street and a few people pushed carts out of the local grocery store. I pulled into the school parking lot just as the last busses pulled out. A few students hung around in front. I looked for Tess hoping she was back and okay, but I didn't see her. Now the challenge was to see if Bill the security man would let me in. As I approached the door, a group of lingering students stared at me. I walked over to them. "Hi, I'm Jamie Forest. I'm doing a story for *The New Yorker* on Mr. Vincent from the shooting."

One of the students, a girl with shoulder-length blonde hair and a tiny jewel in her left nostril stepped forward. "We heard about you. What's *The New Yorker*? Is it like a magazine or something?"

"Yes. You probably have a copy in your library. It's read by a lot of people."

A boy with a mocking grin and long dark hair that fell over his eyes punched her in the shoulder. "Amy, you dummy. It's like that *Inquirer* that's at the checkout in the grocery store."

"Josh, you are such a dork."

I laughed. "Actually, it's not. The stories in *The New Yorker* aren't made up."

Amy pushed a wisp of hair out of her face, frowning at the boy. "I knew that, stupid."

Before they got into a spat, I asked. "Did any of you guys have Mr. Vincent as a teacher?"

None of them spoke up. Once again, I felt like the town was closing in and protecting a secret.

"I hear he was a good math teacher," I prompted.

The other boy in the group answered in a raspy voice. "He was decent."

The mocking expression on Josh's face disappeared. "Phil's right. He was good. I liked him because he could explain stuff—you know. He didn't just stand in front of us and drone on."

"Do you know why Neil Kavanaugh would want to shoot him?"

They all looked down at their feet.

I gave them a moment and forged ahead. "I heard that you were all told not to talk about the shooting. That seems dumb to me."

Amy's expression turned serious. "It is lame. But if we get caught talking about it in school, Mr. Whitacre puts us in detention."

"Really?" What kind of adult behavior was that?

The level of discomfort rose. "Listen, if any of you want to talk with me, here's my card. I promise that I won't put you in detention. What I want to do is get a picture of Mr. Vincent. It sounded to me like he was a good guy."

I took out my card and handed it to them, noticing how quickly they stuffed it in their backpacks or pockets like they didn't want anyone to see that they had it. "Thanks. And by the way, do you guys know Tess Bolton?"

Amy answered in a soft voice, "She hasn't been in school this week. We heard she was sick or something."

Before I could ask them anything else, the front door of the school opened, and Bill stepped out. "You kids go home now. School's over." He glared at me. "What are you doing here?"

"I have a meeting with Mr. Whitacre. Maybe you could show me to his office." I didn't like the tone of his voice. As I walked by Amy I whispered, "I won't tell him anything."

Her shoulders relaxed. The group moved as one down the street.

At the door, Bill blocked my way. "Sorry, can't come in. Mr. Whitacre went home. You can't be here without an escort."

"Can you escort me to the office then so I can find out when he can meet with me?"

"Nope. Not allowed." He closed the door before I could reach it.

I could understand a need for security, but this was ridiculous. I thought about pounding on the door until someone came but decided that would be useless. I waited until Bill was out of sight and walked around the building to the gymnasium. As before, the door was propped. Slipping inside, I decided to take my own tour of the school. Behind me, a deep gray cloud obscured the sun.

Chapter Twenty-Two

The Lone Teacher

The gymnasium was deserted, but the lights were still on. I wondered about after-school activities. Why was it so quiet? The last time I was here was a Friday and I understood how people would clear out for the weekend. Today was Thursday, and yet the place felt a little like Cascade itself, abandoned.

Walking along the edge of the basketball court, I listened for sounds of people but heard nothing but the quiet whirr of the ventilation system. Outside the wind picked up, blowing leaves against the side of the school.

The hallway on the other end of the gymnasium was lit. I made my way to it, remembering that Matt's office was at the far end. Red-painted lockers lined each side of the empty corridor. As I walked, I noted a sign for the cafeteria pointing to the left of his office. Taking the turn, I walked into the room where the shooting had occurred. A row of windows let light into the room. Tables, seating four to six students, were arranged in neat rows with the chairs stacked on top so the janitor could clean the floor.

A door with a red exit sign stood in the back corner. The description of the shooting indicated Neil Kavanaugh had run out this door and disappeared into the woods behind the school. I stared at the area where the shooting had taken place. A table, perhaps the one Tony Vincent had sat on, was positioned near the exit door. If that's where he sat, he had a clear view of anyone who walked into the room.

I saw no evidence of a shrine or a memorial or anything to commemorate the death that happened in this room. Again, the school seemed strangled in its silence. I walked over to inspect the wall, curious to see if it had been damaged by the gunfire. Something was tucked into the corner. When I stooped to inspect it, a gust of wind rattled the cafeteria windows. It was a black, silk rose sitting in a small vase. I peered at it wondering if this was a tribute to the fallen or a warning.

"Excuse me?" A voice called from behind me.

Startled, I quickly stood up and turned around. A woman in her mid-twenties stood at the door of the cafeteria, with her hands clasped as if in prayer. In the gloom, I couldn't read the expression on her face, but her body language told me she was as startled as I was.

"Sorry," I walked toward her with my hand out. "I'm Jamie Forest. I was supposed to meet Matt Whitacre this afternoon, but they said he had gone home."

When I reached her, she took my hand in a limpid grasp. "Oh. I'm Carin Anderson. I teach English." She studied me for a moment. "How did you get by Bill our watchdog?"

I shrugged, not wanting to explain how I'd gotten in the building. "He was distracted, I guess."

"More like he was drunk."

"The school seems deserted. Aren't there any after-school activities?"

Carin shook her head. "Only football, and they don't practice on Thursdays because of the Friday games."

"What about other sports?"

"They say we're too small for other sports. Girls get bussed to Killdeer for volleyball."

My school in Manhattan had a number of after-school options—everything from the chess club to soccer. "You don't have other things like speech or debate?"

"Sadly, no. I tried to set up an after-school group to do a literary journal, but it didn't get approved."

"Has it always been this way?"

She shrugged. "This is only my third year."

Down the hallway, I heard footsteps. "If that's Bill, he'll probably escort me to the door."

Carin sized me up. "You look safe enough. Come on down to my classroom, and we can talk. I get pretty lonely here when the last bell rings."

"All the other teachers leave?"

She didn't reply as she led me down the corridor away from the footsteps.

Carin's classroom was in a corner at the opposite end of the corridor from Matt's. The walls were covered with posters from plays. She had everything from *Les Miserables* to *King Lear*. Many of them had been produced for the Guthrie Theater in Minneapolis.

I pointed to them. "You like theater?"

Her face lit up. "It's a passion of mine. When I was a teenager, I went to New York with my parents and saw *Cats*. I was hooked."

She motioned to a wooden chair next to her desk. "I've heard about you. There's a rumor going around in the teacher's lounge that a reporter from New York is trying to do a smear piece on the school." She rested her clasped hands on the desk. "It's about time. How can I help?"

I told her about meeting Joe and about getting the transcripts of interviews from the late editor of the *Killdeer Times*. "I thought I could do an in-depth piece about the school shooting—something that hadn't been done before. I wanted to profile Tony." I gave her a rueful expression. "It was never meant as a 'smear' piece. Plus, I'm not sure I can do it, because no one will talk with me about it."

Carin nodded as she picked up a pencil, and absently tapped it on the desk. "People are scared. The teachers who have been here for years are afraid they might lose their jobs. The ones who might be willing to talk have all left." She gazed up at the ceiling. "This school is broken."

I took out a notebook and jotted down the phrase "broken school." Outside, rain tapped against the window.

"I'm done after this year. I came here on a three-year special program for schools in high-poverty areas. If I finish the year out, half my student loans get paid off. That's why I stayed after the shooting."

"Can you tell me about Tony? Was he a good teacher? Do you think he was targeted because he was Native American?"

Carin picked up the pencil and made little doodling figures on a piece of paper as she talked. "I came here the fall of the shooting, so I didn't know him well. He was one of the nice ones. You know. Showed me around, made me feel welcome. The others, the teachers who had been here awhile pretty much kept to themselves."

I was getting a picture of a poorly functioning school. Teachers escaping as soon as the bell rang. Teachers afraid of losing their jobs. This could have been its own story. But it wasn't the one *The New Yorker* editor wanted me to write.

Carin told me Tony worked especially hard with the kids who were Native American. "He could relate to them. He pushed them but also spent a lot of time after school tutoring them." She stopped doodling. "I thought he was a great role model. I wanted to do the same—you know inspire the students."

"It must have been hard to be here after he was killed."

"Weird. You know. It was weird. People acted like it didn't happen." She turned to me with tears in her eyes. "Can you believe that? The word went out not to talk about it because it would give the school and the community a bad reputation. Even today, it's like an open wound that was never allowed to be healed."

I pictured the black silk rose crammed into the corner of the cafeteria. Someone wanted to create a memorial.

She told me many of the teachers who didn't have serious ties in the community quit at the end of the school year. "It's like we have two separate faculties—the old guard and the new ones right out of college. The new ones only stay for a year." Her voice dropped off.

This was not what I expected to learn. Nor was it getting me any closer to the essence of Tony Vincent. "I heard the shooting might have been motivated by something that happened between Tony and Neil Kavanaugh's sister Marla. Do you know anything about that?"

Carin blinked at me in confusion. "Marla? Really?"

With the rumor mill that any institution has, I was surprised by her reaction. "Someone said he was dating her."

"What?" Carin sat back in her chair with an amused look. "I can't imagine where that rumor came from. Marla Kavanaugh is, ah, mentally challenged. You know—slow."

Again, not what I expected to hear. "So as far as you know, he wasn't involved with her."

"Here, look." She pulled a yearbook out of a drawer in her desk, flipped through some pages until she found the photos of the school administrative staff. Marla was overweight, wore thick glasses, and had a blank look. "She worked for Mr. Whitacre under a special program with the state. I'm not even sure what she did."

The rain let up and a sickly, yellow beam of wan sunlight lightened the gray skies. Carin slipped the yearbook back in her drawer.

"Does she still work here?"

"Oh no. After the shooting, she and her mother moved. Poor Mrs. Kavanaugh. She lost her son and wanted to protect her daughter."

I thought about the conflicting picture of Neil Kavanaugh. Said to be friendly and open and then suddenly changed. "Did you know Neil at all?"

"The shooting happened about the third week of school. I barely knew the names of my students by then. I remember he missed some classes and when he did come, he sat in the back and never said anything."

"I heard he changed from being friendly to keeping to himself."

She nodded sadly. "Something happened, I guess. At least, that's what Winnie thought." She blinked away a tear. "He was one of the few good people around here. What a loss. I still can't believe it."

I wasn't sure I should share that I might have been the last person to talk with Winnie, but I sensed Carin would want to know. I told her about meeting him at the restaurant and about how he enjoyed the cheeseburger.

She was quiet, drumming her fingers on the desk. When she looked at me, several tears cascaded down her cheeks. "You know, he thought something was fishy about the shooting."

"Really?" Maybe I could finally get some solid information. I readied my pen.

Carin stopped me. "Please, don't write this down, but Winnie came to me before...before he...uh, had his accident. He wanted to know if I'd seen anything unusual the day of the shooting." She wiped her eyes with the back of her hand. "Everything from that day was such a blur. I told him I didn't remember much. He asked if I'd seen anyone in the halls who shouldn't have been there."

"Like a stranger in the school?"

"Maybe, but he wouldn't tell me why he was asking."

Footsteps approached from the corridor. Carin sat up straight, her eyes wide. "If that's Bill," she whispered, "I'll be in big trouble."

The classroom had a little supply closet. I pointed at it and made a dash to hide behind the door.

Bill's voice boomed from the classroom doorway. "Thought I heard voices. Time for you to go home before I lock up."

"On my way," Carin called back to him.

It occurred to me that this school felt a little like a prison. Carin walked by the closet and whispered, "Leave as soon as he's gone."

She took her coat from the hook by the door and pulled it on. Snapping off the light, she chatted loudly to Bill as their footsteps echoed down the hallway. As soon as I heard her say, "See you tomorrow, Bill," I slipped out of the closet. Creeping quietly to the door, I listened for Bill. I heard nothing.

The only light in the corridor came from the red exit sign. In order to slip out, I needed to pass by Matt's office. Hopefully, he hadn't come back. I made it halfway down the corridor before I heard voices. One was Bill's. He spoke loudly like someone who was hard of hearing. The other might have been Matt's.

"That sneaky reporter was around again. Said she was coming to see you." I heard a laugh. "Dodged that bullet."

A door closed as the two continued to talk. "Nothing else to report, Matt. That English teacher left late again."

"No worries about her."

It sounded like they were coming closer to me. I had two choices. I could step out and tell them I was in the building, or I could try to hide. A prickling sense in the back of my neck told me to hide. I didn't want to get Carin in trouble, and if they knew she'd talked with me, well, I wasn't sure what that meant.

By the sound of their voices, they were about to turn the corner into the hallway where I stood. I looked around for a place to hide. Just ahead of me on the right appeared to be a door. I dashed to it, hating that my boots didn't have a soft sole. The noise of my footsteps seemed thunderous.

"Did you hear something?" Matt asked.

Just as they were turning the corner, I slipped into the closet. It was pitch dark and smelled of polish and floor cleaner. I didn't dare pull the door shut for fear of making noise. Pressing against a shelf, I made myself as small as possible.

"Hey," Bill said. "Looks like Ed forgot to lock up his closet."

"I'll talk to him tomorrow. He's getting too careless."

The door clicked shut. I was locked in.

Chapter Twenty-Three

The Closet

The closet had little ventilation, and it didn't take long before my head started to pound from the smell of the cleaning chemicals. I had to get out of this room. The darkness pressed in on me. A little sliver of light shone through the bottom of the door. It was enough that when my eyes adjusted, I saw I was in a small room surrounded by shelves of cleaning products, toilet paper, paper towels, and greasy rags. In the corner stood a janitor's broom, a mop, and an empty pail.

When enough time had passed that I was sure Bill and Matt were gone, I tried the door. It was firmly locked. Fighting off panic, I dug through my bag for my phone. If all else failed, I could call for help.

When I turned on the phone, three text messages popped up. Two were from Jim letting me know that he couldn't make it back this weekend. The first said, **can't come back. Jake not doing well.** The second asked me to respond. **Did you get my message???**

The other message was from Travis. **Let me know you got home safely.**

Sure. I planned to get home safely as soon as was out of this closet. If I called for help, how would I explain myself? Uh oh, sorry. Accidentally locked myself in the janitor's closet? Oops?

Sighing, I called Travis feeling very sheepish. Nothing happened. Staring at the phone, I saw I had no bars. I was locked in a room filled with toxic air and my phone had no bars. My chest tightened like someone held me in a bear hug. I started to pant. Ever since I'd been locked up in that crowded holding cell in Queens, I had a fear of enclosed places. I needed to calm down.

"It's okay," I whispered. "Worst case scenario, you'll be stuck here until morning."

The thought of being in this closet until tomorrow did not settle me down. "You're smart. You've got an MFA in poetry. Can't you figure out how to get the door unlocked?"

Emily Dickinson was not going to get me out of this jam. I thought about Florice and her milkmaid. What would Rose do? She'd dream about Thorgest, knowing he'd eventually come to rescue her. None of the possible rescuers in my life knew I was locked in a closet at Cascade High School.

"Guess you are on your own."

I used the flashlight on my phone to survey the room. Maybe Ed the janitor had something I could use to pry open the door. I searched the shelves but found no prying tools. On a high shelf, though, I spotted a red baseball cap. It had the confederate logo on it.

"Is everybody around here part of the militia?" I took a breath of the rancid air and tried to relax my tensed-up shoulders.

Maybe I could use my credit card to slip the latch on the door. After fumbling for several minutes to wedge the card between the lock and the doorframe, I gave up. What worked in the movies wasn't working for me in real life.

By now, I was overheated and sweating. On top of that, I had to pee. Florice's heroines never had to deal with bodily functions, like full bladders. I sank down to the floor and muttered, "Hopeless." I prepared myself for a long night and hoped I didn't die of toxic fumes before morning came.

At some point, I dozed off, dreaming I was back in the Queens holding cell. Except, instead of the poor downtrodden women stuffed in the cell with me, I was surrounded by men in red caps. They grinned at me with dark, glowing eyes. One of them opened his mouth and giggled.

I snapped awake. Did I hear a giggle, or did I dream it? I crawled over to the door and pressed my ear against it. Nothing but the sound of my breathing. And yet...another faint giggle.

This was time for action. I shed my cloak of dignity. I didn't care if Bill the Bully or Matt the Wimp found me. I pounded on the door yelling, "Help! Help! I'm locked in."

The giggling stopped, but I was sure I heard the squeak of footsteps on the floor. I yelled and pounded again. This time voices approached. With my ear pressed against the door, I listened. The voices sounded young, and at least one was female.

"Help! Help! I'm locked in the closet."

The footsteps stopped. More whispering that I couldn't make out.

"Please, can you figure out how to open this door?" I worked to keep my voice calm. "I can explain myself if you can get me out."

The voices came closer. One of them, a boy with a raspy voice called out. "Who are you?"

I recognized him from earlier this afternoon. "Phil?"

Someone gasped as Phil asked. "How do you know me?"

"It's Jamie Forest. I, um, got lost in the school, and this door accidentally closed."

I heard more whispering followed by the sound of a key in the lock. The door swung open, and I breathed in the fresh air from the hallway. "Thank you." I gasped, stumbling out of the closet.

Phil, Amy, and Josh stood gaping at me. I could have hugged them all, except I really needed to use the bathroom.

"Excuse me." I pointed down the hall to the restroom sign. "I need to make a little stop, and then we can talk."

When I came out of the bathroom, the three stood clumped against a row of lockers. In the dim light of the hallway, I noted how they nervously shifted as they stared at me. Josh stepped forward, pushing hair out of his eyes. He wore a T-shirt that said, "The Truth is Out There."

Pointing to the T-shirt, I said, "Winnie Starling had a shirt like that on the night he had his accident. It means something, doesn't it?"

Amy made a shushing sound as she stepped next to Josh. "We don't know anything."

I sighed. I was tired and stressed and wanted nothing more than to sit in front of my fireplace and pretend that I'd never set foot in Cascade county. "Here's the deal. I shouldn't be here, and you shouldn't be here." I pointed to the ring of keys that Josh held in his hand. "You're breaking in and I'm trespassing. Looks like we have something in common. So, what's your story?"

No one responded.

Amy finally broke the silence. "Um, we've been meeting with Mr. Starling to talk about everything. He and Miss Anderson were the only teachers who seemed to care." She picked at a ring on her finger. "After...after what happened to Mr. Starling, we wanted to make a little memorial to him, but Mr. Whitacre and some of the other teachers said we should leave things alone."

Phil added, "Yeah. It's like something is wrong with this town and Mr. Starling wanted to make it better."

I sat down cross-legged on the floor and motioned for them to join me. "Okay, guys, tell me what you know."

For the next half hour, we sat in a semicircle while they filled me in. Poor kids; they needed to talk, and the adults had left them adrift. They were juniors, so they had been at the school two years ago when the shooting occurred.

"I heard the shots. Miss Anderson closed the door to her room and had us all cram into the supply closet. It was awful."

"Mr. Mayor made us stay in the locker room." Phil shook his head. "I was pretty scared."

"They closed school for two days, and when we went back, everyone acted like nothing had happened—except that they hired Bill the Bully."

They all agreed that Bill was not only a bully but a strong one. "I saw him throw a kid up against the lockers once. One of the teachers was watching and walked away without saying anything."

Amy added, "Sick."

"They told us the school didn't have resources for counseling, so if we wanted to talk with someone about the shooting, we should talk to our ministers." Josh rattled the keys he held in his hand.

"Yeah, as if Reverend Carlson would know what to do. He's half deaf and dresses like it's the sixties or something."

It was clear that the kids felt a conspiracy of silence from the teachers and the adults in the community.

"Did anyone suggest talking with Mr. Starling? He was the guidance counselor."

Josh picked at the shoelace on his Nikes shaking his head. "They said he was too new, and we shouldn't bother him."

Bother him? Wasn't he paid to counsel the students?

Amy pulled the ring off her finger and slipped it back on. "Even my mom acted like she was afraid to say something. All we ever heard was that Neil was, like, crazy and that's why he did it."

Josh added, "As if we didn't notice that all the people who were shot were Indians. That's sick."

"Everyone said Neil was mixed up with those militia guys. You know, the ones who wear the red baseball caps." Phil pointed to his head. "They're bad news."

"But that didn't seem right," Amy added. "He was nice even to us freshmen."

Josh stared at his feet. "Mr. Starling figured out something. We think it had to do with the shooting. He found something, a clue or something."

"How do you know?"

Fidgeting with his shoelaces, Josh said, "Tess told us before his accident. She said, 'He's on to something.'"

"But you don't know what it is."

"No." Amy shook her head. "And we don't think he was in an accident. Like someone forced him off the road."

I thought about my experience with the banged-up SUV. Could this all be tied together?

Josh continued to pick at his shoelaces. "It was like déjà vu all over again. Mr. Starling dies, and old Whitacre makes an announcement about thoughts and prayers for his family and nothing. No memorial, no nothing."

"That's why we're here. We wanted to check out Mr. Starling's desk before they clean it out. Maybe there's a clue."

They looked so fresh-faced and eager. I worried about them. I held my hand up. "Wait. I agree that something isn't right here, but I think you should be careful. Two teachers and several students have died in the last two years." I paused, remembering the phone call from Tess. "Tess was part of your group, right?"

They all nodded.

"And you haven't seen her?"

Amy frowned. "We got together last Friday to talk about stuff, but she was acting kind of weird—excited like. She asked Phil to drop her off near her house. We haven't seen her since."

They weren't telling me the whole story. "Has she called or texted or sent any messages?" They wouldn't meet my eyes when I asked the question. I gave them a few moments before I said, "She called me."

"Really?" Amy's eyes widened.

"I told her uncle, the sheriff, about the call and he assured me that she was fine."

Phil mumbled "Bullshit." He began to wheeze and quickly pulled an inhaler out of his pocket.

My phone buzzed as I watched him to make sure he was breathing okay. I had three bars now that I was out of the closet. A text from Travis demanded.

Where are you!

At the school. Leaving Cascade in a few minutes.

Amy leaned forward, trying to read my text. I hit Send and said, "It's from a friend, wondering where I am." I smiled at them. "By the way, if you ever get stuck in that closet, it doesn't have any cell reception. You'll need a walkie-talkie."

They didn't pick up on my attempt at humor. These kids were serious and reckless. I didn't know what to do with all of this information. Kids liked intrigue, but I was afraid they might have stepped in something big. Or maybe not. I wasn't sure what to believe.

"Listen, if anybody ever asks, I've never met you and I had no idea you had keys to the school. Right?" They nodded in unison. "But please, go home.

Let me mull this over. I don't think sneaking around the school is going to get you any answers." I made a mental note to talk with Clarence and maybe Travis about the situation.

In back of me, I heard voices. Leaning close to them I whispered, "Someone is here. Can we get out without going back down that hallway?"

Josh led the way back to the gymnasium. Before we got to the door, Amy whispered, "Wait. I have to put this out." She took a little vase with a back silk rose out of her backpack. A second memorial. Now I knew where the first one came from. Without another word, she dashed toward the cafeteria.

The voices grew louder. I was sure one of them was Bill's growl. We hurried into the gymnasium. The windowless room was now lit only by the red exit signs.

Bill's voice grew closer. "You sure that car belongs to that reporter? I didn't let her in."

The voice that answered was too muffled to understand. The boys had scared expressions as they pressed against the wall of the gymnasium, trying to stay out of sight. Phil gripped his inhaler as if it was a talisman.

It hit me that my car was probably the only one left in the parking lot. Bill and someone else knew I was in the building.

Chapter Twenty-Four

Escape

B ill and the other person drew closer. I prayed Amy heard them and had tucked herself away in the cafeteria.

"Bitch. She'd probably go for Whitacre's office and snoop around there."

In order to get back to the gym, Amy had to pass by Matt's office. Silently I willed her to stay put.

We huddled near the gymnasium door listening for the men. At the corridor leading to the gymnasium, their footsteps stopped. Bill's voice boomed, "Wanna look in the gym? Could be she's hiding there."

The other man mumbled a reply. They were quiet for a few moments. "Let's check out Matt's office first."

"I hope Amy heard them," Phil's rasp had gotten worse.

"Maybe you two should get out. I'll wait for Amy. If she's caught, I'll come up with some excuse." I wasn't confident of my story-telling ability, but I worried about the two boys after hearing how Bill threw a kid against the lockers.

"No way," Josh whispered back.

I heard the faint jingling sound as Bill unlocked Matt Whitacre's office. His voice was muffled. "Closet. Check the closet. He keeps stuff there."

What stuff?

As soon as the voices went silent, footsteps came running down the corridor.

"Did you hear that?" Bill's voice was louder.

Amy skidded around the corner. "Let's get out of here!"

We ran for the exit. Behind us, we heard shouts. "Who's there! Stop or I'll shoot!"

Bill either had a gun or had he simply watched too many clichéd television programs.

I wasn't about to find out. I didn't know I had it in me to run as fast as I did across the gym floor. Still, I couldn't keep up with the kids. Behind me, the sound of the two men running grew. I heard them huffing as they picked up speed. All three of the kids were out of the exit before I reached the door. It slammed shut in front of me. I pushed on the metal latch and nothing happened. Somehow the door had gotten jammed shut.

"Damn it!" My breath came in sharp stabs. Would Bill really shoot?

My pursuers closed in. I risked a look back and saw through the dim light of the gym that they had made it to the doorway. With all the strength I had, I rammed my shoulder into the door. The pain nearly knocked the wind out of me as the door flew open. I stumbled onto the concrete of the sidewalk scraping my knee. Behind me, Bill roared, "Stop! Stop whoever you are!"

He didn't know it was me. With strength I didn't know I had, I shoved the door shut hoping it would jam again. I ran like I used to when I was a kid on the playground. In my mind, I saw Bill pointing a gun at me. Faster, faster I chanted under my breath. My chest hurt, but I kept on.

By the time I made it to my car, I heard the thump of someone kicking at the gymnasium door. Digging in my bag, I gripped my keys, hit the button on the fob, and took a forward dive into the driver's side of the car. Thank god the Subaru was a reliable car. It started immediately and like a teenager, I peeled out of the parking lot with a screech of the tires.

I don't know if Bill saw me driving away. At that point, I didn't care. It was time to get out of town and regroup my thoughts.

When I reached the highway, I finally took a deep breath and tried to relax. I went over my narrow escape and one thing stuck with me. When I'd looked back to see where Bill was, the person with him wore a baseball cap. In the dim lighting with only a millisecond glance, I couldn't be sure of the color, but my intuition said it was red with a confederate logo.

Rain spit at the windshield as I drove down the dark highway. A car approached me, its headlights on high beam, nearly blinding me. The driver dimmed just before he passed by. I felt wobbly as I drove, all the adrenaline draining out of me. Behind, in the rearview mirror, the highway remained deserted. The drive seemed to take forever.

To my surprise, with the rhythmic slap of the windshield wipers and the warm air from the heater on my feet, I grew sleepy. How could someone feel sleepy after narrowly escaping a goon like Bill? For a moment, the car drifted over the center line. I snapped back into wakefulness when a large semi-truck approached me with its horn blaring. It was like a jolt of caffeine.

My darkened, unheated cabin never looked so welcoming as I pulled up to park. I didn't care if it was only 50 degrees inside. I didn't care if I might not be able to afford my electric bill next month. I didn't even care that I'd run out of beer. I was home.

Bronte greeted me with so much enthusiasm she almost knocked me over. "Am I glad to see you." She licked my face as I knelt down to hug her. Inside my bag, my phone buzzed, stopped, and then buzzed again. Once I'd settled Bronte and let her out, I looked at it.

I had several more texts from Jim. I replied. **Got your message. Sorry. In a dead zone. Back home now.**

He texted back. **Glad you are okay. Worried.**

He didn't know the half of it. **Sorry to hear about Jake. Hang in there. Miss you.**

From the refrigerator, I took out a bottle of white wine. Jim had bought it for me before I confessed to him that I was more of a beer person than a wine aficionado. When I opened it, the cork came apart. I ignored the little pieces that floated in the glass. The wine tasted vinegary. At this point, I didn't care.

Instead of building a fire, I unpackaged the little heater, set it up in front of the couch, and plugged it in. Within minutes it glowed red and sent heat up my legs. Bronte yawned and curled up next to me on the couch. Normally I would shove her off. Today I needed her reassuring sigh as she rested her head on my lap.

I sipped my wine and tried to empty my brain of anything relating to Cascade. "I'm in over my head, girl." I stroked the top of Bronte's head. She looked at me as if to say, I hear you. I tried to make a list of all the things I needed to do tomorrow. Florice expected her manuscript to be edited by the end of next week. I wasn't even close to correcting her commas and her semicolons. I was still working to finish the second reading.

"Then, of course, I'll have to take up the vampire story."

To my surprise, the wine went down easily. I poured another glass, feeling that little uptick of euphoria as the alcohol made its way through my system. As my cheeks grew rosy, a sense of well-being drifted through me. I would be all right. I'd get the proposal for *The New Yorker* done, Rose would be appropriately plucked, and Vladess the Vampire would find a man to suck dry. The euphoria only lasted until my phone binged with another text. This one was from an unknown number. I expected it might be from one of the Cascade kids making sure I got out. Instead, it simply said. **Locked in plz help**.

Who is this? I texted back but got no answer.

Chapter Twenty-Five

Consultation with Clarence

W as this from Tess? The kids at school? Betsy Latelle? I stared at
the phone. Why had I been anointed to deal with the mystery
in Cascade? All I wanted was to give a voice to the people who
died in the horrific shooting. Instead, I'd found a community that appeared
to be bent on burying that voice. Grabbing a notebook, I made a list of
everything I knew about the shooting and the people involved. Three things
jumped out that me.

First, the conspiracy of silence. Why was everyone so reluctant to talk?
I felt like the town had wrapped itself in a dark cloak. Why wouldn't they
acknowledge the horror of the shooting and support the students? Were
people in Cascade afraid? If so, why?

Second, the death of Winnie Starling. A young school counselor dies in
an automobile accident, and no one talks about it. I'd checked the local
newspaper and found only a brief mention of the accident. No memorial
service, no acknowledgment of what he had done for the students. In my
short experience with small communities, the death of someone young
tended to make big news. On top of that, the question remained, *was it really
an accident*?

And third, the existence of the Red Cap Militia. Were they the key? Did
the militia have some kind of hold over the community?

After that, I listed questions: What happened to Tess? What about

Gravediggers Island and Nearbow Lake? Where was Jay Bolton in all of this? What about Betsy Latelle's assertion of the second shooter? Plus, lurking in the background was the question about Marla and her relationship to Tony. By the time I was done, I'd filled up several pages of the notebook and was no further along in writing my article outline.

I scratched Bronte behind her ears and sighed. "Let's go to bed and worry about this tomorrow."

With the help of the electric heater placed at the foot of my bed and away from anything that would catch on fire, I slept fairly well except for waking up at three in the morning with a furry tongue and a vinegar taste in my mouth from the wine.

The morning sun drifted through the bedroom window as Bronte danced by the bed. I'd slept until after nine, and the poor dog needed to go out. "Sorry girl." My head felt like it was stuffed with cotton. When I sat up, an ache radiated through my bruised shoulder where I'd jammed it against the school door.

Bronte dashed out to her spot at the edge of the woods when I opened the door. The air was clear and the sky a deep cloudless blue. As the sunlight sparkled off the dewy ground, yesterday seemed like a bad movie. Did I really get locked into a janitor's closet and escape with kids who had broken into the school? What seemed so dramatic last night felt silly today.

Steam rose off the mug of coffee as I sat on my rock listening to the gentle pulsating of the lake. With the sun warming my face and Bronte at my feet, I took a deep breath of the fall-scented air. Maybe I could sit here all day and leave the worries of the world and the worries of my life behind me. I took off my shoes, rolled up my jeans, and waded into the water. The cold stung my feet and sent a shiver up my legs. No, I couldn't spend the day basking in the sun. I had work to do.

With the notes from last night in front of me, I called Clarence.

He answered after only two rings. "Engstrom."

"Clarence, it's Jamie. I have a whole notebook here full of problems, and I need some sage advice."

"Hmmm. I'm looking around and don't see any sages, just a cantankerous old lawyer."

"Then I'll settle for the old lawyer." We set up a time to meet in early afternoon. "If you see Joe, could you have him join us?"

"I sent him off to see that physical therapist this morning. I think he's kind of sweet on her." He chuckled. "Good for the boy to have a little love in his life."

I could hardly argue with that. I had love in my life—sort of. Thinking about Jim and what he was dealing with gave me another dose of reality. Whatever problems I might have, they hardly compared to a gravely sick child.

Instead of spending more time thinking about Cascade, I took out the vampire manuscript. After reading the first chapter, I set it down with a huge sigh. Letty DeVoss had paid the first installment of my fee. I either needed to plow through the rest or refund her money.

"Winter is coming," I said out loud while I finished my coffee and soldiered on. Where Florice wrote in choppy sentences that needed smoothing out, Letty wrote sentences that stretched into paragraphs. It left me breathless with the effort to finally find the period.

"Listen to this," I read to Bronte. "Vladess, her ruby lips sucking the blood out of Troy the groomsman with his shoulder-length hair cascading down his shoulders and his bulging biceps, encircling her, helpless to fight off the nectar of her kisses and the rubbing of her pointed nipples hard against his muscled chest while below his manhood stood at attention even though the life drained from his body..."

Bronte's tail thumped against the floor. I wondered if she was happy with the prose or happy because I paid attention to her.

"Really. Who would name a character from the eighteenth century, Troy?"

The phone saved me from chapter two where I assumed we would find Troy drained and spent on Vladess's bed.

"Hello, Travis. You just saved me from slitting my wrists."

"What?" His voice rose in concern.

"Sorry. I was joking. I've been editing a manuscript." The last page floated to the floor. I was tempted to stomp on it.

Travis cleared his throat. "I, uh, was just checking on your trip to Cascade."

Should I tell him about my adventures? I hesitated because he was a lawman, and I didn't want the kids to get into trouble. I tried to keep my response carefully worded because I thought he should know about Winnie. "I met some of the high school kids. Interesting conversation. They said Winnie was meeting with them and they suspected he knew something." I paused. "They're convinced that it wasn't an accident."

Travis whistled. "Do you know why?"

"I can't piece it together. That's all I can tell you."

"I'm on duty until five. Would you like to have a beer and we can talk?"

I had mixed feelings about meeting with him. On one hand, it was nice to have someone to talk to. On the other, was I being disloyal to Jim? The desire to talk won over. "I'll be in town this afternoon. We can meet at the Loonfeather, if you'd like."

After I ended the call, I felt a pang of regret followed by a pang of excitement. I laughed, wondering how Letty DeVoss would write the scene.

By midafternoon I'd plowed through fifty more pages of Letty's writing. The plot was going nowhere. How can you have a romance when you kill off all the men you take to your bed?

I left Bronte with a new rawhide chew, stopped outside for a moment to breathe in the crisp pine-scented air, and headed for Killdeer. The maple in Clarence's yard glowed in a red splendor with the slanting rays of the sun. The grass was still a deep green, despite the frost of the other night, and his hanging flower baskets still held a colorful array of blossoms.

Joe greeted me at the door. Every time I saw him, he looked healthier and more relaxed. The physical therapy—or therapist—clearly helped him.

We sat in the kitchen. Lorraine had baked brownies before going home. The room smelled of sweet chocolate and fresh-brewed coffee. It would have been an idyllic scene except for my anxiety over everything to do with Cascade.

Joe poured coffee while I settled in with my notebook full of questions. I told them everything about my visit yesterday except I left out the part about being locked in the janitor's closet.

"Cascade High School has this security guard named Bill, who looks like pro-wrestler gone to seed. The kids are scared of him. And, I think the teachers are too."

Joe wrinkled his brow. "He wasn't around before the shooting, I don't think."

I told them about my conversation with Carin Anderson, the English teacher, and how new teachers don't stay. "It seems to me the school is a toxic place."

Joe shrugged. "I didn't get much involved with the school when I went. I mostly wanted to get good grades and play football."

Clarence bit into his brownie with relish, a few crumbs spilling down the front of his shirt. "What about your coach, Mr. Mayor? He wasn't a bad guy, was he?"

"I liked him. Maybe I would have stayed in school after the shooting, but he left."

"Really?" The brownie was so rich I had to keep myself from groaning as I bit into it.

"They cancelled the rest of the football season and he left."

With a pencil in one hand and a second brownie in the other, I made a note about the coach. "Do you think Mr. Mayor knew something?"

Joe leaned back from the table stretching out his legs. "I think something weird was going on before Neil shot us. Kids talked to Coach. Maybe he'd know something."

Clarence brushed off his neatly pressed shirt with a paper napkin. "Well, then, we should talk to him." He pointed to me. "Use that great investigative tool you have and find him. We'll give him a call."

"No need," Joe raised his hand in a stop gesture. "I have his cell phone number. We've stayed in touch—sort of. He teaches in Fargo now."

Joe took out his phone and airdropped the contact information into my phone.

Clarence watched in amazement. "You mean those phones talk to each other without talking?"

I laughed. "Welcome to the new century. I'll give the coach a call tomorrow when school isn't in session."

Outside, a small plane buzzed overhead. Killdeer had a municipal airport that was mainly used by the wilderness guiding companies to fly hunters and fishermen into remote lakes.

I looked at Clarence. "Have you had a chance to think about my question from the other day? What if there was a second shooter? Who would I tell?"

Clarence frowned. "It's hearsay, of course. I doubt anyone, especially Jay Bolton, would reopen the case for that."

"I reread the newspaper report on the shooting. They found one gun that they assumed Neil had dropped when he ran out the exit." I turned to Joe. "Did you see it?"

Joe winced. "It was all a blur. I remember reaching for my brother…" he paused, his voice tightening. "I saw Neil. I saw him run out the door." He stopped, biting his lip.

Clarence watched him with a sympathetic expression. We both waited for him to speak again.

"Um…I think he was carrying a gun when he ran. I have this little flash of a memory. Something about someone wearing a ski mask." He took a long, deep breath. "But I can't be sure."

I remembered picking up a ski mask for Winnie just before he left the restaurant. What had he said? Something about "winter coming." I tucked the thought away for the time being.

A clock in the kitchen ticked in a regular rhythm, filling the silence in the room. I closed my eyes trying to picture the scene. If there were two shooters, what happened to the second one? And if there were two shooters, why didn't the police identify two different weapons?

Clarence must have picked up on my thoughts. "What if one of them never shot his weapon?"

This was taking me way deeper than a human-interest piece on Tony or even a human-interest piece on the surviving students. I rubbed the tension out of my face. "Are we being 'conspiracy theorist' crazy, here?"

Again, the room filled with the sound of the kitchen clock. Joe finally broke the silence. "If somebody else was part of this, we need to know.

They're out in the world and my brother will never play another football game."

It felt like all the air had been sucked from the room. Joe and I watched Clarence as he wrinkled his brow and made a few clucking sounds. "Seems to me," he said, "We need more information."

For the next half-hour, we talked about what to do next. I watched Joe's body language and saw a crack in his normal reserve. I didn't want him to have to relive the worst moments of his life, but it seemed to me that as we talked, he became less reserved and more animated.

"I'll talk to my cousins up there and see what they know."

Clarence cleared his throat. "I'll tap into my old crock network and see if I can get my hands on the investigative report." He winked, "Unredacted, of course."

I studied all my notes. "I'll give Coach Mayor a call. And try to talk with Matt Whitacre again."

We agreed to get together again later next week. "One more thing," I raised my hand, "Red Cap Militia. Who wants to tackle them?"

"No way," Joe shook his head. "I'll see what the cousins say about it."

I remembered the other thing I wanted to ask Clarence. "Joe and I talked about Charity Whitacre helping with the diversity program. This might be completely off the subject, but I heard she runs a business of some sort. Do you know anything about it?" I was still stuck on how someone in Cascade could afford a Hermes handbag.

"Wait," Joe stood up. "I'll be right back."

He returned with a laptop. He googled Charity Whitacre and came up with *"Charity's Americana. Handmade American Crafts."*

I studied the website. It looked like she sold a variety of crafts—everything from turquoise jewelry to kitschy pottery. The items listed were guaranteed handmade and some were quite pricey.

"If her purse is any indication, she makes more with her online store than I do with my off-line editing." I needed to talk with her about Tony. Maybe using her expertise as an independent businesswoman might be my way in. I felt a slight tingle in the back of my neck. I recalled the photo in Matt's office of her and the other hunters. Something about Charity didn't add up.

Chapter Twenty-Six

Uncle Sam

Checking my watch, I saw I had a little time before meeting Travis at the Loonfeather. I parked in front of the restaurant and walked the two blocks to the *Killdeer Times* office. Jilly was getting ready to lock up when I walked in. No one else was in the building.

Jilly had worked at the *Times* since high school. Twenty years later, she kept the place afloat as the paper went through one novice editor after another. I hadn't met the newest editor yet.

"How are you?" Jilly called out from behind the counter. "Still editing those romances?"

I came close to complaining to her about the Vladess but decided anyone who could write a 400-page manuscript deserved respect. "I'm checking in to see if you found anything out about Sunny Morne."

She laughed. "I'm sure she's not the sister of Cloudy Day."

"Or Starlit Nite," I added.

"Unfortunately, my spies had nothing to report. Sunny doesn't spend any time at the salon, isn't active in church, and doesn't drink at the Loonfeather."

Behind me, the door opened. The amused expression on Jilly's face faded. I turned to see a woman in her mid-twenties wearing leggings with knee-high boots. Her longish brown hair fell loosely around her shoulders. She could have been pretty if her face didn't have such a sour expression.

"Hello, Jeanine."

Jeanine nodded and walked directly to the desk that housed the editor.

"Jamie, this is Jeanine Sanders, our new editor."

Jeanine seated herself without acknowledging me.

"Nice to meet you." I raised my voice like I was talking to someone hard of hearing.

She nodded and switched on the computer. "Likewise."

Jilly rolled her eyes, and I took this as a cue to leave.

"I'm late," I pointed to my watch. "Let me know if anything comes up."

In the darkening afternoon, it felt good to be outside and away from the tension in *The Times* office. Poor Jilly. She'd have to put up with Jeanine until the next editor came long.

The Loonfeather was Friday-afternoon busy. Travis had not arrived when I made my way past the bar into the dining room and found a table for two out of the noise of the patrons and the television set. The craft beer I ordered came in a frosty glass and had the good IPA taste of hops I'd learned to savor. While I waited, I reviewed my notes.

Travis arrived in jeans and a long-sleeved T-shirt with a Grandma's Marathon logo. When he sat down, I pointed to the shirt. "Did you run that?"

He straightened his shoulders. "You betcha. Finished in four hours."

In my youth, I'd watched the New York Marathon and remembered how miserable some of the runners looked. It was not a sport that I found appealing. "That's good, right?"

He grinned. "Good enough to get me this shirt."

When the waitress came, he looked at me. "Should we get a pitcher?"

I held up my beer. "I'm good."

I ordered a chef's salad and he ordered a steak dinner. I'd found that people in this part of the country liked their beef.

Before the food arrived, I filled him in on what I'd learned in Cascade. I left out the speculation about the second shooter and spent most of the time telling him about the kids and their connection to Winnie. "They thought he was on to something that had to do with the shooting."

"Winnie and I hadn't talked much in the last couple of years. I wish we had." Travis leaned back and looked up at the ceiling as if he were trying to pick out the right words. "I'm sorry I didn't warn him about Cascade. Winnie was obsessed with the death of his father and with Stone Kavanaugh. He'd talk about it over and over. He thought Kavanaugh should have gotten life in prison, and that he was into some bad things when he shot his dad."

"Interesting. I guess he was right about the 'bad things' considering what they found out about stolen goods." I sipped my beer. "I thought you said you didn't know why he wanted to go back to Cascade to teach."

He shrugged. "I didn't put two and two together until recently. He applied for the job in Cascade a few years after Stone was released from prison."

Something in the tone of his voice bothered me. Travis struck me as being intelligent, yet he didn't wonder more about why his cousin would go back to the town where his father was murdered.

I moved my beer glass around on the table, watching it make little circles of water. "I don't know what to do with all this information, Travis. It might mean something, and it might mean nothing."

"Are you sure you want to pursue it?"

"The people who died, they should have a voice..." I stopped. Was that really the reason I kept at the story? Was I sincerely being altruistic about giving a voice to those who died? Or was it the basic need for money? I had an editor who was interested. The magazine paid better than Florice or Letty, and I was pretty sure I could produce something that had quality and depth. Maybe it was the need for recognition as a writer. My poetry had gotten me nowhere.

Travis peered at me. "And?"

I opened my mouth and shut it again, at a loss for words.

"I...I think I have to do it. That's all." I looked down at the table, shaking my head.

"Sounds like you're not sure."

I saw concern in the way he looked at me. Instead of answering, I raised my glass. "Here's to figuring it out."

Before Travis could say anything more, the food arrived. He dug into his steak like he hadn't eaten in a week. Maybe this conversation was a little too serious for him. I picked at my salad mulling over his question. Why pursue it?

We spoke little during the meal. The lettuce in the salad tasted like it had been dried and reconstituted. The tomatoes were hard and tasteless, and my mood had plunged to new lows.

When he finally came up for air as he cleaned the last of the baked potato off his plate, he said, "I was just thinking. My parents were closed-mouthed about the death of Winnie's dad Sam. I overheard them one night when they thought I was in bed. My mom said, 'Do you think Sam was in cahoots with Kavanaugh?' I don't remember what Dad said, and I never heard them talk about it again."

"You mean your Uncle Sam might have been into something illegal, too?"

Travis shrugged. "It was odd when I look back. Uncle Sam was the banker, so you expected that he had some money. But it seemed like they had a lot more than usual. They had a huge house with horses, expensive new cars and they travelled a lot." He looked at me. "We're talking about Cascade, one of the poorest counties in the state. Even a banker wouldn't be that rich. Where did he get all that money?"

"Interesting." I wasn't sure what to make of this information.

"Even before they were caught, there were rumors the Red Cap Militia was selling stolen goods. I doubt John Bolton ever investigated. In fact, if they were, he was probably in on it."

I'd once read an article on stolen goods and money laundering. In order to 'clean' the money, it was helpful to have a cooperating bank or at least someone inside the bank who wouldn't question the infusion of cash. Maybe Uncle Sam was involved.

"Was Winnie trying to find out if his dad was involved?" My beer was almost gone. I decided not to order another.

Travis stared down at his empty plate. "I don't know. Maybe we'll never know. Uncle Sam is dead and now Winnie, too."

We sat in silence while the crowd in the bar erupted in response to the baseball game.

"Here's something I don't understand. Your Uncle Sam made a visit to

Kavanaugh to get money the bank was owed. I didn't think bankers made home visits."

He shrugged. "It's a small community. Maybe that was part of Sam's job."

"The land must have been valuable." I poured more dressing on the salad, hoping to make it palatable.

"Hard to believe Kavanaugh's land was worth anything. It abutted Nearbow Lake which is an unpleasant place. No beaches; probably polluted from old mining operations. I fished there when I was a kid. Never caught anything. No one goes there. The Natives think it's haunted."

I let it all sink in. "Maybe Winnie got in over his head trying to track down dirt on Kavanaugh."

"I don't know. But if someone ran him off the road..."

A roar rose up from the bar as someone called out, "By God, he just hit a grand slam." Sadly, I didn't care that the Minnesota Twins baseball team was headed for the playoffs. Dad had been a Yankees fan and even hauled me to a couple of games. Despite his enthusiasm, I found baseball to be boring.

"Dessert?" The server swept in looking at Travis with a big smile emphasizing the dimples on her cheeks. She was young, maybe just out of high school, her blonde ponytail bouncing when she walked.

"Sorry, I'm filled up to here." He brought his hand up to his chin. "Maybe some other time."

The server didn't even look at me before she giggled and turned away.

"You have a way with women," I commented.

Travis grinned. I liked the way his eyes sparkled when he was amused. For a moment, I felt the kind of rush Rose the milkmaid must have had when she first spotted Thorgest. As if my body was telling me to cool it, I bumped my empty beer glass and nearly knocked it over. Both Travis and I grabbed for it at the same time. His hand brushed mine, and again, I felt that longing.

"Oops," I said. "Looks like I've had enough."

He laughed. "One beer and you're tipsy?"

"You should see me after two beers." I laughed. "I really need to go. If I hear anything else, I'll let you know."

"Wait." He raised his hand. "I just thought of one more thing to add to the mix."

"Oh?" I took out my wallet to pay the server.

"I talked with Mom the other day. She said she had an odd call from Winnie two weeks ago."

Travis turned his attention to the main room as the bar crowd roared once again. I heard the sound of hands slapping.

When the noise died down, I prompted. "You said she had an odd call?"

"Winnie wanted to know how to reach Marla Kavanaugh. My mother and Marla's mother, Aggie, were good friends back in the day and they've kept in touch. Aggie divorced the idiot of a husband, a few years before the shooting and moved to Duluth with Marla after the shooting."

I wondered how that fit in. I thought about the woman who lost her son Neil and had to live with the knowledge of what he'd done. "Do you know why Winnie wanted to talk with Marla?"

Travis shrugged. "Not a clue."

I stood up. "Interesting. I'll add it to all the other random pieces I have."

He smiled. "Keep in touch. I think I'll stay a little longer. Belly up to the bar, as they say. Find out what's happening with the Twins."

When I walked out, I didn't look back to see if he was watching me. Once in my car, I sat for a few moments before starting it up. A piece of me wanted to go back into the Loonfeather and belly up to the bar with Travis. Another told me to go home and pet my dog.

As if to settle the conversation my phone pinged with a text from Jim. **Alone in the apartment having a beer. Wish you could join me. Hope to be back soon.**

I wanted to text back and tell him I needed him in my bed right now. Instead, I sent him a smiling emoji.

"Coward," I muttered as I pulled onto the street.

Chapter Twenty-Seven

Coach Mayor

Saturday dawned clear and sunny. I gazed at the lake and at all the leaves that had fallen since Jim and I had raked. I wanted to text him and demand that he come back and rake with me. Instead, after breakfast, I called Coach Mayor.

He answered on the third ring. "Mayor here. If you're selling, I'm not buying."

"Not selling, honest." I introduced myself, told him I'd gotten his number from Joe, and explained I was planning to write an article about the shooting.

"Well, it's about damn time someone did something about it." His voice had a gravelly quality about it as if he was a longtime smoker.

"Joe told me you left when they cancelled the football season."

"Couldn't stand Matt Whitacre. He wanted to push the whole thing under a rug." He coughed. "Sorry, I've got a little bug of some sort. Anyway, Whitacre was a fool if he thought people wouldn't talk."

"Joe said the kids were comfortable talking to you."

He laughed and it turned into another cough. "Hell, I don't know if they were comfortable or not. But the day Whitacre announced the end of the football season, a few of the boys came to me. They weren't happy."

"I can imagine." I grabbed a pen to take notes as he spoke. Bronte sat calmly next to me with her ears pricked up. I resisted the temptation to put him on speaker. Who would do that so their dog could listen in?

"They weren't upset about the end of the season. They'd lost their two main players—Joe and his brother Frank. Those two held the team together."

"What were they upset about?"

"They were mad because Whitacre and the other teachers shut them down whenever they tried to talk about what happened. Geeze, think about it. A major shooting, classmates, and a popular teacher killed—all of them Native Americans. Had hate crime written all over it. But Whitacre didn't do a damn thing except for a prissy little announcement from the principal about 'thoughts and prayers.' That place was sick. I was happy to walk out the door."

"Were the other teachers supporting Whitacre in this? Nothing I've ever read about dealing with a tragedy like this says to not talk about it."

Coach Mayor let out a sour laugh. "Whitacre told me his wife had some kind of degree in counseling. She told him that new research on school shootings says the best way to get over it is to 'move on.' That's pure bullshit."

This was the first time I'd heard anyone mention Charity's role in the campaign of silence. "Was Mrs. Whitacre a counselor at the school? I know she runs an online store and was helping Tony with the diversity program."

"Hah! I think she was helping Tony with something else."

"Excuse me?"

"Whitacres own a big house and horse ranch outside of town. I guess it used to belong to the banker who was killed—Winston Starling's dad."

Matt owned Uncle Sam's property?

"Tony worked for Charity the summer before the shooting. I heard they got along good."

"An affair?"

"Just talk. It died down quickly after he was killed."

I scratched my head. None of these pieces of information formed a picture of Tony the teacher.

I told him about Winnie's death but didn't mention the rumor that it wasn't an accident.

Coach cleared his throat. "Sorry to hear it. Didn't know Winnie well, but he seemed like an okay kid." The background noise over the phone sounded like cheers from a television broadcast.

"What did you say to the kids who came to you?" I asked.

"I let them talk. They wanted to talk about why Neil would shoot. It didn't make sense to them."

"I've read profiles on shooters in some of the schools. I didn't think he fit the others."

Coach sighed heavily. "You're right. Neil was a good kid. And he was well-liked in school. I never had any problems with him except that I couldn't teach him to sink a basket. Too bad because he had the height, but not the coordination."

"Do you have any idea what drove him to do what he did?"

The line was silent for a few moments except for the muffled noise of the game.

"Cascade has a history of bad characters. You've heard about the Red Cap Militia? White supremacist group?"

I pictured the men in the bar with their baseball caps. "Yes, a couple of people have told me about them. I've seen some men in Cascade wearing red baseball caps with a confederate flag."

"God damn. They're like a jock itch that won't go away. That's another reason I think Whitacre didn't want to make noise about the shooting. People in town might be goddam bigots, but they're touchy about being labeled kin to the KKK."

Bronte stood up and sauntered to the door. I followed her and let her out to roam in the woods by the cabin. Taking a deep breath of the brisk air, I asked, "Did you see any prejudice against the Native students?"

Coach paused as if choosing his words carefully. "It was there, of course, but I've seen worse. Kids like Joe and Frank really helped to dampen it. They were both very popular."

I watched through the screen door as Bronte chased a squirrel up a tree. I wished I felt that much exuberance so early in the morning.

"One more question for you. What can you tell me about Tony as a teacher? I was planning on focusing the article on him as a Native American schoolteacher in an almost all-white school, but I'm having trouble finding people who will talk about him."

Coach whispered something to someone before he came back on the line. "Sorry. You wanted to talk about Tony?"

"How was he as a teacher? Is there anything I should know about him?"

"Good guy. Students liked him, and many of the teachers did not."

This was the first time I'd heard anything negative about Tony. "Why didn't the other teachers like him?"

Coach laughed. "He made them look bad, I guess. I used to call the teachers who had been around for a while the 'old guard.' They didn't like change, they didn't like the energy he put into teaching, and mostly, they didn't like how he was working with the kids from the reservation. Old prejudices die hard. Ruffled a bunch of feathers. The old guard took it as an insult to their teaching, I guess."

Insult to their teaching? That seemed strange to me, but I let it go.

"One more question for you. Did you ever hear about something going on between Tony and Marla Kavanaugh, Neil's sister?"

Coach sounded confused. "Marla? The one who worked for Whitacre? Good God! That has to be one of the most asinine rumors ever. Do you know anything about Marla?"

I played dumb. "Only that she worked for Matt."

"That poor girl was a walking poster for why you get your kids vaccinated."

Bronte bounded to the door with something in her mouth. I opened the screen long enough to see that it was a dead bird. I shoved her away as I asked. "What do you mean?"

"The story I heard was that her parents were either against doing the vaccinations or just too dumb to get around to it. She got the measles after a trip to Minneapolis to the Mall of America when she was three or four. Ended up with encephalitis that damaged her brain."

"Oh. I didn't know that."

"Her dad, who was an idiot, went around blaming those damn 'illegals' for bringing it across the border. Marla could barely read. The only thing I can tell you is that Tony was nice to everyone including her." He paused. "I do remember walking by his classroom that fall, and she was sitting at a desk in the front talking to him. I thought it strange at the time."

"You don't know what they were talking about."

"Nope. And I never saw her in the classroom again."

Coach started coughing again. This seemed like a good time to end the conversation. I asked if I could contact him again if I had more questions.

He responded, "Anytime. Hope you do a great exposé on the incompetence of that school." He ended the call.

Bronte woofed at the door. This time her mouth was empty. She walked in, her tail wagging.

"Well, girl, I can see that Coach Mayor has no regrets about leaving Cascade. I wonder if I could find another former teacher who could corroborate what he said."

Bronte licked my hand before going to her water dish. I took it as an affirmative. I'd have to check with either Joe or Carin to find someone else.

I sat in the quiet of my kitchen trying to plug in what he said to what I already knew. Still nothing really fit together. If I could catch Matt, maybe I'd get his side of the story on the reluctance to talk about the shooting. Maybe he could tell me more about Marla and her relationship to Tony. And maybe, just maybe, I had nothing cohesive to write.

"Damn, now what?"

Instead of pondering it more, I took out Letty's manuscript. I was halfway through the first read, and by my count, Vladess had sucked the life out of four lovers—Troy, Joshua, Eric, and Mark. She was now on her fifth one, her ruby lips whispering a spell into the ear of Count David, owner of a castle near Transylvania.

I sighed. "Okay, Count David. Are you going to stand up and salute while she drains you dry?"

Ten pages later, Count David was alive and charming Vladess. Was he a vampire as well? Finally, we had a plot. Maybe the day would go well for me.

Clarence called near lunchtime. I filled him in on what the coach had told me.

"This Whitacre sounds like an idiot," he commented.

CHAPTER TWENTY-SEVEN

"I wonder about his wife. Was Tony having an affair with her?"

"Ah, the plot thickens?"

I waited for Clarence to say more, but the line was quiet. Thinking back on the conversation at the Loonfeather with Travis I remembered what he'd said yesterday about Sam Starling. I asked Clarence, "I heard there was some speculation that Winnie's father had more money than you would expect of a small-town banker."

Clarence chuckled. "Heard the same thing myself back then. There was nothing to prove it, of course. The rich have ways of hiding their money and their sources."

"He might have been involved in something illegal?" Perhaps that explained Winnie's fascination with his father. Perhaps he learned something that got him into trouble.

"I'm getting too old to speculate on that. I called for another reason. My friend Peterson hasn't seen his Sunny for several days and he's worried about her."

"I haven't been able to find anything on her—she's not on social media and my confidential informants don't know anything. My guess is that Sunny is an alias."

Clarence laughed a deep amused sound that made me smile.

"Can you get me a photo of her? Maybe I can try some photo recognition apps."

Still laughing, Clarence said, "I'll see what I can do. I'll also find out if he's missing more money."

I thought about Vladess and how she sucked her lovers dry. Sounded like Pete Peterson had found himself a vampire.

Chapter Twenty-Eight

Call from the Kids

I finished the first read-through of Letty's novel by midafternoon. I felt more drained than the victims. Fortunately, Count David was smarter than Troy and the others. Instead of being seduced, he seduced her. Who knew a vampiress with no soul could fall in love? In the end, Vladess figured out how to join him as a mortal and transformed from Vladess the vampire to Valerie the Countess. I imagined that she and Count David were destined to live happily ever after in his dank, dreary castle on the border of Transylvania.

"Well, girl, I think I have this one figured out." Bronte raised her head from the cushion where she napped. "Letty DeVoss decided to write a revenge romance. She'd probably been jilted at one time by Troy, Joshua, Eric, and Mark before she met David, her true love. What do you think?"

Bronte sighed, got up, and trotted over to her empty dish.

After I fed her, I brewed a fresh pot of coffee. With a mug in hand, I walked outside to my rock. Two loons paddled on the quiet waters of the lake. One ducked its head into the water to retrieve an afternoon snack. I watched them savoring the moment. I'd read that with climate change and warming, the loons might soon disappear.

As the sun bathed my face in warmth, I decided, despite my financial trials and my iffy love life, the cabin was where I wanted to be. Bronte lay at my feet chewing on a stick. All that was missing was the sound of Jim's pickup truck rattling down the driveway.

Closing my eyes, I thought about where I was this time last year. As the trees in Central Park turned their autumn golds and yellows, I'd sat on a bench hardly aware the seasons had changed. Too much had happened in a short period of time. My father, my only family, had died. My husband, who had once pledged eternal faithfulness, had left me, and my job was on the line because I suddenly couldn't make the deadlines.

"It was a terrible time for me," I explained to Bronte as she ripped the bark off a birch branch. But the trauma had been far worse than those losses. It was on the eve of the final divorce decree that the drug enforcement task force had kicked down the door of my Queens apartment and ripped me out of bed. Twenty-four hours in a Queens holding cell had turned me into a zombie, afraid of anyone in a uniform.

"I don't live in constant fear anymore," I explained to my dog. "Instead, I'm sitting here, now, having a one-way conversation with an animal who brings me dead birds. Still, it's an improvement."

Bronte sat up and deposited the stick at my feet with a nod of her head that meant, "Throw it for me." I picked it up and hurled it into the lake before it occurred to me that I would have to contend with a wet dog.

We kept up the fetch for several more rounds until I heard the sound of a car's wheels crunching gravel as it neared the cabin. Bronte barked, loping up the hill toward the car.

"Who is it, girl?" I followed her.

Travis pulled up, parked, and slid out of the driver's seat. He reached in the backseat and brought out a six-pack of beer. "Need some refreshment?"

He wore faded jeans and a long-sleeved flannel shirt. If anyone fit the image of a Northwoods Minnesotan, he did. Blonde hair, muddy blue eyes and all.

"You're taking a risk showing up unannounced."

"Jim assured me you would be chained to your cabin over the weekend."

"Oh?"

Travis must have seen the skeptical expression on my face. "He said you texted him that you were working on some book. I thought you might need a break."

Bronte sniffed at him, accepted a pat on her wet head, and trotted to the back door. "Oh, no. Not until you dry off."

"I hope you are referring to the dog and not me."

I laughed. It was nice to have company.

We sat on the rock together watching the water ebb and flow against the little sandy beach. Travis drank a beer while I finished my coffee. I told him about my phone call with Coach Mayor.

"I didn't know the coach," Travis said, idly throwing a little rock into the lake. It made a plunking sound when it hit the water. "He came after we moved. I heard he had a reputation for producing good teams."

"He wasn't a fan of Matt Whitacre. He thought Whitacre handled the shooting stupidly."

Travis emptied the beer. "If I recall right, Whitacre was hired several years before the shooting. He replaced the old fossil who had been there since the American Revolution."

A grayish-white cloud obscured the sun and the temperature dropped. Goosebumps rose on my arms. I was glad my coffee was still hot. "Did you know Matt bought your uncle's house?"

"I heard Mom say something about it—like Whitacre's wife had some money."

"Whitacre's wife, according to the coach, was the one who advised him to tell the students to 'move on.'"

"Hmmm." Travis stood up and pointed to the cabin. "I'm getting a refill. Do you want one?"

I pointed to my coffee mug. "I'm going to finish this first." At the rate he was going, there wouldn't be any beer left for me.

When he came back, we chatted about the cabin, the weather, and the upcoming winter. I told him I was getting a new furnace next week.

"Have you ever experienced a Minnesota winter?" He asked.

"No. But I know cold. I can't imagine anything worse than the freezing wind whipping through the skyscrapers in Manhattan."

Travis laughed. "You're in for a surprise."

I found it nice to have a human being close to me but worried about how good the heat of his body sitting next to me felt. Was he interested in me now that Jim was away? When he leaned over to pick up another pebble to toss in the lake, his arm brushed mine. I should have pulled away, giving him the message that I wasn't available, but I didn't

If I had been Vladess, I would have been all over him by now, sucking the honey-sweet blood from him, feeling the surge of power and excitement as our bodies touched.

The sound of my phone snapped me out of my thoughts. My cheeks heated with embarrassment as I stood up and pulled out the phone. "Sorry, I'd better take this."

I walked away from the rock as I answered. I didn't recognize the caller ID. "This is Jamie Forest. Can I help you?"

"Ms. Forest?"

The sound was so soft I could barely understand the words. "Can you speak up?"

"This is Amy, you know, from Cascade High School?"

"Yes, Amy." The line crackled. "We have a bad connection."

"Please," her voice faded for a moment. ". . . hasn't come back yet... Scared. Something isn't right...Nearbow Lake..."

Raising my voice to a near shout, I asked. "Are you talking about Tess?"

"...Don't know where she is...think she knows something important..." The phone went dead.

In contrast to the ominous message of the phone call, the cloud moved away from the sun, and bright rays glinted off the water.

I tried redialing the number, but nothing happened. Next, I tried texting Amy. The text failed.

"Problems?" Travis walked to me as I worked the phone.

I told him about the call. "Tess's friends are worried about her. I think Jay is holding something back."

"Could it be a prank? You know, teenagers getting the nosy journalist?"

I thought about the students. They seemed too serious to be playing some kind of joke. "No, I think their worry is real."

We walked inside. Travis helped himself to another beer and offered one to me. We sat at the kitchen table with a plate of cheese and crackers.

"I think I should call Jay again."

Travis frowned. "He already told you she was all right. I'm guessing that won't change."

"Then what should we do?"

Travis finished the last cracker. "Jay and I aren't exactly friends anymore, but I could give him a call."

"And what would you tell him? That I asked you to call?"

Bronte sat at Travis's side hoping for a crumb. She knew better than to ask me.

He finished his beer before he replied. "I'll tell him I pulled over some teenagers from Cascade the other day and they told me they were worried about a classmate."

It sounded sketchy to me, but I shrugged. "You go."

Travis took out his phone and scrolled through until he found the number for the Cascade sheriff's office. He hit speaker. The phone rang until it went to a voice mail telling us that if this was an emergency to call 911 and otherwise leave a message. He hung up before the beep.

"Forgot it's the weekend. I'll try his personal cell."

This time Jay answered after two rings. Travis told him the story of the teenagers and their concerns. The line was quiet before Jay said, "They don't need to worry about Tess. She's fine. Home with the flu is all." He hung up.

Travis stared at the phone. "Geeze, for a man in a political office, he doesn't have much finesse."

Even with the poor quality of the speaker, Jay's voice sounded strained. "I think he's worried or scared."

Amy had said something about Nearbow Lake. I retrieved the box of Tony's things and took out the crude map of the lake and Gravedigger's Island. I pointed to the circled area. "Could there be a cabin or something here?"

Travis studied it. I noticed he squinted like he was having some trouble focusing. Two beers remained of the six-pack, and I was only halfway through my first beer. At this rate, I couldn't let him drive anywhere.

He looked up from the map. "I called my dad last night to ask about Kavanaugh's property by Nearbow Lake. He said he thought the militia had some kind of a hideout on Gravediggers Island back when they were active."

He went to the refrigerator. "Want another?"

I held up my half-full bottle and shook my head. He uncapped the beer and sat back down gazing at me. When he spoke, he had a slight slur to his speech. "I have something to tell you."

Red flag, the little voice in my head said. The last time a man used that phrase with me, it was Andrew, my ex. He'd ended the phrase with, "and now you know why I'm leaving."

Travis must have read something into my expression because he smiled. "You look like I'm about to tell you the diagnosis is terminal."

I didn't say anything. Andrew hadn't smiled, he'd simply blurted out that he had found someone else.

"It's about Winnie," Travis continued. My shoulders relaxed as he watched me. "Even though he was younger than me, I spent a lot of time at his house. I've always said he was a nice kid, but—odd."

I picked at a crumb on the table. "What are you trying to say?"

"If there was something not right about the shooting or something not right in Cascade, I think Winnie knew more than he was saying."

Travis went on to tell me he saw Winnie as a manipulator. "Even in grade school, he got kids to do things for him. My parents used to say, 'he's got his father in him.' They didn't have a high opinion of Uncle Sam."

Thinking about my brief encounter with Winnie, I realized he'd made me a little edgy. I'd assumed it was because I'd finally found someone to talk with me and didn't want to spoil it.

It was dawning on me what Travis was trying to say. "You think he used those high school kids to find out something?"

I felt like a darkness had descended on the room. Bronte felt it too because she walked to the door and whined to go out.

We talked a little more about what the kids had told me but came up with nothing. "I don't think they uncovered anything." As I thought about it, though, I pictured the ring of keys in Josh's hands. "I'm sure Winnie got the keys to the building for the kids. If they got caught, Winnie could claim he knew nothing about it."

"It gave them access to all the offices."

Outside the sun was setting. Travis peeled the label off his beer bottle, rolling up the little pieces of paper and placing them in a neat row.

As I thought about Winnie, I remembered what Travis had said at the bar. "Winnie was looking for Marla. Do you know if your mother has a phone number for her? If he talked with Marla, maybe she could shed some light on all of this."

Travis raised his eyebrows with a shrug. "I'll ask, though I can't see what Marla has to do with any of this."

I told him what the coach had said about Tony and Marla. "Maybe she found something on Whitacre because she did filing in his office." Pushing back my chair, I stood up and stretched. "Too much information going nowhere. Let me make some supper, okay?"

Travis studied the map while I quickly scrambled some eggs with broccoli and cheese.

While I fixed the food, he turned the crude map several times. "I think I know where this is. I can get us there." He pointed to the line drawn on the map. "If you take a canoe and follow this line, it will get you across the lake. Must be a landing on the island."

We ate the eggs in silence. Once he cleaned his plate, he leaned back. "I should go there. Maybe I'll find something interesting."

I brewed a pot of coffee to go with ice cream and chocolate sauce. Travis had two helpings of ice cream and two cups of coffee. The way he gazed at me had me wondering if he was hoping for an invitation to stay. I knew coffee didn't actually sober a person up, it simply made them more alert. Still, I didn't want to signal to him that it was okay to stay, even though a part of me wanted it.

"I have more work to do tonight," I pointed to the manuscript stacked neatly on the counter. "I hate to, but I should send you your way."

He nodded. "Guess so."

CHAPTER TWENTY-EIGHT

"You sure you're okay to drive?"

"Never better." At the door, he hugged me. It was nice to have the warmth of his body against me. When I pushed away, I saw something in his eyes that Rose, the fictional dairymaid, would have called 'an earthy need.'

Definitely time for him to go as I guided him out the door.

Bronte and I stood on the step watching as his car disappeared down the driveway. I worried about Travis and his alcohol consumption but decided it wasn't my problem.

The night chill was coming on. Time to build a fire.

Chapter Twenty-Nine

Tess's House

After Travis left, I built a fire and sat on the floor in front of the fireplace with a cup of tea. Bronte settled next to me chewing on her rawhide. As I watched the flames, I wondered if I'd made a mistake by sending Travis off. If he was with me, would I feel the same as I did with Jim?

As I tried to shake those thoughts the phone buzzed, and Jim's face came up on the caller ID.

"Hey," he said. "What are you up to?"

The sound of his voice triggered an ache in my chest. I fought to keep my voice from breaking. "Just drinking tea and watching the glow of the fireplace." I longed to say *and missing you*, but the words wouldn't come. Instead, I told him about Travis.

"Hmmm...he showed up with a six pack?" Jim's voice sounded amused. Didn't he realize Travis was an attractive man?

"And he drank most of it himself." I shook my head thinking about how fast the beer disappeared.

"I hope you didn't try to keep up with him."

"You know me, two beers and out."

He laughed.

I filled him in on my progress with Vladess. "Now that I know Vladess will become Countess Valerie, I can move on to stage two of the edits."

"Glad I'm not there to hear you muttering."

He told me about Jake's progress. The pneumonia had cleared, and his counts were going up. They planned to discharge him tomorrow. "Maybe I can make a quick trip up to see you next week. I'll have a few days off."

"I could use you tonight. No furnace and the temperature dropping."

I reached over and poked the fire before I told him about the phone call from Amy. The fact that the kids hadn't seen Tess in a while caused my stomach to tighten. "Jay isn't worried. Or so he says. I think something is really wrong."

Jim thought for a few moments. "What about her parents? Could you call them?"

"Maybe I'll try tomorrow, although I'm in a very weird position with this. I've only met her once. What would I say to them?"

Beside me, Bronte pushed herself up and sauntered toward the back door. I hated to end the call, but it was late, and I was exhausted. Between Letty DeVoss and her vampires and the Cascade mess, my body felt drained.

When I said goodbye, I added, "Love you." The last time I'd said that to a man, he'd left me for his Venezuelan make-up artist.

Jim cleared his throat, paused, and finally said, "Sleep tight." I set the phone down, poked the embers of the fire, and decided, best not to get too attached to anyone right now.

In the night, the temperature dropped to near freezing. The little electric heater barely kept me warm even with all the covers and a dog next to me. Maybe Travis was right. I didn't know cold yet.

The day dawned with a thin layer of clouds that kept the sun from fully heating the earth. A mist rose from the lake. I watched it from the kitchen window while the oven heated the kitchen area.

"Well, girl, that furnace can't get here fast enough. How did people survive before propane?"

After breakfast, I called Travis. It went directly to voice mail. "Travis, it's Jamie. I talked to Jim last night, and he thought I should call Tess's parents and confirm that she is homesick, like Jay said. I tried to find them in the white pages but couldn't find a number. Any thoughts?"

Travis called back an hour later. He sounded groggy and tired over the phone. We discussed contacting Tess's parents, and Travis suggested that we drive to Cascade together. "We can stop by their house and knock on the door, just like real investigators." He had an odd edge to his voice when he said this. I wasn't sure if he was mocking me or mocking himself.

That little voice in the back of my head repeated several times, *are you getting in deeper than you should?*

If we were going to be in Cascade, this might be a good time to talk with the kids again. I tried the number Amy had called me with last night, but it wouldn't go through. Rummaging through my bag, I found Josh's number and called it.

"Hullo?" He sounded like he was half asleep.

"It's Jamie the writer. I'm wondering if you, Amy, and Phil could meet with me today to talk about the shooting and the article I want to write?"

I heard voices in the background when he replied. "I guess."

We agreed to meet at a public access to Nearbow Lake because he said it was little used. I suspected he didn't want to be seen in town with me. This would give me the chance to get a look at the mysterious Gravediggers Island. I pictured it as a barren mound filled with gravestones.

When I called Travis back with the plan, he sounded less groggy. "Meet me at my place in Killdeer in an hour." He gave me the address. It was one of the only regular apartment buildings in town. Most of Killdeer was comprised of single-family houses. I'd heard that many of the new teachers rented apartments in that building. If Jeanine Sanders, the new editor, lived there, perhaps I could introduce her to Travis. If anyone could wipe the sour look off her face, he would be the person.

Killdeer was Sunday morning quiet. I was the only car on the main street. In the summer, every day was busy in town because of the tourists who came to enjoy Lake Larissa and the nearby state park. The Loonfeather was usually packed. Today, a few cars were parked by the café, but nothing else stirred.

I pulled up in front of the apartment building. Travis stood on the front step, shading his eyes as the sun came out from under the thin layer of clouds. He looked surprisingly untouched by all the beer he had consumed last night.

Walking up to him, I pointed to the building. "Is the new *Killdeer Times* editor one of your neighbors?"

"You mean the woman in 216 with the perpetual frown?"

I told him my experience meeting her. He agreed that she was particularly unfriendly. "I can usually get a smile out of anybody. But not her."

On the way to Cascade, I told him about my phone call with Josh. "He seemed less than enthused to meet with us. How can a town produce so much fear?"

"It wasn't always that way. At least I didn't see it when I was growing up until the mines closed and property values dropped. I look back at when my family moved to the Twin Cities and remember a feeling of defeat."

"Defeat?"

"Like the bad guys had won." He glanced at me with a serious expression. "The militia scaring people, Uncle Sam murdered, and a sheriff that no one trusted."

"That's a lot for a kid."

"Maybe that's why I eventually went into law enforcement."

Interesting how people like Winnie and Travis were drawn back to this community. If I'd grown up in Cascade, I'd have headed for other parts as soon as I could.

Cascade was even quieter than Killdeer. The only evidence of people were a few stragglers coming out of the church near the courthouse.

"If I remember right, Tess's parents live near the school."

We drove by the abandoned motel. A pickup truck and the battered SUV were still parked at the side of the motel. I pointed to them, "I think that's the car that tried to run me off the road. Do you think someone is squatting in that building?"

The windows were all boarded up and the motel was surrounded by a ten-foot chain-link fence. It was hard to imagine anyone inside. Travis shrugged but made no comment. He turned down the street by the school and drove another block. The four houses on this block were all midcentury ranch style with picture windows looking out onto the street. Two of them had For Sale signs. Travis pulled up to the one on the corner. The front drapes were pulled shut.

"Looks neglected." I noted the tall weeds growing up in the flowerbeds in front of the house. A hanging planter by the door held the browned remains of a dead flower. "Are you sure this is Tess's place?"

Travis didn't reply. He appeared to be lost in thought for a few moments. When he turned to me, I saw sadness in the downturn of his mouth. "Our house was a couple of blocks from here. This part of town was filled with kids. It used to be a riot of ghosts and goblins on Halloween. It looks so dead around here now."

We walked up to the door together. I had decided I would tell the Boltons I'd interviewed Tess last week and wanted to verify some things. It was almost true. When Travis knocked, I was ready with a notepad and a pencil.

After the first knock, we waited. I heard a faint sound that could have come from a television set. When no one answered, Travis knocked again, harder. He had a determined set to his jaw like he was tracking down a lead.

Still no answer. This time Travis called out, "It's Travis Booker. I used to play with your brother Jay. Can you open up?"

His voice was answered by the creak of floorboards as someone approached the door. Without opening it, a male voice called, "Yeah. What do you want?"

"Can you open the door?" I asked. "We're looking for Tess."

"What the hell?" The man who unlocked the door was unshaven with a mop of greasy hair hanging over his forehead. Even from where I was standing, I smelled his unwashed odor. Peeking out at me he demanded, "Who the hell are you?" When he caught sight of Travis he added, "And what the hell are you doing here?"

His tone seemed to be a mixture of anger—maybe even rage—combined with fear. Growing up in New York, I was used to loud conversations and shouting, but this was something different. I fought to keep the nervousness out of my words. "Mr. Bolton, I had a few follow-up questions for Tess on a story I'm doing. She hasn't been answering her phone so I thought I'd stop over to see if she could talk with me."

Travis smiled and added with a shrug. "Jamie needed help finding your place, so I volunteered."

"You wanna screw it up for her? Get the hell out of here. Now!" He slammed the door.

I felt the vibrations from the impact of the door on the frame. "Wow."

As we walked to the car, I glanced back at the house and saw a face peeking out from the drapes. For a moment I thought it was Tess until I realized it must have been her mother. I almost turned back, hoping she'd open the door, but the face disappeared inside.

Once we were back in the car, I asked Travis, "What do you think?"

He frowned, pressing his lips together. "I don't know. Let's hope the kids have some information that will make sense of this."

I felt a sinking sensation in the pit of my stomach that Tess was in trouble for something connected back to the shooting two years ago.

Chapter Thirty

Dead Man's Curve

On the way out of town, Travis turned to me. "Before we head for the lake, do you mind if we take a little detour to see Uncle Sam's place?" He paused, clearing his throat. "And where Winnie went off the road?"

"Uh. Okay." I wasn't sure I wanted to see where Winnie met his death, but it was clear to me that it was important to Travis.

He took the main highway north toward Nearbow Lake and about a half-mile out of town, turned onto a gravel road leading into a thickly forested area. Ahead, the road took a sharp turn around a swampy lowland.

"Dead Man's Curve." He pointed. "That's where they found Winnie. The report said he missed the curve and ended up rolling the car."

I shivered as we neared the curve. Ruts in the gravel and tire tracks showed where Winnie's car had gone off the road. I closed my eyes and for a moment relived my experience as I faced the curve with the SUV forcing me toward the ditch.

"I..." Words wouldn't come out.

Travis slowed then stopped. He studied me as I fought back tears. When I looked at him, I saw a grim set to his mouth. Without speaking, I opened the car door and stepped out. The air smelled of the dampness of the swampy area. I expected to hear the chirping of the frogs and insects. Instead, I was met with silence—not even a whisper of a breeze through the brown, weedy expanse.

Travis joined me as I surveyed the area. I turned to him. "Do you think someone ran him off the road?"

"I don't know."

I tried to picture how the car must have landed. A few shards of broken glass glinted in the sunlight. As I squinted at them, something dark caught my attention. "What's that?"

Near where the car must have landed was a piece of fabric. I picked my way through the weeds and muddy ruts. Travis followed. Partially buried in the trampled grass was a black ski mask.

"Oh my god! Winnie had that with him at the restaurant."

Travis stooped down and gingerly picked it up. "I have a plastic bag in the backseat of the car. Can you get it for me?"

When I brought it back, he carefully dropped the mask into it.

"What…what are you going to do with the mask?"

Travis studied it. "Nothing right now." Abruptly he turned back to the car. "We should get going."

Back in the car, Travis reached under the driver's seat and brought out a flask. Uncapping it, he offered it to me. "At toast to Winnie."

I took a small sip. "To Winnie." The bourbon burned my throat and I fought not to choke. My eyes watered. Travis didn't appear to notice as he took a long pull on the flask.

He turned to me. With his sunglasses on I couldn't read his expression. "Ever since the accident, I've beaten my head against the wall trying to figure out why Winnie would be out on this road. He lived in town."

I told him about how Winnie saw Charity and left shortly after. "Maybe he had a meeting with her?"

He shrugged. "Doesn't make sense."

I mentally added this piece of information to everything else I'd learned. Travis was right, none of it made sense.

"Should we turn back? I don't need to see your Uncle Sam's place."

Travis had a grim set to his jaw. "I'd like to see the old place." He took one last swig on his flask and tucked it under the seat.

Chapter Thirty-One

Nearbow Lake

We continued to Uncle Sam's old place. Two miles beyond Dead Man's Curve, the woods opened up to a clearing. On one side of the road was a cemetery that looked abandoned. Weeds and grass grew tall and dead leaves piled up against the headstones. My body did an involuntary shudder as I thought about all the dead who were now forgotten.

Travis must have noticed my reaction. "This place hasn't had a burial in fifty years. There's a newer one closer to town. When I was a kid, we used to bike here to scare ourselves. Jay and I dared each other to spend a night alone by that mausoleum." He pointed to a gray, granite building about the size of a tool shed. "I made it until just after dark, sure I'd heard someone inside. Jay claimed he slept the whole night, but I never believed him."

"You two really were friends."

He sighed. "A long time ago. People change."

I wasn't sure if he meant Jay or himself.

A quarter of a mile from the cemetery on the other side of the road was an open pasture surrounded by a white wooden fence. A sign arched over the driveway announcing, "Whitacre's Acres." At the end of the drive stood a large brick house with a wraparound veranda overlooking a well-kept yard and the pasture beyond it. Two horses grazed in the cool sunlight.

Travis pulled to the side of the road. "That was Uncle Sam's place except back then it was wooded all the way to the house. Whitacre must have cleared out the trees to make a place for the horses."

"It reminds me of Graceland. My Dad took me there once. I thought I'd be bored, but it turned out I liked the music and the history."

"My grandparents were Elvis fans. Me? Not so much."

The house and grounds should have been set in the South, not in Cascade. "Seems like Whitacre would need a lot of money to keep this place up."

"The last time I saw it was a couple of years after Uncle Sam was killed. Sam's wife had put it on the market and moved with Winnie. It stood empty for a long time. It almost burned down when kids were using it for a party place and set the kitchen on fire."

Considering how much money I had spent to make my little cabin habitable, I couldn't imagine what Whitacre put into fixing this huge house. "Charity must be making a lot of money with her business."

Several buildings stood behind the house. One was a low, white structure that must have been the stable. Another, a large wood-sided garage. The third, closest to the house was structured like an old carriage house complete with dormers. "Could that be the office for *Charity's Americana?*" The parking area in front of it was empty.

"Could be. I hear she employs people from town."

"Doing what?"

Travis grinned with a shrug. "Making Americana?"

I laughed and it felt good after the grim scene at Dead Man's Curve.

In the slanting light of the sun as it filtered through the windshield, I thought I detected an expression of envy on Travis's face. "Would you like a place like this?"

He didn't respond. Having lived in cramped apartments all my life, I found large houses made me nervous. I was happy for the tidy nest of my cabin.

As we were turning around to go back to the highway, a woman riding a horse emerged from the woods across the road from the house. She rode tall moving with the horse in an easy gait. When she neared our car, I recognized Charity. It was hard not to appreciate the way she carried herself and the way her ponytail swayed with the rhythm of the horse.

DEATH OF A STARLING

She trotted up to the car as Travis rolled down his window.

"Hello, Mr. State Trooper." She greeted Travis with a slight accent that I couldn't place.

"Hello, Mrs. Whitacre. Beautiful day for a ride."

Her smile could have dazzled a Hollywood producer. I was impressed and also uncomfortable with it. My ex's girlfriend had a smile like that.

"What brings you out here?" She leaned closer to the car. I guessed her riding outfit cost more than my furnace.

"Just a Sunday drive. Showing my friend the sights." He pointed down the driveway to the house. "I like what you have done."

She dazzled him with another smile.

I leaned over and introduced myself. "I met your husband the other day when I talked with him about Tony Vincent. I understand you were working with him on the Native American project."

The smile disappeared. "So sad. Tony was a good teacher. But everyone must go on."

"I'm doing a story on Tony. I'd love to talk with you about him. Maybe we could set up a time?" I really wanted to ask her about Winnie and if he was meeting her the night he died.

The horse stamped his hoof on the gravel with an impatient whinny. "Sorry, Beauty here is restless. I must go." She waved at us as she urged the horse down the driveway. An image of Vladess flashed through my head. Could she suck the life out of men?

Travis stared at her long enough that I cleared my throat. "Notice how she avoided my question about setting up a meeting?" I paused, thinking about the interchange. "She called you Mr. State Trooper. What was that all about?"

"I stopped her for speeding once."

"Oh?"

He put the car in drive and headed down the road without responding. When we reached Dead Man's Curve, he slowed for a moment. I wondered if he was going to stop, but he drove on, the gravel of the road spitting against the bottom of the car.

The highway to Nearbow Lake took us past Eyeman's Corner. When we reached the little country store, it looked as abandoned as it had earlier. I pointed to it. "Odd place in the middle of nowhere."

"Not for me. When I was in junior high school, this was the only place a kid could buy cigarettes. We'd bicycle out here in the summer and hang around smoking like we were really cool."

"But it was illegal, wasn't it?"

He laughed, "So was the beer they sold to the older kids."

"Did George Big Horse own it then?" I thought about how protective he was of Betsy Latelle and the other victims of the shooting and couldn't picture him selling to underage kids.

Travis's expression changed. "Believe it or not, John Bolton owned the store although officially it belonged to Stone Kavanaugh."

"That's why there are still militia caps in his office, I'll bet."

"Could be. Once Kavanaugh went away and they finally got Bolton, the place went up for auction. George Big Horse must have been the buyer."

I pictured the empty shelves. "Looks like he closed it down."

"They say he keeps it open in the summer for people heading back from the lakes further north. It's the only gas pump between here and the Canadian border."

Just beyond Eyeman's Corner a brown sign with a number of bullet holes in it pointed to a gravel road. "Public launch."

Travis turned. "This is the only public access to Nearbow Lake, not that anyone would want to launch a boat onto the lake."

"Why not?"

"You'll see. It's one of those Minnesota lakes that wouldn't make it in the outdoor magazines. It's not a good lake for canoeing. Much of it is too swampy and the water around Gravediggers Island is deep with choppy currents. Quite frankly, it's ugly."

Whoever thought a lake in northern Minnesota could be ugly?

The landing was nothing more than a graveled area with a small parking lot. A rough wooden picnic table stood askew at the edge of the parking area under a large pine. Next to it was an overflowing garbage barrel. A firepit near the picnic table was strewn with empty beer cans and bottles.

Travis pointed to it. "When I was growing up, this was the place the high school kids came to party." He gestured to the area around the firepit. "No one lives near here. You can make as much noise as you want, and no one will report you."

The area appeared cold and neglected. I thought about the keg parties we had in college. None of them happened in such a desolate spot.

When we stepped out of the car, the silence was eerie. No hum of insects, no low rumble of traffic, no rhythmic slapping of the water on the shoreline. I felt the tingle on the back of my neck.

"This place doesn't have a good feel to it."

Travis nodded. "The Indians believed it was haunted with bad spirits. That's how it got the name Nearbow Lake. It's from the Ojibwe word *nibo* meaning dead. They believed that anyone who ventured out on it came back tainted—if they came back at all."

"Interesting." I walked down to the water. Instead of the clear water of Lake Larissa, the water was murky and smelled a little like the sewer gas that emanated from the grates in Queens. I turned back to Travis. "You said it was rumored the militia had some kind of a meeting place here."

He pointed across the water to an island with a high rocky edge. "Gravediggers Island."

I grimaced. "Nearbow Lake with a Gravediggers Island. Doesn't sound very welcoming. Why is it called Gravediggers?"

"My dad told me it was because a hundred years ago when the KKK was active around here they used it as a burial ground for people they didn't like."

I shuddered. "Like the Indians?"

"Most likely, however, this part of the state also had a growing Jewish population. Antisemitism didn't start with Hitler. Anyway, the story goes that the Klansmen would make their captives dig their own graves before they killed them."

I took a few steps closer to the water, studying the island. Contrary to my preconceived image of a barren land, it appeared to be thick with trees and underbrush and had an unwelcoming rocky, craggy shoreline. I remembered the map in Tony's possessions. As I scanned the shoreline, I spotted the boat landing indicated on the map.

Pointing to it, I said, "I see where boats could land. Do you suppose the Red Cap boys got over there by canoe?"

Travis laughed. "I seriously doubt it. I'm sure they used motorboats although it would be tricky getting over there especially in the fall when the lake is shallower."

We stood together at the edge of the water, close enough that I smelled the perfumed detergent of his laundry soap on his shirt and the hint of bourbon on his breath.

I checked my watch. "The kids are late. I wonder if we'll get stood up."

Travis squatted down and picked up a small rock. He tossed it into the water and watched while it landed with a low splash. "They're scared, you know." He turned to me. "And if they aren't, they should be."

He had a strange expression I couldn't read. My gut said he knew or suspected more than he was telling me. But what was it he knew? Before I could ask, we heard the rumble of a car as it approached the landing.

Chapter Thirty-Two

The Flyer

They arrived in the car I'd seen at the school. It roared to a stop, the broken muffler dragging on the gravel road. Travis and I stood still, watching as Phil stepped out of the car followed by Amy and Josh. The three stood near the car as if they wanted to be sure of their escape. They were dressed alike in skinny, faded blue jeans and hooded sweatshirts.

I waved at them. "Hi. Thanks for meeting with me."

They didn't move, their gaze fixed on Travis. "Who's he?" Josh asked.

"A friend. You can trust him." I turned to him. "Can't they?"

He smiled and shrugged. "Hey, guys, I'm just her chauffeur. Chauffeurs never talk. I signed a confidentiality agreement."

Good line. At first, the kids looked perplexed, then Josh grinned. "Oh, I get it." They relaxed as I gestured toward the picnic table. The three sat on one side of the table while I sat on the other. In the outdoor lighting, the tiny jewel in Amy's nose sparkled. For a second I wondered how her parents let her get away with a piercing like that.

Travis stood with his arms folded.

Josh squinted up at him. "You're the state cop, aren't you?"

"Off duty and not interested in your busted muffler."

A little breeze wafted from the lake bringing with it the smell of algae and stagnant water. I pondered how to start the conversation when Amy spoke up.

"That Friday before the football game, Tess told us she thought she had some big news for us, but she had to check it out first. She gave us this flyer. She said she found it in a wastebasket at school and showed it to Mr. Starling."

She handed me a folded piece of paper. It was printed on an expensive, creamy bond and announced a pop-up store for *Charity's Americana* at the Rosedale Mall in Minneapolis beginning the end of October for the Christmas crowd. It was dated two years ago.

Puzzled, I asked. "Do you know why she gave it to you?"

"Read the bottom. I think it was Mr. Vincent's handwriting."

I looked at the note scrawled in pencil that read, "Cash from RCs?" Below it, a word was erased. Holding it up to the light I could barely make out the letters "laundry."

"Do you know what it means?"

They all shook their heads. As I reread the flyer, a cascade of thoughts ran through my head. Was something odd going on with Charity's business—like the Red Caps were paying her for something? Before Kavanaugh went to prison they were supposedly dealing in stolen merchandise. Maybe *Charity's Americana* was some sort of front. It was hard to think the elegant woman riding a horse today was involved in criminal activity. Then I remembered the photo of her holding a rifle. Still not likely.

I handed the flyer to Travis. He read it and gave it back to Amy, commenting, "I can't imagine Tony would be interested in Charity's pop-up store."

"What about the word laundry?" I asked as I took the flyer from Travis and straightened it out on the table.

Everyone looked blank.

"Could it be money laundering?" I tapped my finger on it as if it would reveal its secret.

Travis laughed. "Come on, Jamie. This is Cascade. Sounds far too sophisticated for this crowd."

Amy bit her lip. "Tess said she found something else, but she wouldn't tell me anything more. She said she gave it to Mr. Starling, and she thought it was important."

"You don't know what it was?"

"No, except she said it was 'hidden away' and she'd have more answers soon."

Phil added, "She was real excited about what she'd found."

I tried to imagine what it might be but came up blank.

Josh worked his phone until he found what he was looking for. "Here. This was her last text. She sent it after we dropped her off near her house that Friday." He handed me the phone.

Found him. BIG NEWS!!!!

"I texted her back but never heard anything more. That's the last text I got from her."

I looked at the other two. "Who did she find? Any ideas?"

Amy drummed her fingers on the table in a marching cadence, her face pale in the fall sunlight. "The last couple of weeks she'd talked about getting into trouble with her dad for spending too much time on Facebook and Instagram."

Travis slid onto the bench next to me. "Do you know what that was all about?"

A look of distress crossed Amy's face. "We were helping Mr. Starling. We think it might have had something to do with him."

"What happened that Friday night?" I leaned forward to make closer eye contact.

"We picked her up at school before the football game, like usual."

"Yeah, since coach Mayer left, our team sucks, so we usually go somewhere else and hang out." Josh snapped a little twig as he talked.

"We drove around for a while and she kept looking at her phone. She got a text and said she had to go home. So, we dropped her off," Amy added.

Phil nodded. "We figured she'd gotten in trouble with her parents or something."

"Except it was weird. She didn't want us to take her right to her house." Amy pushed a wisp of hair away from her eyes. "I kind of thought maybe she was meeting someone."

A couple of gulls circled overhead squawking as if we had invaded their territory. A gust of wind picked up the flier and blew it off the table. Phil leapt up to grab it.

I was puzzled. "You haven't seen her or heard from her since a week ago Friday?" Over a week was a long time for a teenager to be out of communication.

"We've texted and called, but she hasn't answered." Amy took out her phone and scrolled through it as if suddenly she would hear from Tess. "I even called her mom, but she didn't answer."

I pictured Tess's mother peeking out from behind the curtain. Was Tess home and her parents were trying to protect her? From what? And what about the text I'd received? Maybe this was completely unrelated to the shooting or Winnie. Maybe Tess found an online romance. I was about to ask the kids when a vehicle rattled down the gravel road. All of us turned in the direction of the sound.

Phil picked up his backpack, his brow wrinkled. "I...I think we should go."

The fear in the group was palpable. I stood up. "Listen, will you tell me if you hear anything from Tess? The sheriff and her parents say she's okay. I guess we'll have to believe them for now."

Without answering, all three made a dash for the car. Before the approaching vehicle could reach the parking lot, they pulled around and gunned the car onto the road.

"Those are some scared kids," Travis said.

"You think? They're holding back on something, but I don't know what it is." Their fear penetrated through me. I wanted to leave this place with the ugly lake as soon as possible. A four-hundred-page manuscript about female vampires looked good to me right now.

Before we could talk about what we'd just heard, a mustard-colored pickup truck pulled into the parking area. It was old, with rusted wheel wells and a large dent in the passenger door. Travis moved close to me as the truck stopped. The driver turned off the ignition, and the truck continued to ping and rumble for a few seconds before it quit.

The driver slowly opened the door. I held my breath hoping he wasn't wearing a red militia cap. I needn't have worried as George Big Horse stepped out of the truck. He waved and slowly walked over to us.

Travis extended his hand. "Long time, George. How are you?"

They shook hands. "I'm good. Fishing's not so hot, though." He gestured to the lake.

"Never has been."

George eased his way onto the picnic bench. "Saw you drive by the store and then saw the kids. Having a little powwow here?"

His expression was difficult to read. Why had he come?

I sat down across from him. "I'm still working on my story."

"And the kids know something?"

I shrugged. I wasn't sure if this was a friendly visit.

Travis stood behind me. I felt like I had a bodyguard. "What brings you out here?"

"Saw the traffic jam and wondered if it was part of the night activity."

"Night activity?" Travis sounded puzzled. "What do you mean?" He moved around and slid in beside me.

Rain clouds slowly gathered over the lake. With the sun obscured, the air chilled. I hugged myself, sorry I hadn't brought a heavier jacket. I still didn't know how to dress for these sudden temperature changes.

George pointed at the lake. "Week ago, or so, I heard activity on the road. Car with a big noisy engine and a couple of motorcycles. Wondered if kids were partying here." He pointed vaguely at the firepit. "But nothing happened."

He shrugged. "This lake is a dangerous one. It doesn't like people. I stay away from it." He gazed at us with his deep brown eyes. "You should, too."

We sat in silence for a few painful moments as more clouds rolled in. A gray, misty veil rose up from the lake dampening my face. As hard as it was for me not to jump in and ask more questions, I waited. I was learning to be patient with silence, but I couldn't stop my feet from making circles in the sand beneath the table.

Finally, I gave in, "I know you suspect something bad is happening around here. I can feel it in your silence. What do you know?"

George studied his hands on the table. They were callused like my friend Rob's—a man who built things. "This lake. We were taught to stay away from it. My father said it was haunted. Do you know why?"

"Evil spirits?" Travis ventured.

George tsked. "You white men. What is this, 'evil spirits'?"

In the graying light, Travis blushed. "Sorry."

"I don't know any evil spirits. I only know evil and greedy men." He waved at the lake. "It was white men, Klansmen back in the 1920s who spread the word the lake was haunted." He leaned forward. "You know why?"

I thought about Travis's story of the gravediggers, but I shook my head interested in what George had to say.

"They had a bootleg operation out on the island. Invented all sorts of stories to keep people away."

"Like people digging their own graves?" I asked.

He chuckled. "Graves, evil spirits, haunting, my ass."

Travis laughed. "So that's where it got its reputation. When I was a kid trying to fish the lake, I always felt like someone was watching me."

George's voice turned thoughtful as he watched a gull circling above us. "My grandfather said that in the time of his grandfather the lake was a place of beauty filled with the best fish. Then the loggers came and took the trees and the miners came and poisoned it. Cut off its lifeblood." He took a deep breath and closed his eyes. "All part of the haunting. That's why they call it Nearbow Lake, a bastardization of the Ojibwe word for dead. In my great grandfather's time, it had an Ojibwe name that meant 'handsome waters.'"

His sadness was tangible. The weedy lake with its shoreline thick with brush and brambles gave me the shivers.

A few raindrops plunked on the table as the air grew chillier. Before it started to seriously rain, I needed to know if he had information on Tess. "Those kids we were talking to, their friend is missing. Do you know anything?"

George kept his gaze on me. "I know the lake is unsettled. Maybe there really are evil spirits. The Red Caps are up to something since Stone got out of prison. Too much activity. I hope their friend isn't mixed up with it."

Light rain began to fall in a steady pattern. He looked up. "Skies are going to open. Best if we all get going." He groaned as he stood up, one hand holding his lower back. "Old war injury." He limped back to the pickup. "My advice. Stay away from the lake and let nature take care of it."

The pickup started with a clunk and a roar. Travis stood next to me watching George drive away. The rain came down a little harder. "I guess we should go before we get soaked." He pointed up to the clouds.

Once in the car, the rain now pouring out of the sky, Travis reached under his seat and pulled out the flask. "A little hair of the dog?"

The only dog hair I wanted was Bronte's head resting on my lap. "No thanks."

He took a slug. "Something wicked this way comes."

"No kidding." Outside the rain obscured the boat landing. I wondered what all the activity was about. "Should we tell someone about the kids?"

Travis tipped the flask again. "Won't do any good." His voice was filled with resignation.

Chapter Thirty-Three

In the Quiet

I kept an eye on Travis as we drove away from Nearbow Lake. The flask was tucked between the driver's seat and the door. If he had taken more shots, I would have said something. Instead, he concentrated on driving through the downpour, windshield wipers slapping away the water as it cascaded down. We said little as he drove through the rain.

It poured until we reached Jackpine County. As if the rain god had tired of soaking us, the clouds lifted, and the sun poked out. I pointed to the little beam of light. "Really, I think all of Cascade County is haunted."

By the time we reached his apartment building in Killdeer, sunlight sparkled off the wet fallen leaves and the outdoor temperature was a comfortable sixty-eight degrees. Once out of Travis's car, I took off my jacket.

He pointed at it. "Enjoy the warmth. It won't last much longer."

It seemed he was always reminding me that winter was coming.

We stood in the parking lot of his building. I wasn't sure what should happen next. Part of me wanted to invite Travis back to the cabin and part of me wanted to escape to the world of milkmaids and vampires.

Travis broke the silence. "I'd ask if you wanted to grab a beer at the Loonfeather except I have paperwork to do. Night shift tonight."

"That's okay. I have to think all of this through and see what I can sort out." I patted my bag with the notebook. "I'm really worried about Tess, but

193

I'm not sure she has anything to do with the article I want to write."

Travis furrowed his brow. "I loved living in Cascade when I was a kid. I hate seeing what it's become." He fingered his sunglasses. In the sunlight with his light complexion, he looked young—at least younger than me. "I'm not sure they have much law enforcement up there right now."

I turned to leave when he caught my arm. "Wait." He let go quickly when I stiffened. "Sorry. I forgot to tell you. I talked with my mother. She gave me Aggie Kavanaugh's phone number in Duluth if you want to ask her anything about Marla. Mom wasn't sure she'd talk to you, but I guess it's worth a try."

He airdropped it to my phone. I smiled, recalling the look of wonder on Clarence's face when Joe and I had done an airdrop. "Thanks. I'll call you or text you if I hear anything else from the kids."

"Ditto if I hear from Jay about Tess."

Back at the cabin, as the sun slanted downward in the west, I sat on the rock by the lake, drinking coffee and idly throwing a stick for Bronte. A breeze gently rippled the waters of Lake Larissa. I watched, taking in the contrast between my lake and Nearbow Lake. Would the mining operation that was trying to start up again here in Jackpine County do the same thing to Larissa as it had to Nearbow?

Jim called as I tried to redirect my thoughts to something more pleasant. He said Jake was continuing to improve, and he hoped to get away later this week. "I could use a dose of fresh northern air." He didn't say he missed me, nor did he commit to coming to the cabin. It left me feeling unbalanced.

Before we ended the call, I told him about the trip to Cascade, Dead Man's Curve, and the missing Tess. His advice, "Have you considered that you might be trying to connect imaginary dots?"

Nothing I'd learned painted much of a picture, except an overriding sense of evil in Cascade. I kept my voice light. "You might have a point. Right now, I need to focus on keeping the cabin warm. Tomorrow—a new furnace. Cabin should be toasty in time for winter."

When the call ended, I wondered about my reaction. Using the word "toasty" was not part of my usual vocabulary.

With the darkening sky, and day merging into night, I sat with Vladess and my blue pencil. Letty DeVoss loved adverbs and endless sentences. If she had a spare space in a sentence, she inserted a word ending in "ly." On top of that, she hyphenated words that didn't need it and left alone words that did. At page twenty of the copy edit, the words began to swim in front of me. I was grateful when my phone rang. Caller ID unknown name, unknown number. I should have learned to leave those calls alone, but I thought it might be one of the kids—or even Tess. When I answered, a deep harsh voice whispered, "Leave it alone or we will find you." In the background, I thought I heard the sound of a pool ball slamming against another.

"Excuse me? Who are you?" I stared at the phone, my hands shaking. The call ended abruptly. Something malevolent oozed from the whispered voice, and I wasn't sure if I shivered from fright or anger. Moreover, the voice had a familiar gruffness to it. Bill the Bully?

"I will not leave it alone!" I hissed into the dead phone. Bronte raised her head in concern as I slapped the phone down on the table.

The air cooled as darkness enveloped the cabin. I sat in front of the crackling fireplace with my laptop. The first thing I did was look at *Charity's Americana* website once again. As I paged through her offerings, I saw she had a line of inexpensive crafts like embroidered aprons with catchy sayings and baseball-type caps with inscriptions like "Favorite Grampa." It was the kind of thing that might sell well in a booth at an art fair or a pop-up at a mall. The website listed several upcoming pop-up sites for the merchandise, including one at the Mall of America.

"So why did Tess have the flyer, and why had Tony written on it?" Bronte offered no answer.

Next, I checked out her business listing with the secretary of state's office. *Charity's Americana LLC* listed Charity Whitacre and R.C. Associates as owners.

"I wonder who R.C. Associates are?" I googled them but found nothing.

As I tried to make sense of all of it, I wondered more about Neil. The article on the shooting indicated that he had committed suicide. Where had this happened? Had he been in hiding? Did he shoot himself? His death certificate might tell me more if only I knew his birth date.

I texted Amy. **Who would know Neil Kavanaugh's birthdate?**

To my surprise, she texted right back with the date. **I remember because he was born on 9/11.**

This time I went to the Minnesota Department of Health's webpage and filled in Neil's birthdate. Nothing came up. I tried several different years and still found nothing. "Curious. They would have a record of his death somewhere." *Unless he didn't die.*

Could that be? I must have entered something wrong. Yet when I tried again, I came up blank. I called Travis and filled him in on my research. "This is what I know. Charity's business partner is something called R.C. Associates and the department of health has no record of Neil's death. My head is swimming."

"Interesting. I can't believe Neil is still alive. How could a community keep that kind of a secret? And why?"

"It's Cascade, remember."

"Well, don't do anything rash, okay? I'm on shift tonight, but we should talk tomorrow."

Unnerved, before going to bed, I made sure both the back and front door were locked.

* * *

Monday dawned clear and crisp. I woke to the little sounds of birds chirping and the rumble of a vehicle approaching the cabin. Checking my phone, I saw I had overslept. Cal arrived with the new furnace as I was pulling on jeans and a sweater.

"I should have 'er all installed by early this afternoon."

A helper who looked like he was just out of high school stood behind him nodding. "Cal, he's quick, don't cha' know."

Bronte waggled her tail at both of them indicating that she thought they were safe to come in.

I spent the morning at the kitchen table with Vladess, adding commas and removing adverbs. One of my challenges in copyediting was to try not to insert myself into the actual writing—bad as it was. If I became too critical, I insulted and even hurt the author. Yet, they paid me for my opinion and expertise. How could I tell Letty DeVoss her novel was badly written, boring, despite all the sex scenes, and way too long? I still needed to pay utilities, pay off my student loans and buy food. Oh, to be back in the world of *The New Yorker* and professional writers.

Putting down the blue pencil, I wandered back to the utility room to check on Cal's progress with the furnace.

"How's it going?"

He grunted. "Got a little problem here." He pointed to the floor. "Board's rotting. Must have gotten wet at one time. We'll need to drive into town and get wood to replace it." He turned to his helper. "Hopefully we won't have to do the entire floor."

I didn't ask if it would add to the expense because I already knew the answer. Five Letty DeVoss manuscripts wouldn't be enough to pay for all of this. After they left, I stared at the mess of papers on the kitchen table covered with blue ink.

"I've got to figure out this article or we will starve this winter." Suddenly this wasn't about giving a voice to the Cascade victims, it was about my survival in the cabin by the lake.

Cal and his helper spent the entire day working on the flooring before he could install the furnace. As the light faded from the sky, he came out to the kitchen. "Guess we'll be back tomorrow. But I think we got the floor all squared away. You should have your furnace going good by tomorrow night."

A cold mist rose from the still waters of the lake as I sat shivering on the rock. Bronte crashed around in the woods chasing a squirrel that hadn't bedded down for the night. The dampness of the lake seeped into my bones. Could I make it here? Would I need to go back to New York? I could eke out a living there by cobbling together freelance and fact-checking jobs until I found something permanent. Did I want to go back to the city? Sometimes the noise and the rhythm of people and the cars was comforting. Was it as comforting as the lap of water against the shoreline here or the call of the loon? And what about Jim? Would he object if I said I was going to leave?

None of these questions had easy answers. Time to build a fire and look at my finances.

The fire crackled and spit, throwing off enough warmth that I could take off my thick woolen socks. I sat on the rug in front of it with the laptop and a glass of merlot. The wine had been gathering dust on my counter since last summer, but despite the lack of temperature control, it tasted okay. By my calculation, if I had no income for the next month, neither Bronte nor I would starve. After that, I was in unknown territory.

"Time to launch this project." I opened a blank Word document and typed, *In the quiet of Northern Minnesota, on an ordinary September school day, the shots fired in the high school cafeteria killed a popular teacher and two students. They were all Native American.*

It felt good to finally get something down on paper.

Chapter Thirty-Four

Aggie Kavanaugh

Bronte's woof woke me in the middle of the night. She pricked her ears and sat up. A low growl rumbled through her throat.

"What is it, girl?"

In the darkness, I held my breath and strained to hear an unusual noise. Nothing appeared out of the ordinary. Outside, a night breeze swept through the trees and stirred the leaves. I couldn't remember if I'd locked both doors before going to bed.

"I don't hear anything." With a sudden chill, I remembered the threatening phone call. Holding my breath, I tiptoed quickly to the kitchen. The floor was icy beneath my bare feet. Bronte trotted ahead of me, still growling. "Shhh..."

Peeking through the kitchen window, I saw a dark shape, silhouetted by the moonlight. Bronte barked. The shape raised itself up and I saw the outline of a small bear. When Bronte barked again, it lumbered off into the woods.

"You're a brave dog—at least when you are inside." Bronte wagged her tail at the door and continued to woof. "No, I'm not going to let you outside. That guy would claw you into little pieces."

After a few moments, she stopped growling and followed me back to bed. Once under the covers, my heart pounded. I curled up and wished Jim was next to me, not a canine with a low, rumbling growl. It felt like my whole

199

life since I took on the Cascade project was like the bear. Something dark in the woods. Something not right.

My head filled with everything I knew about Cascade. If I was going to do the article, it was clear I needed to know more about Tony, starting with the rumor about Marla. Did I have the guts to call her mother, a woman whose son was involved in a horrific shooting?

I closed my eyes with the photograph of Tony and his brother in my head. Marla might be a key or simply another meaningless thread. Maybe she knew something about the darkness in Cascade. I drifted off to sleep with the image of an animal clawing at me.

* * *

Cal and his helper finished installing the new furnace Tuesday morning. When he turned it on, it hummed, and heat poured out of the ducts.

"You're all set for winter. Could get down to thirty below and this baby'll keep the place warm."

"My loan should come through by the end of this week. Send me the bill." I winced, wondering if I could make the monthly payments on the loan.

Once again, it was a clear, sunny day. As we moved deeper into October the sun slanted more, and its rays didn't warm my sitting rock like it had in the summer. Living in the lights of New York, I'd never noticed how the quality of the sunlight changed with the seasons. Now I was getting used to it and liked how it showcased the turning of the trees.

After Cal left with the furnace warming the cabin, I brought out my notebook, turned to a blank page, and jotted down a list of questions. Taking a deep breath, I called Aggie remembering the many times I'd called sources to fact-check articles. I told myself it would be like I was back at my New York job.

"Hello?" The woman's voice sounded tentative.

I debated how to introduce myself and decided to be straightforward. "Is this Mrs. Kavanaugh? This is Jamie Forest, I got your number from Travis Booker's mother."

"Yes?" I heard a little tremor as she spoke.

"I'm wondering if I could ask you a few questions for an article I'm doing on…on Cascade." I couldn't bring myself to talk about the shooting. At least not yet.

"I'm not talking about Neil. People need to leave us alone." She sounded less angry and more afraid.

"Actually, I want to talk to you about Marla."

The silence was so long I thought she'd cut me off. My phone indicated she was still on the line.

"Mrs. Kavanaugh? Are you still there?"

"You people should leave Marla alone. She's not right, you know."

The call was going as badly as I feared it would. I tried a different tack. "I'm trying to write a piece on Tony Vincent, the teacher who died. I'd heard that he was kind to Marla. I just wanted to check it out. Do you think I could talk with her about him?"

Again, more silence. In the background, I heard, "Ma?"

She muffled the receiver and said something I couldn't hear. When Aggie spoke again, her voice sounded strained. "He was nice to Marla. That's what I told Winston Starling when he called."

I waited, hoping she'd say more. In the background, I heard the voice again. "Ma. Tell them I was only trying to help with the laundry."

I sat up a little straighter. Why did laundry keep coming up?

"They shouldn't have yelled at her like they did. She's a good girl."

None of my written questions addressed this odd conversation. I cleared my throat. "Was someone yelling at Marla? Kids teasing her or something?"

Aggie covered the phone and heard her shush the voice behind her. "If I tell you what I told Winston, will you leave us alone?"

Outside, Bronte scratched at the door. When I let her in, it was clear she'd rolled in something. A dead fish odor followed her to her water dish. With the phone in one hand, I grabbed her collar and dragged her to the door. "Go," I hissed, pushing her out.

"I'd like to hear what you have to say. It sounds like someone wasn't being nice to your daughter."

Aggie's voice filled with indignation. "I told Winston what Marla said to me. She was so upset, crying, and worried she'd lose her job at the school. She overheard some people talking about the pile of dirty laundry at the motel. She thought she could help because we have a washing machine." She paused. "You know, Marla takes things as they're said."

"I see." I didn't see.

"She told Mr. Whitacre that she could help with the laundry and he got really mad at her. Said she should never talk about it again or she would lose her job. That job was really important to her—made her proud that she could help out."

Outside Bronte whined at the door, not understanding how bad she smelled.

"Mr. Whitacre threatened to fire her over some remark about laundry?"

"That's what Marla thought. She was so upset she told Mr. Vincent about it. I don't know what happened after that except..."

Except your son shot him. I waited for her to finish the sentence. Instead, she said, "That's all I have to say. And I won't talk about Neil. He was protecting his sister like he always did."

"He was protecting her?" My voice rose. "Protecting her from Tony?"

"Don't call back!" The phone clicked off.

I stared at the darkened screen. If the story was muddied before the phone call it was completely mired now.

Setting the phone down, I went to the door where Bronte stood waiting to be let in. Her back was slick with whatever she'd rolled in. She reeked. I put on my jacket, filled a pail with soapy water, and set to the task of cleaning her up. As I washed her down, I wished I could clean up the dead fish of the Cascade story as easily as I could hose down my dog.

Chapter Thirty-Five

Charity's Americana

I t was early afternoon by the time I finished washing and drying Bronte. She appeared disappointed when I shoveled up the dead fish left by the bear last night and dumped it in the compost box.

I pointed to her, "No more fish rolls. Okay?" What was it about dogs and the need to smell like something rotten?

Once I showered and settled at the kitchen table, I jotted down what Aggie Kavanaugh had said. "Dirty laundry? Sounds like something political. Did someone have some dirt on...who?"

I remembered the flyer from Tess. It, too, said laundry. Maybe it was time to explore *Charity's Americana* a bit more. My thoughts were interrupted by a phone call from Clarence.

He wasted no time with pleasantries. "Sunny Morne got Pete to give her $20,000 to 'fix her teeth.' Now she's disappeared again."

"I thought they were reconciled and living blissfully together."

"Seems she shows up when she needs cash, cooks him a nice meal, and gives him a good cuddle. Then she's off again. Can you find her?"

I sighed. I didn't have those kinds of private eye skills. "Why doesn't he report her to the sheriff?"

"Hah! And let the world know he was snookered?"

I smiled to myself. This was a small community. I guessed the world already knew. "As I said before, if you can get me a photo of her, I'll try a facial recognition search. Barring that, I think he's going to have to hire a private investigator. And good luck with that."

"Good advice. I'll see if Pete has one he's willing to part with."

"If she's a smart con woman, she won't have too many photos hanging around." I said this with the sleuthing wisdom of someone who used to watch reruns of *Murder She Wrote* to avoid schoolwork.

Clarence cleared his throat. "If I recall, the *Times* had a photo last summer that she was in. A group shot of some sort. Can you find out? And remember to keep track of your time."

Outside, a flock of geese honked noisily overhead. I watched them as I talked. It appeared they were heading north. Could that be right? If so, climate change was definitely on fast forward.

I skimmed my notes about Cascade. "On a different matter, I'm wondering about Charity Whitacre. Do you think there's something strange about her business?"

"Why do you ask?"

I told him about the flyer and Tony's cryptic message.

Clarence was quiet for a few moments before he spoke. "Well, we could pay Charity a visit. A successful business like hers must need a lawyer, and I'm looking to build my practice." He laughed. "Or maybe I just want to go back to that place in Cascade for another cheeseburger."

It sounded like a possible way to get some information from Charity. I could ask her about her advice on not talking about the shooting and whether she met with Winnie the night he died. And I could also ask her if her Hermes was real.

"Do you want me to set up a time to meet her?"

"Oh no. I think we need to ambush her." Clarence chuckled. "She won't have time to hide the loot."

We decided to take a trip to Cascade tomorrow morning and have lunch on the way home.

"If they don't kidnap us," Clarence added.

I spent the rest of the day with vampires, attempting to smooth out sentences and plot lines. If I applied myself, I could send the manuscript off tomorrow, along with Florice's plucked Rose. Two checks might get me through until another manuscript arrived.

* * *

The next morning dawned sunny but cold. The ground sparkled white with frost. For the first time since moving here, I had to scrape the windshield of the car. I found it rewarding to run the scraper over the glass and have the frost peel off like plastic wrap.

Bronte watched me with her tail wagging. "Who but a New York City girl would find this fun?" I'd already heard tales of having to chip the ice off windshields in twenty-below weather. "I guess this is good practice."

I dropped both manuscripts, complete with invoices, off at the post office. Several people came in to get mail from their boxes while I waited for the packages to be weighed. Much as I disliked editing manually, I loved going to the post office. With its WPA murals and the old-timey smell of cigar smoke and dust saturating in the creaky wooden floor, I felt transported to a different era.

Clarence was ready and waiting when I arrived. Once again, Joe helped him to the car. As Clarence slid in Joe looked at me with a worried expression. "Are you sure this is a good idea?"

Clarence replied. "Young man, I have my weapon." He indicated his cane. "I'll fight off any and all attackers."

Joe didn't smile and neither did I.

As I entered the highway to go north, I felt like my car could navigate this stretch on its own. So much had happened in the last two weeks, and yet I knew only a little more than when I'd first met with Winnie.

On the way, I told Clarence about my phone call with Aggie. "It's at least the third time I've heard the word laundry. Tony had it in his appointment book. I wonder if someone had 'dirty laundry' on someone."

Clarence pulled out a crisp white handkerchief and blew his nose. "Sorry. Fall allergies. Either that or the 'old man drippy nose' syndrome."

I laughed. "Never heard that one before."

205

When we passed the county line into Cascade, I half-expected the clouds to erase the sunshine, but it stayed bright with a light blue sky.

"You say Marla talked about dirty laundry at the motel."

"Could it be a code word or something? Maybe stolen goods?"

Clarence wiped his nose once again. "It's a puzzle. Let's concentrate on Charity before we tackle the laundry."

We devised a game plan of sorts. We'd boldly drive to Whitacre's Acres, knock on the door and ask Charity about Tony. Clarence would sneak in some questions about her business, and we'd be on our way.

When we passed the boarded-up motel, I noted the chain-link fence around the building also had rolled barbed wire at the top. I slowed down and pointed it out to Clarence.

"Isn't it strange to have that much security for an abandoned building?"

"Maybe they're protecting their piles of dirty laundry." His eyes sparkled. He was clearly enjoying himself. I wished I could feel the same.

For the first time, I noticed several security cameras attached to poles around the periphery of the building. The SUV was parked in its usual spot, but the place looked deserted. I glanced over at Clarence. "Should we take a peek?"

"Not before we see Charity or have that cheeseburger."

As we approached Dead Man's Curve, I told Clarence about finding the ski mask. "Travis put it in a plastic bag and kept it."

Clarence peered out the window at the spot where Winnie died. "I handled a lawsuit once where a kid was killed going too fast on a curve. He was drunk and his parents sued the liquor store."

"Did you win?"

"I guess you could say that. I represented the liquor store. The parents couldn't prove their case." He turned to me with a look of sadness. "Nobody really won. The reputation of the liquor store was ruined even if it wasn't found liable. And the parents...well the parents still lost their son."

I found I was holding my breath the whole time I drove around the curve. I finally took a gasp of air when the road straightened out.

Two horses grazed in the pasture in front of the Whitacre house. Clarence squinted out the windshield as we approached the turnaround in front. "Looks a darn sight better than when I last saw it."

"Pretty upscale for this part of the world."

A driveway around the side of the house led to the carriage house in back. Several cars were parked in front of the building. We decided to start with the main house, and if no one answered, drive to what must have been the shop.

"Stay in the car and I'll go ring the bell."

As I walked up the steps, I suddenly felt like an unwelcome solicitor. I pressed the bell by the large, dark-oak door and heard it chime inside. Footsteps approached the door. When it opened, I expected to see Charity. Instead, the woman who greeted me was middle-aged, overweight, and wore baggy knit pants and a flowered top. I'd half-expected any staff to be in uniform.

"Yes?" She peered at me.

"I'm here to see Charity. Is she in?"

I expected her to at least ask who I was and if I had an appointment. Instead, she gestured to the back. "You're supposed to go to the shop."

The door closed before I could say, "Thank you."

By the time I reached the bottom of the steps to the veranda, I heard the sounds of a vacuum. I must have been talking to the cleaning lady.

We pulled around to the building behind the house. Up close, I was surprised at how small it was. I was expecting a large warehouse for all of the "Americana." Instead, the building was about the size of the tourist shop in Killdeer. One car, a dark Mercedes SUV, stood out.

As I helped Clarence out of the car, I pointed to it. "Those aren't cheap vehicles."

"Charity is clearly doing all right with her business."

A small plaque on the door said, "Charity's Americana. Receiving in Back." Nothing else indicated this was a business.

When we walked through the door, we were greeted by a young receptionist who sat behind a desk with two monitors. She wore earbuds and was bobbing to music as she tapped on the keyboard. The reception area was decorated in muted brown and red earth tones. In the corner, opposite the receptionist, was a coffee table and a couple of upholstered chairs.

She looked up with an annoyed expression. "Deliveries in back."

Clarence stepped forward. "We're here to see Charity." He paused. "About charity."

"What?" She pulled off her earbuds.

I wanted to ask the same thing. What was he talking about?

Clarence cleared his throat in an officious way. "We represent Wildlife Without Borders. Would you tell her we're here?"

I pressed my lips together to avoid giggling. Wildlife Without Borders? Really?

"I...she...uh...isn't..."

The receptionist was saved from finishing her sentence when Charity swept into the room from a hallway behind the desk.

She wore a long colorful tunic with black leggings and ankle boots. I recognized the brand as Gudrun Sjoden, the eco-friendly Swedish designer. Even in the loosely fitting clothes, she had an elegance about her. She was the kind of woman who carried herself with such grace, she would probably look good wearing a feed sack.

I found myself tongue-tied.

Clarence saved the day. "Charity Whitacre, so pleased to finally meet you. I'm Clarence Engstrom, the Killdeer barrister."

Barrister? I was still trying to recover my voice.

Charity smiled with a puzzled expression, and I wondered what product she used to whiten her teeth. Up close she was older than I expected—probably in her late forties or early fifties.

She studied me. "I've met you, yes?" Again, I noted the slight foreign accent. It sounded eastern European to me.

"I'm doing a story on Tony Vincent and hoped you could tell me more." I extended my hand, but she ignored it. Instead, she turned her attention to Clarence. "And you are here because?"

"Just out for a ride with my friend, here. Nice estate you have here." He gestured toward the house. "I hear you have a thriving online business."

I stood glued to the spot, watching as Clarence worked his charm. If he could soften her up a bit, maybe I could get some answers on Tony and her advice to not talk about the shooting.

"I remember when this belonged to Sam Starling. We thought it was a pretty fancy setup back then, but it was nothing like what you have. Did you use the Houmas House in Louisiana as your model?"

Charity wrinkled her brow in confusion. "What is this Houmas House?"

"It's a classical revival mansion built in the 1800s by a sugar baron." Clarence recited like he'd just looked it up on Wikipedia. "Built on the backs of slave labor, of course. Sugar plantations were notorious for the worst working conditions."

Charity continued to stare at him while I took the opportunity to peek behind the desk into the hallway. It looked like it led to a back workshop of some sort. I interrupted Clarence's lecture about the evil injustice of slavery to point down the hallway. "Is that where you make the Americana?"

Charity shot me an expression of annoyance. "Some things are made here. Others I acquire." Her tone was abrupt. I felt like she'd slapped my hand and told me to sit down.

Clarence pulled out his handkerchief and politely coughed into it.

Folding her arms, Charity said, "I don't want to be rude, but you are interrupting a busy day. What do you want to ask me?"

I took my notebook out. "Just a few questions about Tony Vincent and we'll be on our way."

She narrowed her eyes. "I hardly knew him. Perhaps you should talk with my husband?"

"That's the problem. I'm having a hard time connecting with him. However, I was told Tony worked for you over the summer before he was... ah...shot."

"My foreman can tell you more than I can."

Of course, she'd have a foreman. Who else would manage the beautiful horses grazing in the pasture?

I forged ahead. "I also heard you were working with him on a diversity project."

She drummed her manicured fingers on the desk. "Yes?"

Clarence had stepped over to the wall and was admiring a landscape painting. I recognized it as one my friend Rob had done.

"Nice art," he remarked while I waited for Charity to say more about Tony.

Her lack of response gave me the impression she had something to hide. The receptionist watched from behind her desk, wide-eyed as if she'd never seen a customer before.

The front door opened before I could prod Charity for more information. Stone Kavanaugh walked in wearing a red militia cap.

The spider tickled my neck as I watched him approach. He had a cruel set to his lips, which twitched as he stared at me before turning to Clarence. "You," he hissed. His voice was surprisingly high and raspy like a vocal cord had been damaged.

"Hello, Mr. Kavanaugh." Clarence's expression turned steely. "I see you are out and about."

Kavanaugh took a menacing step toward Clarence who held his ground. "Engstrom, you are trespassing."

"What's it been? Twenty-some years since we put you away?"

The spider was no longer tickling my neck, it was clawing at it. Time to act. I interrupted. "Excuse me. Can I finish my questions?" I tapped at the notebook hoping the shaking in my hands didn't show.

"What questions?" Those eyes bored into me. I could have sworn they glowed red like some kind of a demon. Letty DeVoss would have loved this scene.

I willed myself away from his gaze and looked directly at Charity. She appeared to have diminished in Stone Kavanaugh's presence. Glancing at my notes, I blurted out, "Tony wrote down something about pop-ups and cash for RC. Do you know what he meant?"

The color drained from Charity's face. "I...uh...don't know." In that moment, her façade of sophistication appeared to flake away, and her accent grew thicker. A look of fear crossed her face as she turned to Stone.

"Get out!" Stone rasped, pointing a finger at me. "This is an unwarranted intrusion!"

I backed away from him, dropping my pen. When I stooped to pick it up, Stone moved closer to me. I felt the threat as his boots approached me.

Clarence saved the day by striding over, holding firmly to his cane. "I think we have what we need," he leaned down and whispered, "Best not to taunt the bear."

I straightened, gritting my teeth, and choked out, "Thanks for all the information. I'll call you if I need more."

Clarence and I nearly toppled each other hurrying out the door. It was not a graceful exit. Behind me, I heard the high, malevolent voice. "What information?"

Charity replied in a hissing tone but I didn't catch what she said.

Once safely in the car and rolling down the driveway I turned to Clarence. "Were you trying to get beat up back there?"

He spoke in a tense voice. "He's an example of why we need life without parole."

I was too busy watching the rearview mirror to argue or respond.

Once on the main road, I said, "Perhaps we should lunch at the Loonfeather in Killdeer. I'm not feeling particularly welcome right now."

When we approached Cascade, I half-expected to be greeted by a road-block manned by the Red Cap Militia. Without saying anything to Clarence, I prepared to speed through town chased by battered SUVs. The town, however, was late morning quiet. Even the parking lot at the bar and grill was nearly empty.

Once we were back on the highway I glanced at Clarence. He had a pensive expression. "What aren't you telling me?"

Clarence pulled out his white handkerchief and dabbed at his forehead. "I'm thinking about dirty laundry."

"What? Doesn't your housekeeper take care of that?" I tried to laugh, but it came out in a strained voice.

"Money laundering."

"Like what they do with drug money?" For someone who sounded like a Mafia mol to Minnesotans, my knowledge of that kind of illegal activity came mainly from watching television crime shows when I was in high school.

"I have a notion, but I need to check with some experts before I say more."

"But you think Kavanaugh is involved in it."

"Up to his neck."

I couldn't get anything more out of him. After we had lunch and I dropped him off I drove through the array of fall colors haunted by Stone Kavanaugh's eerie voice and the way Charity seemed to shrink when I told her what Tony had written.

Money laundering? What did that have to do with the killing of a teacher and two students?

Chapter Thirty-Six

Travis is Missing

Jim called in the afternoon. I filled him in on our visit to *Charity's Americana*. "Clarence and Stone Kavanaugh nearly got into a shoving match."

He laughed. "My money would be on Clarence. I bet he wields a wicked cane."

I smiled imagining Clarence clobbering the icy-eyed Stone. "On the way back to Killdeer Clarence said something about money laundering, but he wouldn't tell me anything else. What do you know about it?"

"Hmmm. My know-how is with drunken drivers and broken taillights, but I do recall a lecture on it back in my college days. Want the Twitter version—280 characters or less?"

I poured leftover coffee into a mug and slipped it into the microwave to reheat. "Sure."

He hesitated as if to put the words together. "Drugs or stolen goods are sold for cash. It's suspicious if someone walks in the door of a bank, for instance, with a bagful of money. In fact, we have banking laws that require reporting large amounts of cash. The bad guys need to find a cash-intensive business to launder it. Once they do that, they can invest in legal businesses—often real estate."

The microwave pinged, and I burned my hand when I accidentally tipped the mug, pulling it out.

"Ouch!" I quickly ran my hand under cold water from the tap.

"You okay?"

"That's me being a klutz. You were saying something about a cash-intensive business?"

"Massage parlors are a good example. A legitimate business—sort of—with a lot of cash flowing through it. You take the dirty money and claim it came from the parlor, create the books to make it look legitimate, and deposit it in the bank. Presto! It's clean."

I pictured Charity's online store and couldn't see how it would launder money. "*Charity's Americana* doesn't fit the description. She wouldn't be dealing in cash—Paypal, checks, and credit cards mainly."

"Maybe they have a massage parlor business going in Cascade."

"And you law enforcement people wouldn't know about it? Come on!"

I thought about the phrase he'd used, *imaginary dots.* This was too confusing. It was time to drop the sleuthing and simply tell the story about Tony. Still, Charity's Hermes bag came back to me. What if she bought it with tainted cash and turned around and sold it on her online store? Could that constitute laundering?

Bronte barked from the front of the cabin. When I looked out the window, I thought I saw something brown disappear into the woods.

"Sorry, I have to go. Bronte is after a four-legged creature. She probably needs saving."

After talking with Jim, I pondered the idea of money laundering but couldn't put it together into a cohesive story. Better to keep the focus on Tony and his achievements.

Later, Travis called. "I wanted to tell you I have some business in Cascade. I'm going to try to talk to Jay about Tess. I might even stop in at the bar and shoot some pool with Roger and his Red Cap pals. Maybe I'll check to see if they have clean laundry and if they've been wearing ski masks lately." He laughed, but the sound had a bitterness to it.

I shuddered as I pictured the men with their red caps. "Hey, you be careful. People there aren't very friendly, and we've been seen together. I got a nasty anonymous phone call from them warning me away. And now I'm really on

Kavanaugh's bad side."

"I figure I'm still a hometown boy—grew up with a couple of those guys. I'll be okay. In fact, I'll tell them to leave you alone."

I thought I heard a little slurring in his words. Had he been drinking already? "Travis, are you sober?"

He didn't answer my question. "I'll call you when I get back tonight."

When the call ended, I had that spider crawling up my neck feeling. I should have tried to stop him. Would I have been able to talk him out of the trip if I'd invited him over for dinner or something? Just the thought of him mingling with the Red Caps in the poolroom made me a little sick to my stomach.

Jamie, what's wrong with you? Call him back. I ignored the voice by saying out loud, "Not my problem."

Feeling guilty I concentrated on an outline for *The New Yorker.* So far, the story was pretty thin, but maybe with an outline and subheads, I could focus. As I jotted down my ideas, the piece that kept coming back to haunt me was the effort to silence any talk about the shooting. What had Whitacre said? Everyone would heal better if we simply moved on?

He might have had a point. I spent some time on the internet researching the aftermath of school shootings. Gun rights conspiracists, fueled by fringe social media, took it so far as to claim the children who were killed in school shootings never existed in the first place and schools like Sandy Hook were a giant hoax. I was shocked and appalled by the websites I uncovered. One father who'd lost his son was stalked on the internet and the conspiracists not only threatened to kill him, they found his home address and published it.

"This is obscene," I said, staring at the screen. "People actually believe this crap." No wonder Whitacre wanted to keep a low profile on the shooting. I thought about Joe and how he would have reacted if someone accused him of making up his twin brother. It was hard to imagine evil people like that existed.

As I thought about Whitacre and the town's quest to keep silent, though, it still didn't seem right. The shooting had happened two years ago, yet the conspiracy of silence continued to have an element of fear to it that didn't make sense. Were they trying to protect the students and the families of those killed and injured, or were they covering something up?

I took a break and called Jilly about the possible photo of Sunny. She told me she would look through the archives and see if she could find something. "I know what old Pete Peterson looks like. I'll check out group shots from this summer." She chuckled, "It will give me something to do while my editor scowls through getting the next edition out." She lowered her voice. "She's refused to ask for help, and I'm done trying to be polite and offer."

I didn't envy Jilly working with her. Something was amiss with Jeanine and I was glad I didn't have to work with her.

Late in the afternoon, Jilly emailed a photo with a note. "This was from the July fish fry. The old guy with the glasses is Pete. The woman standing next to him might be the mysterious Sunny."

The photo had four people lined up by an outdoor picnic table. They held paper plates in one hand and plastic cups of beer in the other. The headline said, "Another Successful July Fry."

I enlarged the photo until I had a good shot of Sunny. She was short and sturdy-looking with dark hair. She might have been Jilly's age. It was hard to tell. What surprised me most, however, was that I had seen her before. I closed my eyes and pictured the night I'd met with Winnie. She'd been seated at a table behind him. I was sure it had been her because I remembered the thick mascara and the low-cut blouse she wore. Was she sitting with Bill the Bully? I remembered the man at her table spoke with a low growl. At the time, I didn't think more about it because of Winnie's abrupt departure.

"I don't believe in coincidences, Bronte." Bronte stood up yawning and sauntered to the door.

At bedtime, as I settled under the covers, I checked my phone in case I'd missed any messages. The text from Travis had come in the evening when I'd stepped out with Bronte to look at the stars.

trouble

I texted back. **What's wrong???**

He didn't reply. I stared at the phone looking for the floating dots that told me he was writing back. Nothing happened. I called and the phone went directly to voicemail. "Travis, I just got your text. Is everything okay?"

Bronte, settled in comfortably beside me, raised her head with a concerned expression. I ran through all the possibilities. He could simply be drunk, so wasted he didn't know he texted. He could be in a ditch somewhere.

The phone rang and I answered it without looking at the ID. "Are you all right, Travis?"

"Uh...uh this is Madelyn. You know from the bar in Cascade?"

"Is Travis all right?" I jumped in before she could say more.

She whispered into the phone. "Something is wrong. I overheard those Red Cap guys talking in the pool room. They said they got the trooper, and then one of them slammed his pool cue against the table and they all laughed."

I sat up, my heart pounding. "Did you see him today?"

"He...he came in earlier and asked a bunch of questions of the guys, and then he left. I'm scared for him. Those guys are creeps."

Handling distress calls like this was not one of the skills they taught in my MFA program. I was at a loss. "Did you call the sheriff?"

Her voice trembled as she lowered it to a barely audible whisper. "Um, I think he's part of whatever those Red Cap guys are doing." I heard loud voices in the background and someone calling, "Hey Madelyn, bitch. Wanna come home with me?" Drunken guffaws followed.

"I gotta go." The phone went silent.

I threw the covers off, pulled on a robe, and walked into the kitchen. While the water boiled for tea, I listed my options. I could try the Cascade sheriff's emergency number. But what would I say? My friend sent a text and isn't answering his phone? I could keep trying Travis's phone. Or I could call Jim and ask him what I should do.

My call woke Jim up. "Hullo."

"It's Jamie and I don't know what I should do."

"What?" His voice was gravelly from sleep.

I explained the situation, the text, and the call from Madelyn. "My gut is telling me Travis is in big trouble."

Jim listened patiently and finally cut me off. "Hey, first of all, Travis isn't your kid. He's a grown-up and he can take care of himself. Second, knowing him, he tied one on and is sleeping it off."

Though he meant the words to be reassuring, they didn't help me to feel better. "But I'm worried."

Jim's tone had a condescending note to it. "Listen, you can't do anything about this tonight. Give it a rest and see if he gets back to you tomorrow." He yawned. "I'll call you in the morning."

Great, I thought. What kind of help is that?

That night I kicked at the covers, unable to get comfortable in bed. I was restless enough that Bronte finally gave up and settled on her rug on the floor. I kept going through everything I knew about Cascade and what Travis had told me he was planning to do.

When I finally slipped into a troubled sleep, I had murky dreams about slogging through a swamp trying to catch up with someone wearing a black ski mask. It wasn't clear exactly who I was chasing—Travis, Jim, Tess, or a Red Cap. I woke up with a start just before dawn when my phone rang again.

"Jamie? This is George Big Horse. I'm down at the access to Nearbow Lake. That car you were in the other day is here and the window is bashed in. Looks like blood on the driver's seat. That's why I called."

Now I knew Travis was in trouble.

Chapter Thirty-Seven

The Abandoned Car

In less than half an hour I was showered, dressed, and pouring coffee into a thermos. I'd told George I would drive to the lake access and meet him there. On the table, I had the map I'd found in Tony Vincent's things. I took a photo of it to bring along.

This time I took Bronte with me. I needed a companion who wouldn't scold me for doing something that might be either dangerous or simply stupid. She jumped into the car with so much enthusiasm she crashed into the dashboard. "Settle down girl. I don't need you to knock yourself out."

It was all I could do to keep her from trying to crawl behind the wheel as I drove. "This was a dumb idea," I muttered after I pushed her away once again. "Good way for both of us to get killed."

I pulled over to the side of the road and pointed at her. In a firm voice, I told her, "You stay sitting or you go home." She wagged her tail.

Taking out my phone, I texted Jim. I didn't think he'd be any help, but at least I would let him know what was going on.

Travis's car found at Nearbow Lake. Smashed window and blood. Going to check it out.

He did not immediately reply. Before pulling back on the road, I called Travis. This time when I pressed send, it didn't ring. Instead, the phone registered a "call failed" message. "Damn it, Travis. Where are you?" I texted, and again the text failed.

Tucking the phone in my bag, I set it on the floor of the passenger seat. "If it rings," I told my dog, "Answer it."

Early morning fog obscured the highway. As the sun rose, it slowly burned off the gray veil. Bronte, to my relief, stayed put, her attention fixed on the window.

Over the hum of the fan blowing warm air on my legs, I heard the ping of my phone. Probably Jim was texting me back, no doubt to tell me to stay home.

"I can't," I gripped the steering wheel. "If Travis is in trouble it's because I asked for his help."

Bronte slapped her tail on the seat at the sound of my voice and turned back to the window. At least she wasn't telling me what a bad idea this was.

Cascade was waking up by the time I drove through it. A few cars were out in the chill, foggy morning. I noted the parking lot next to the courthouse was empty and the sheriff's car nowhere in sight. Maybe he was checking on Travis. Maybe he was holding Travis for ransom. I didn't know how to read Jay. Why had he been so anxious to talk with Stone Kavanaugh when he was hospitalized? Conspiring? Investigating?

A few cars were parked in front of the Cascade Bar and Grill. A man in a white chef's apron swept broken glass from the near-empty parking lot beside the building. It looked like there had been an outdoor party last night with glass and other debris scattered over the pockmarked tar.

I realized as I drove by, that I had neglected to eat breakfast. Hopefully, this would be a quick trip to the lake where I would find Travis safe and sound. As I passed the abandoned motel, I noted several more cars and two white vans parked in front of the boarded-up building.

"See that place?" Bronte pricked up her ears. "The old sheriff used it as a jail. I wonder what's going on inside. Maybe they're doing the laundry."

Bronte woofed in reply.

The fog thickened as I travelled north to the lake. I met one car and it startled me as it emerged from the curtain of gray with its bright lights on. I remembered the driver's manual telling me that in foggy weather you should keep your lights on low beam. Now I understood why. The lights reflecting off the fog nearly blinded me as the car passed. I had to blink away the spots in front of my eyes.

Bronte whined as I struggled to get my bearings. The closer we came to the lake the thicker the curtain of fog. I nearly missed the turn to the lake access because the visibility was so poor. Navigating through fog was not an experience I'd grown up with in New York. Even when it was misty, I knew where I was in the big city. For a moment, I missed the crowded sidewalks and the people bumping into each other as they stared at their phones.

The back of the car skidded as I braked hard just before the turnoff. When I pulled onto the gravel road, I saw several deep ruts cut into the ditch. Someone had taken this turn too fast. No vehicles were in sight.

At the lake access, Travis's Focus sat in the middle of the lot. It appeared, by the position of the car, as if it had been hastily parked. Had someone been chasing him? Or was he drunk when he drove here?

I stopped close to it and grabbed my bag with the phone. The ping I'd heard was a text from Jim.

Stay home. Coming this evening.

I was tempted to text, "too late." Instead, I tried calling Travis, but I had no bars. I sat behind the wheel and wondered what to do next. A piece of me was reluctant to get out of the warmth of the car. What would I find? And where was George? In my haste, I'd expected he would stay here, but I saw no evidence of his banged-up truck.

Bronte rubbed her paw on my arm. "You want to go out?" I sighed and opened the door. Bronte nearly knocked me over with her enthusiasm as she scrambled over my lap. "That wasn't polite," I called as she leapt onto the ground. Her enthusiasm did not reassure me.

Outside in the damp, chill air, I shivered in my windbreaker and jeans. I should have put on warmer clothes. Again, I cursed my haste in leaving the cabin. This was the kind of dampness that crept under the skin and into the bones. I heard no sounds other than the scrabble of Bronte's paws as she danced across the parking lot. Gripping my bag, I walked to Travis's car, my mind filled with possible scenarios. Passed out in the back seat. Passed out near the water. Body hidden in the trunk.

What did I expect to find?

George had described the car accurately. The driver's side window had been smashed in. When I peeked inside, I smelled a combination of spicy deodorant, locker room sweat, and something else. The something else was clear on the seat of the car—glass from the smashed window and big splotches of blood staining the fabric of the driver's seat.

Gasping, I drew back. What had Madelyn told me last night? Something about getting the trooper? Jim had been right. I should have stayed home and called Jay Bolton even if I didn't trust him.

I dug my phone out of the bag and hit 911. Nothing happened. I tried again. Of course, I had no bars. I stood on the shores of a lake named after the word for dead in a dead zone. It was time to go back into Cascade and get help.

"Bronte." She was nowhere in sight. "Come on girl. Time to go." In the grayness surrounding me, I couldn't see her. "Come on." My voice rose, and I swallowed, fighting back the urge to run to the car and speed away. Not without my dog.

I whistled and heard rustling sounds near the old picnic table. "Come on! Come on!" I ran toward the table. The rustling grew louder as I approached. "Bronte?" Overhead a solo crow cawed a warning. I backed up. "Bronte?" For a moment, it felt like the fog had its arms around me, encasing me in its chilly depths. The crow cawed once again as the rustling grew louder.

To my relief, Bronte emerged from a tangle of trees and underbrush. She had something in her mouth. "What have you got? It better not be a chipmunk." I squatted down as she dropped it at my feet.

"Oh no!" I picked up the leather case with Travis's phone inside. The case had a red smear on it. "It's blood, isn't it?"

Behind me, I heard the rattle of a vehicle. Several crows now circled above me, floating in and out of the fog. "Let's get the hell out of here." I grabbed Bronte's collar and tugged her to the car.

Chapter Thirty-Eight

Gravediggers Island

Bronte pulled away from me and ran toward the sound of the approaching vehicle. "Bronte!" I chased her, praying she wouldn't get hit by whoever was turning into the access lot. She stopped as the rattling old pickup truck's horn beeped. George Big Horse had arrived, and Bronte greeted him like an old lost friend.

He stepped out of the truck, stooped down, and held his hand out to her. She sat, her wagging tail sweeping the gravel beneath her. "Nice dog," he said as he stood.

"She's not usually this friendly with strangers."

"We're not strangers. She and I have this earth in common." His hand swept the foggy landscape.

I laughed, mostly in relief because he wasn't one of the Red Cap men. "Well, she's been known to bark up a storm at others who also have this earth in common."

He walked over to me, one hand massaging his upper arm. "Glad you could come. We have to untangle the mystery of the car with the broken window."

"Bronte found this in the woods near the picnic table." I showed him the cell phone. He touched the leather case and looked skyward with a thoughtful expression.

"Man's in trouble I'd say." Without explaining, he walked slowly toward the water studying the gravel beneath his feet. Bronte trotted beside him, and I followed feeling a little left out. What was he looking at?

At the water's edge, he squatted, peering into the gray fog covering the lake. The heavy curtain of air held the odor of rotting vegetation and scummy water.

"Boat launched here. See the tire tracks where they backed the trailer into the water?" He pointed to marks in the sand where the lake met the shoreline.

"Do you think Travis went out on the lake?"

George continued to study the sand. "Maybe taken on the lake. Can't tell."

I dug out my phone once again, searching for bars and cell service. Nothing came up. "We should go into town and tell someone."

Groaning, George stood up. "My gut, the one my wife once said was the gut of a fool, tells me the law will be of no help here. Your phone says it, too. No service."

The fog was slowly lifting. George glanced over at Travis's car and said more to himself and me, "I wonder..." He limped up the incline to where the Focus was parked and stooped down, studying the ground.

"Did you find something?"

"Tell me again where your dog found the phone?"

I pointed to the area beyond the picnic table. "She was out in the weeds by the sumac."

Still reading the ground, George walked slowly toward the picnic table. "Hmmm." Once again, he stooped down. "What's this?"

I trotted over to him. He pointed to something that looked like a blotch of blood. "You think he went into the woods?"

Not for the first time in my life, I wished Bronte could understand and speak English. "Is he out there, girl?" Maybe he had crashed into the woods and was unconscious somewhere in the thick underbrush.

I ran over to the edge where the sumac and a tangle of raspberry bushes formed a wall beyond the clearing. I saw no evidence of anyone going into the woods here. George had his eyes closed and his face to the sky as if awaiting some telephonic transmission.

"We should put the canoe in the water and check out the shoreline here. Maybe he followed the lakeshore to the woods."

George had brought an old battered Grumman aluminum canoe in the bed of his pickup. "If you can help me get it out and launched, I can navigate. We'll look along the shoreline."

Between the two of us, we got the canoe and paddles to the landing. I noted George winced with movement and in the short time it took us to maneuver the canoe out of the truck and to the lakeside, a sheen of sweat had broken out on his forehead.

"Not the agile injun I used to be," he gasped when we set the canoe down at the water's edge.

All the time we worked on getting the canoe ready to launch, I had a sinking feeling we should go for help. Why was I following this old guy who had a Red Cap in the office of his store? Yet, Bronte trusted him.

"You paddled a canoe before?" He grunted, shoving the canoe into the water.

"Once, very badly." When I was sixteen my dad and I had travelled to Minnesota to scatter Mom's ashes in Lake Larissa off Bear Island across from the cabin. We'd both been inept and at one point nearly tipped the canoe. Dad, usually serious, had laughed as the boat rocked, "Your mother is watching us and getting a kick out of us Yankees in the wilderness."

George pointed to the front of the canoe. "As soon as I get it far enough into the water, you crawl up front to the bow. Stay in the middle and hold onto the sides."

Bronte woofed as he turned the canoe to face the water. "What about her? If anyone can swamp us, I nominate her."

"I'll handle her."

As I wobbled my way to the front of the canoe, I heard him whispering to Bronte. I turned to see her climb in and sit quietly in the stern. George launched the canoe and jumped in before his feet got wet. For such a creaky heavyset man, he looked like a dancer as he settled into the seat in the stern. Bronte sat in front of his legs like she'd been born in a canoe.

Go figure. For a moment, I felt a sharp stab of jealousy.

225

We paddled along the shoreline through the weeds and the rushes. I called out, "Travis? Travis are you there?"

The only sound we heard was the slap of the water against the side of the canoe and the mourning coo of a dove in the woods. We'd paddled about fifty yards through the reedy water calling out to Travis when the sound of an approaching vehicle silenced us. Bronte woofed and moved enough to start tipping the canoe. George put his hand on her back, and she calmed.

"Shhh," he whispered. He motioned me to stow the paddle while he carefully maneuvered the canoe into tall weeds. A hardy mosquito who had survived the frost buzzed around my head. I held my breath, hoping it wouldn't land.

Car doors slammed. Above the lapping of the water against the aluminum canoe rose the sound of a muffled voice.

"Looks like that injun Big Horse's truck. What's he doin' here?"

"Yeah, and the reporter bitch."

Bronte's ears pricked up as George held his hand on her coat.

Please don't give us away. My hands gripped the sides of the canoe so hard my knuckles ached. The voices rose again.

"You sure you left him over there? Got his phone and all?"

"Tossed it in the woods. Couldn't call."

It sounded like they were moving closer to the lake. "God damn it, Roger! Now we gotta get the boat and make sure he's over there. You stupid son of a bitch. Shoulda just thrown him in the lake."

The second voice was familiar. I'd heard it enough times at Cascade High School. Bill, the Bully.

"Hey, you think they went after him?"

"Do you see anyone around? Big Horse knows the lake, damn Indian. Can't mind his own business."

More swearing. Bronte's claws scrabbled on the bottom of the canoe.

"Shit, phone's got no bars," Billy growled. "Gotta go call. He'll be madder than hell. They're packing up."

Car doors slammed again and an engine revved. Just as it pulled away, Bronte broke from George and leapt out of the canoe barking wildly. She nearly swamped us.

"Bronte!" I yelled, but she was paddling toward shore. The noise of the car receded.

"Geeze," I gasped. "What do we do now?"

George pointed to the island. "We go find your trooper. And we move fast. They won't be gone long."

Chapter Thirty-Nine

The Hidden Landing

We found Bronte standing by the driver's side of my car. She'd sensed the danger and looked at me with eyes that said, can't we go home now? I wasn't about to leave her in the car for Roger and Bill to find. Using a chew toy I'd stashed in the backseat, I coaxed her back to the lake and into the canoe.

Our plan was simple, hasty, and ill-conceived. We would canoe to the other side, find Travis and bring him back. Because of the fog on the lake, we thought we could avoid the two men if they came back with a boat.

Once more, I tried my phone, and once more it had no bars and no service.

George and I talked quietly as we glided across the still waters of the lake. "What's going on? Does this have to do with the Red Caps or something else?" I asked.

"I hear things sometimes in the store. Whispers about something big. It all started after Kavanaugh got out of prison."

"Drug dealing? Stolen goods?"

George sighed. "I don't know. Things were pretty calm around here until he showed up again. Wish they'd locked him up and thrown away the key."

I dug my paddle into the water. Neil was related to Stone. Was there a connection between the shooting and the militia? With all this information swirling in my head, I still couldn't put it together into a cohesive narrative.

Bronte whined. When I looked back at her, she was chewing her rawhide but also shivering.

While all the pieces of this puzzle appeared to be scattered, a couple came together. "Tess gave me a flyer about *Charity's Americana* pop-up store. Does that mean anything to you?"

I didn't hear his response as he steered the canoe toward an outcropping on the island.

In tense silence, George guided the canoe. While I splashed and made slapping noises digging my paddle into the lake, George slipped his through the water without a sound. Before we neared the island, I heard a loud vehicle approaching the access.

"They're back." I found I was whispering as if the lake would carry my voice back to Roger and Bill.

George responded by paddling faster, his breath coming in little grunts. My arms ached from pulling the paddle through the water. We tried to speed up and it was as if the lake responded by turning into a thick stew. The nasty little mosquitoes of late fall, too tough to be killed by the frost, found my neck and my arms. "Aargh!" I slapped at one and nearly dropped the paddle.

We needed to get to the island before the fog lifted and revealed us. Ahead, I saw a clearing with a sagging wooden dock. With renewed energy, I dug my paddle in.

"Wait," George called. "They'll look for us there. I know a hidden landing." He pointed to a jut of land to the right of the dock.

It looked so far away. I groaned and Bronte whimpered. We kept paddling, moving closer to the shoreline and closer into the weeds. "A motorboat can't go through this. It will clog up and strangle the propeller."

To me, through the mist, the shoreline looked impenetrable. Where could we land and how would we find Travis?

Behind us, I heard the sound of the truck backing up to launch the boat. Had they spotted us? It felt like we moved in slow motion through the reeds and cattails and the green algae. George guided us around an outcropping of rock. At least for the moment, we were hidden from view. He pointed twenty yards ahead. "There."

With the clearing of the fog, a wind rippled across the water. I looked up to see gray-blue sky and fragmented dark clouds. For the first time, I noticed a growing chill in the air. I felt as if the island was wishing us away. In the distance, I heard an outboard motor sputter to life.

"Quick. Paddle hard," George commanded. Bronte continued to whimper.

The lake water splashed up against the rocky outcropping tipping the canoe back and forth. If we ended up sideways, it would swamp. George fought the current and I paddled with all my strength, sorry I hadn't eaten any breakfast. I estimated the motorboat was mid-lake by now.

With one last heave, we were around the outcropping and in calm, stagnant water. George's breath came in short gasps, and when I glanced back at him, his face was sweaty and an ashen color. Would he be able to hold up? He must have sensed my concern.

"I still have some pop left in the engine." He wheezed. "Let's get to the shore."

Ahead, through the weeds, I saw a very small clearing. Before we could land the canoe, Bronte scrambled out, splashed through the water, and ran into the woods. I didn't dare call to her in case my voice carried across the lake.

George climbed out, soaking his shoes in the scummy water, and tugged the canoe ashore. I stepped out, my shoes sinking in the brown muck. Other than the sound of the motor and the slight whisper of the wind through the trees, the forest was quiet. A little overgrown path led away from the water. We pulled the canoe far enough up the path that it couldn't be seen from the lake.

The trail led through a thick, dark tangle of bushes, trees, and underbrush. Bronte loped back to us, panting. "What now?" I whispered.

George eased himself down, sitting with his back against a small aspen tree. His chest heaved as he worked to catch his breath. "I need to stay here for a bit. Not feeling quite plum yet." He motioned into the woods. "This trail is a backway to the cabin the KKK used ninety years ago. Bootlegged here." He wiped his brow. "If I'm right, Travis would be there."

I dug out my phone noting again no bars. Pulling up the photo I'd snapped of the map from Tony's things, I handed it to George. "Is that what you are talking about?"

He squinted at it. "Looks like someone mapped out the location."

I told him how I'd found it in a box Matt Whitacre had given me. "I wonder if Tony was on to something?"

In the back of my brain, I felt a prickling like something else had fallen in place. "He was meeting someone there, wasn't he?"

George handed me the phone. "I heard rumors of it being a 'love shack.'"

"Tony was having an affair?" I couldn't help but sound disappointed. I had him pictured as a young, enthusiastic teacher, pure as the driven snow.

George shrugged, grimacing as he tugged at the top button of his shirt. Bronte sensed it and pricked up her ears.

"What? What's going on?"

Wiping a sheen of sweat off his still red face, he sighed. "Chest pains. Give me a few minutes and I'll be all right."

Oh my God, he's having a heart attack. I squatted down beside him. I helped him loosen his collar while a flash of high school health class on CPR shot through my brain.

"Bottle in my jacket. Bring it."

His jacket lay on the floor of the canoe. I grabbed it and fumbled through the pockets until I found a small pill bottle. I opened it and handed it to him. He took a tiny white pill out and placed it under his tongue. Bronte and I watched him as his breathing eased up.

"Better," he rasped. "Just a little angina. Nothing to worry about."

The boat motor sputtered and went silent. I looked at George. "Engine trouble?"

"Maybe."

Once they got it running again, we wouldn't have much time if we were going to find Travis. According to the little map, the trail from the regular landing wound through the woods. It wasn't to scale.

"George, you stay here. I'm going to try to find the shack you talk about and see if Travis is there."

George stayed slumped against the tree. He motioned down the path. "It's close, but you'll have to wade through a swampy area. That's why no one uses this trail."

I hugged Bronte and patted her on the back. "I need you to stay here with George. I don't want Roger or Bill to find you."

George grabbed her collar and whispered to her. I didn't look back as I scrambled onto the path. It was rocky and slippery with mud and slimy moss. After about 20 feet, I stopped to listen for the sound of the motor. I heard nothing but the rattle of the wind through the trees.

The forest darkened as clouds obscured the sun. I prayed the shack wasn't too far. I needed to get there before they found me.

The path rose out of the rubble and rocks onto higher ground. It was overgrown and in places hard to see. At one point, I turned the wrong way and found myself in a patch of twisted and thorny black raspberry bushes. Mosquitoes buzzed around me and I pulled my turtleneck up to cover my ears from their high-pitched whirring. Retracing my steps, I wondered if I was on the wrong path altogether. Where was the swamp George warned me about?

Ahead, something snapped in the woods. I heard a low huffing and more crashing noises. Stopping, I held my breath. Could it be Roger and Bill? But the grunt that came from the thick woods ahead of me sounded more like an animal. I stood stock-still, willing my lungs to stay silent. Dead leaves and debris rustled beneath my feet as the sound retreated. With as little noise as possible, I moved on. In my head, I pictured Roger with his greasy hair and shaggy sideburns and Bill with his burly wrestler's build. I hoped the creature in the woods would get them before they found me or before it found me.

By now, I'd broken into a sweat. The air had grown cooler and a little drop of rain dripped through the forest canopy. As I forged ahead, I saw no evidence of a swamp. George must have been wrong. For a moment, some of the stupid things I'd done in my life flashed through my head, like falling in love with an actor and going into significant debt for an MFA in poetry.

"Calm down," I whispered. "You'll be okay."

Another raindrop landed on my arm. I was running out of breath and energy when the path suddenly plunged downward. I stumbled and nearly fell. Below, I saw the reeds and browning grasses of the marsh. When I reached the bottom of the path, the mud sucked at my shoes. I might have stopped. I might have turned back and said, "To hell with this," as I surveyed the slew in front of me, except on the other side, on higher ground, rose a building. More a cabin than a shack.

"Travis, please be there," I said under my breath as I plunged into the muddy water.

Chapter Forty

Red Cap Shack

The mud and muck soaked my jeans to mid-calf. Every time I stepped forward, it was as if the swamp tried to suck me back. Halfway through the mire, I was sure I saw a leech slithering under the murky water. It reminded me of the scene from The African Queen when Humphrey Bogart emerges from the water covered with leeches. I gasped and nearly fell over. Walking through Central Park, even on the wettest and coldest days of the year, had not trained me for this. I closed my eyes and pictured the warmth of my rock by the lake and took a deep breath.

"You can do it." If Rose the milkmaid could survive adversity, including an epidemic of smallpox, to fall into the arms of her Thorgest, I could make it to the rise ahead of me.

Rain scattered down, and the wind rustled through the trees above me. Huffing with exertion, I willed myself forward until I reached the beginning of dry land. Before climbing up the embankment, I stopped to listen for voices. The only sound was the erratic plink of raindrops, making their way to the forest floor.

I scrambled up the rocky path, the cuffs of my jeans dripping and my shoes and socks squishing with water and mud. Ahead, in a small clearing stood an unpainted wooden building. It reminded me of photos I'd seen of houses in the hollows of Kentucky—battered by weather and years of neglect. The shingles on the roof were discolored and mossy with age. Three boards were nailed across the front window overlooking a sagging porch.

A yellowed shade covered the side window of the building. Taking a deep breath, I made my way around to the front of the cabin. With care to stay as quiet as possible, I crept up the rotting steps to the door. It was padlocked from the outside.

I pressed my ear against the door. Silence except for the wind. This was hopeless. If Travis was inside, I wouldn't be able to get him out. If he wasn't, this was a waste of time. Considering all the alternatives, I did what any polite New Yorker would do, I banged on the door and yelled. "Travis, are you in there?"

This time I heard voices. One of them was higher pitched. "Help. Let us out!"

"Who's there?" I hoped my voice didn't carry far enough for Roger and his bully companion to hear.

"It's Tess Bolton! Can you get us out?"

I caught my breath. "Tess, it's Jamie, are you okay?"

Her voice rose. "Please get us out!"

"Is Travis with you?"

"The trooper? He's hurt."

I tugged at the lock as if it would come off in my hand. I rattled the lock again. I'm not sure what I expected to happen, but it remained firmly in place.

"I need to get the door unlocked. Hang on while I figure this out."

Breaking and entering was another one of those skills one doesn't learn in a class on nineteenth-century poets. I studied the lock. I didn't see any way I could get it off.

As panic filled me, numbing my brain, I noticed the hasp on the lock wasn't totally screwed in. Inside the cabin, a male voice that wasn't Travis's said, "Can you pry it off?"

I didn't have time to wonder who he was.

"I can try." I turned, about to run into the woods to find some kind of a stick to use as a lever when I saw a rock by the front window. Maybe I could hammer the lock off with the rock. I stooped to pick it up and to my astonishment, a key was concealed underneath it.

"You've got to be kidding. It's the key under the doormat." What were the odds of that? Maybe Thorgest and Vladess were looking down on me. With shaking hands, I fit it into the lock.

Quickly I twisted the key and the padlock slipped open. "I've unlocked it. We need to get out of here in a hurry. Those Red Caps are back."

I heard a sob from Tess as the door opened. Inside the cabin was dark. A little light filtered through the spaces between the boards of the front window. The one room held a table, a couple of chairs, and a mattress on the floor. The mattress was covered with a sleeping bag. A rusting wood stove stood in the corner.

The kitchen area had a sink, several shelves, and an assortment of empty cans of beef stew and soup. I didn't want to think about how everyone inside managed bathroom duties, but the place smelled of mildew, rotting food, and something else as vile.

In the distance, I heard muffled voices. Roger and Bill were close. "We have to get out of here, now!" My voice came in a panicked whisper.

Travis appeared to stagger as he stood behind Tess and a young man with long light brown hair and the beginnings of a beard.

The young man stepped in front of Tess in a protective gesture. "Who are you?"

"Stop it, Neil. She's the reporter."

Neil Kavanaugh looked older now than his yearbook photo from several years ago. For a moment, I couldn't move. The words came out before I could stop them, "You shot Tony and those students."

Tess moved next to him, putting her arm around his waist. "No, he didn't. That's why he came back—to make it right. Except he went to his uncle, and he locked us up here."

"Why did he lock you up?"

"Protection, he said," Neil mumbled.

I couldn't follow this. Who was protecting whom?

Behind Neil, Travis lurched forward, blood caked along the side of his face. One eye was swollen shut, and he groaned as he moved. "Sorry. Real woozy. They banged me up."

Tess let Neil go and hurried to him. "You have to help him. They beat him up, those bastards."

"We have to get out of here. Can you walk?" I held my hand out to him, and he grabbed it, nearly tipping over and taking me with him.

"Think I'm drugged. Everything fuzzy and dizzy."

The voices outside were more distinct now.

"Help me get him out. I have a canoe by the landing." I pointed in the direction of the swamp. "We need to get the hell off this island."

As if he'd awakened from a deep sleep, Neil moved into action helping Tess with Travis as I led the way out of the cabin.

From the main path, I heard Roger's voice. "Supposed to get rid of all of them."

Bill chortled. "Dig a grave on Gravediggers?"

"Shut up!"

They were getting close. In a few moments, they'd be in the clearing in front of the cabin. "Listen," I hissed. "Get behind those trees. All of you. I'll take care of the idiots." I pointed to a thicket behind the cabin as a hasty plan formulated in my head.

I crept back to the shack and peeked around the corner. They would see the door was open. I counted on surprise and stupidity—hopefully theirs, not mine.

"Hey, look!" Bill pointed to the door. "Someone left the door open."

Roger replied. "I locked it."

"You sure? We wasn't real sober last night."

As soon as they got inside, I planned to lock the door. I prayed they'd both go in at the same time. If not? I didn't have a plan B.

They both trotted up the rotting steps. Bill yelled, "Hey, anyone inside?" He walked in the door followed by Roger.

Go! As soon as I saw Roger's butt slipping in the door, I hurled myself up onto the porch, grabbed the door and pulled it shut. I knew that for a few moments, they'd be in the dark. I picked up the lock I'd dropped and looped the shackle into the hasp. My fingers felt like paws as I pushed the shackle into the locking mechanism. At first, it didn't catch.

"What the fuck! Who's out there? I'll kill you."

The lock caught just as I heard the tug against the door. I leapt off the porch and ran as he yanked at the door again. Between the two of them, they let off a stream of f-words, one after another.

"Need a better vocabulary," I gasped, running to the thicket.

I found Tess and Neil standing over Travis who was sitting on the ground, dazed. "We have to get out of here." Roger and Bill were big men. They'd have the door smashed open in no time.

Tess and Neil pulled him up as I motioned for them to head downhill to the swamp. Behind me, the banging continued. Eventually, the rotted wood would give away. By then, I hoped to be reunited with Bronte and the canoe.

Overhead, beyond the thick canopy of trees, clouds swirled, obscuring the sun. A few icy raindrops pelted us as we stumbled and slid down the hill to the swamp. When we reached the mucky water, Travis sank to the ground, gasping for breath. "I don't think I can do this. Ribs busted."

"You have to move! Those guys aren't playing around."

"Come on!" Tess's voice rose to a sob. "I want to get out of here ."

Neil helped him up, talking in a low calming voice. "You can do it." This was not the voice of a killer.

Perhaps it was the shock of the water or perhaps the chill of the rain, but Travis staggered to his feet. As we slogged through the swamp. Neil kept up his mantra. "Okay, keep going. You can do it."

How I wished to be in front of my fireplace, bundled in a blanket drinking hot cocoa. Instead, I pushed through a leech-infested swamp with a punch-drunk man, a terrified teenager, and a supposed murderer. Neither Florice nor Letty could have used this as a plot for their next romances because no one would believe it. And there was nothing romantic about two dirty, smelly kids and a trooper whose face was unrecognizable and who reeked of blood, alcohol, and vomit.

By the time we reached the rise out of the swamp, the rain had stopped. I got out of the water first, collapsing on the muddy bank. The other three followed. The rain had washed some of the blood from Travis's head. I saw the gash in his hairline.

"Looks like you took quite a beating."

Travis wiped water out of his eyes. He blinked trying to focus. "I was drinking at the bar and talking to Roger, and the next thing I remember is waking up with these guys in the shack. I'm not sure what happened."

"They dumped him in and left," Tess added, still trying to catch her breath. "We'd already been stuck there for days. It's like they forgot about us or something."

This was not a good time for a chat about how they ended up on Gravedigger's Island. "We need to keep going. Roger and Bill will figure a way out soon enough."

"My head is pounding." Travis rubbed the back of his neck. "Maybe I could stay here."

"No way. We need to get off this island."

A weak flash of lightning followed by a low rumble of thunder emphasized the shadows of the thick forest. I felt it—an evilness to this land.

We made our way slowly up the rise and into the forest. About halfway between the swamp and where I'd left George, I heard rustling.

"Stop," I hissed. "I hear something."

Before I could process the sound, Bronte came bounding through the rocky path, panting and woofing at the same time. She nearly knocked me over. I stooped down and hugged her tight, while she licked my sweaty, dirty face.

"Let's get off this lake, girl."

Bronte sniffed at Tess and Travis. I watched her, wondering what she thought of my motley crew. She turned without offering an opinion and headed back down the trail.

We found George still sitting propped up by the tree trunk. His eyes were closed and, for a moment, I thought he might be asleep. He opened his eyes and smiled. "Knew you'd be back. That's what I told your dog here." He didn't seem surprised by the presence of two more people besides Travis.

Bronte wagged her tail. The lake had taken on an unusual calmness.

"The lake is holding its breath, waiting for the big blow." George pointed at it. "It wants us gone."

I wanted to be gone, too. How were we going to get back with a sick old man, a skittish dog, an injured state trooper, and two extra passengers?

A crooked bolt of lightning lit up the sky. The earth trembled and Bronte yipped in fear. I looked at the group, and the first thing I thought was that I was part of the old riddle about a farmer, a fox, a chicken, and a sack of corn. How to get them off the island without the chicken eating the corn and the fox eating the chicken.

Chapter Forty-One

The Fire

I sat down next to George. The skin on his face had changed from ashen to gray. I pointed to the bottle in his hand. "How many have you taken?"

He shook his head. "A few."

"Are they helping?"

He didn't return my gaze.

I took his wrist and felt for a pulse. It was erratic, racing sometimes and slowing others. Dad's was like that before he had his heart attack. I tried to tamp down the rising panic in my chest. Pointing at the canoe, I said to Neil, "We need to get him out of here. Can you navigate it?"

He nodded. I didn't like the uncertain expression that crossed his face, but I felt like I didn't have much choice.

Looking at Tess and Travis I asked, "Which one of you can paddle?"

Tess, with a weary sigh, raised her hand. "I think I can."

Travis had his eyes closed and appeared to be drifting off.

I motioned Neil and Tess over to me. "This isn't a great plan but it's the only one I can come up with. We need to get George and Travis settled in the middle of the canoe. You two paddle like hell back to the lake access. Once you're there, take my car, and as soon as you are in cell phone range, call for help."

They both nodded. I noted that although Neil was only two years older

241

than Tess, he had a world weariness to him. I hoped the maturity I saw on his face was real. If he was a murderer, God help us all.

I leaned in close to Tess. "Don't call your uncle Jay. I'm not trusting him right now." I took out my phone and showed her Jim's number. "Get hold of Jim. Tell him it's an emergency and he needs to get the state patrol involved."

Taking the phone, she nodded solemnly. I wasn't sure I could trust her not to call Jay, but I had to leave it. Motioning toward Travis and George, I whispered, "They need help ASAP. Got it?"

"What about you?" Tess's voice trembled. "We can't leave you here."

"We can't fit all of us in one canoe. You need to go now before the storm hits. You can send someone back for me once you get help."

"Okay." Her voice was small, like a little girl's.

I couldn't read Neil's expression. There was a good chance he'd run as soon as he could. At this point, it didn't matter. George and Travis's lives were at stake.

It took us close to ten minutes to get the men settled into the bottom of the canoe. The way they weighted it down worried me. Would it float? With my legs knee-deep in water, I pushed them off, praying they'd make it across the lake before the storm. If they swamped, I wasn't sure either George or Travis would survive.

"Godspeed," I mouthed. I hoped they had the strength and speed to make it across the lake.

I watched Neil maneuver them around the rocky outcropping and disappear. Almost as soon as the canoe was out of sight, the wind began to rise. I looked up at the threatening sky. "Wait. Please?" I hoped my request could be heard by the spirit of the lake.

Bronte stood at my side, wagging her tail as if this was a great adventure. "Listen, girl. We have to head back to the shack and find the trail to the other landing. If we can get there, maybe we can take the Red Cap boat back." It was a flimsy plan, but the only one I had right now.

Before slogging back through the swamp and up the hill, I sat for a minute to calm myself. Regret washed over me. I'd just sent three people off in the hands of a possible murderer. Before they left, why hadn't I asked Neil what really happened the day of the school shooting? Why hadn't I asked him why he was still alive and Tony and two other students weren't? Bronte pulled me out of my dark thoughts barking at something in the woods. I grabbed her by the collar and shushed her.

If something was out there, we had to get going. Once again today I slogged through the swamp. At this rate, the leeches would begin to recognize my shoes. Bronte trotted ahead, oblivious to the mud on her paws. I was out of breath as the ground rose out of the marshy water.

"Bronte, wait," I called to her. I was out of fuel, my legs soggy logs. I needed to rest before reaching the shack where Roger and Bill were hopefully still locked in. Grabbing my canvas bag, I pulled out a mashed and crumpled granola bar. "Breakfast." Bronte nosed me with a hopeful look. I broke off a piece and fed it to her.

The flash of light, so bright it was almost green exploded just as I was licking the last crumb off my fingers. A bang of thunder shook the earth. Spooked, Bronte jumped up with a wild look in her eyes. Before I could grab her collar, she tore off into the woods her tail drooping between her legs.

By now the woods had darkened as the storm clouds rolled in. The wind picked up and drops of rain began to splat through the pines. "Bronte! Come!" The wind whistling through the trees and stirring up the dead leaves threw my voice back at me. I scrambled to my feet and tried to follow in the direction Bronte had fled.

Calling to her, I stumbled through the underbrush. A low branch caught my face and ripped across my cheek. Another seemed to reach out and catch at my ankle. I tripped forward, banging into the trunk of an aspen. Bronte was nowhere to be seen. Rain began to pour down and a sudden bolt of lightning followed by a crack of thunder sent me to my knees.

All at once, it was too much. I lay on the floor of the forest with twigs and pinecones pressing into my back and sobbed. I was stuck on Gravediggers Island in the midst of an unusual fall thunderstorm, my dog had abandoned me, and I wasn't even sure why I was here. I wanted to go home.

I might have continued in my maudlin weeping until my clothes were thoroughly soaked, except I heard a loud crackle and when I breathed in, I smelled smoke. The lightning must have hit a tree. The sound came from above. What if it was the shack?

Pushing myself up, I scrambled toward the path praying the fire was my imagination. The closer I got to the path, the heavier the smell of smoke. By the time I reached the clearing, the area was clogged with smoke even as the rain came pouring down.

It looked like the lightning struck a tall, dead pine just behind the shack. The fire was spreading to the roof of the building. I heard shouts and rattling from inside. I had to get Roger and Bill out.

They'll kill you. The voice in my head screamed. *Get away!* I gathered myself to dash to the path to the landing, when a second voice, a voice like my father's ripped through my head.

Can't let them burn up!

I had to get the door unlocked. I ran up to the porch and the heat pushed me back. Rain and ash and smoke obscured my vision, but I saw through the tears the padlock with the key still in it.

I shouted, "I'm opening the door!"

From inside came a bang and the splintering of wood. Roger screamed, "You shot me, you idiot!"

I pictured Bill inside in a panic trying to shoot the door open.

The metal on the padlock was already heating as flames licked at the building. I shouted, "Don't shoot! I'll get the lock! When the door opens, run!"

A piece of the porch roof crashed down behind me. A cinder singed the top of my head. I brushed it away and grabbed the lock, twisting the key. The shackle popped up and I pulled the lock out. With my foot, I kicked the door.

"It's open! Run!"

I should have leapt off the porch and run for shelter, but when the door opened, neither of the men rushed out. The room was filled with smoke. Roger was collapsed near the door and Bill was huddled in the corner, holding a gun with a stunned expression.

Pulling the turtleneck over my mouth, I rushed in holding my hand out for Bill. "Get the hell out of here!"

He was like a terrified animal. His eyes, in the blaze of the fire, were big and had a look of panic. No time for coaxing. I grabbed his arm and with a strength I didn't know I had and yanked him to his feet. I screamed. "Run!"

By now the little building was filled with black smoke. I could hardly catch my breath. I ran to the door, my eyes streaming with tears. Roger lay on his side, a bloody hand covering the gunshot wound.

"Roger," I shouted. "Get up!"

Maybe it was the tone of my voice or maybe it was because I kicked at him, but he roused.

"Get out!" I grabbed his arm and pulled. He was dead weight. We'd both soon be dead if I didn't get through the door. Again, from somewhere deep inside me, a strength rose. I dragged and pulled until he lurched to his hands and knees. Grabbing his belt, I tugged him out the door. We stumbled off the porch as I held tight to his belt.

We made it to the trail in the woods just before the roof collapsed. The world seemed to slow as I watched it. The pouring rain dampened the fire as the charred wood hissed and moaned.

Exhausted, I sat down beside Roger who groaned and held his side. "Damn motherfucker shot me."

I guessed he deserved it, but I didn't say anything. "Let me look."

I was truly getting sick of tending to grown men today. I wanted to be home with my dog and my rock and a book of poetry. Carefully, I pulled back Roger's bloody shirt. It looked like the bullet scraped his side, leaving a bloody gouge, but hadn't actually gone into his belly. At least this was the assessment of someone who once took a basic first aid class. "I think it's superficial and you should be okay."

Roger grunted. "Where is that son-of-a-bitch."

Good question. My dog was gone and now an armed, dumbass Red Cap was somewhere out there. This island was damned. An image of Florice's redheaded milkmaid flashed through my head. What would Rose do? She'd go for safety knowing that Thorgest would find her.

I didn't have a Thorgest, but I did know where the Red Caps landed their boat. I needed to find Bronte and get the hell off the island.

Chapter Forty-Two

Help from the Vladess

A rusted utility shed stood on the periphery of the clearing. The fire had not touched it. "I'm going to check out the shed. If it's dry, you can rest in there while I go for help."

Roger was too dazed to wonder where I would go for help. He mumbled, "Watch out for Bill. The man's stupid crazy."

"No kidding." I pictured the wild look in his eyes in the burning shack.

The shed leaned sideways like it was too tired to stand up straight. I sympathized as I tugged open the cheap metal door. The building was empty except for a pile of old cans and bottles in the corner. It had a dirt floor and smelled of garbage and skunk. I didn't care if it housed a whole family of skunks. It was out of the rain. I supported Roger as we stumbled to the shed, the rain still pouring down.

Once inside, I eased him down and sat beside him, panting to catch my breath.

"If I die, I want you to tell 'em I'm not a killer."

In the darkness of the shed, I couldn't read his expression. "What do you mean?"

"I didn't have nothing to do with what happened to Winnie. We was only supposed to scare him. You know?"

"You ran him off the road."

"We was only supposed to scare him 'cause he knew something. Billy said the stupid fucker was gonna blackmail us. Billy just went a little crazy. I tried to stop him."

He groaned as he moved to sit up more. "We had orders for everything."

In this dark, dank place permeated with skunk and dead animal smells, I was finally getting some answers.

"Roger, who gave you orders? Was it Kavanaugh?"

He coughed. "We got good pay, you know?"

"What were you doing?"

"I didn't ask no questions. Made pick-ups in Minneapolis—people Stone knew through prison, I guess. Brung it all back to the motel."

"What did you bring?"

"Cash. Bags of it."

Now I had part of the answer. The town was protecting an illegal operation to keep itself from dying.

He coughed again and let out a big sigh, "Kavanaugh was in business with that Charity woman. Don't know how it worked."

In that dark musty shelter with a man who smelled like he hadn't bathed in weeks, a light went on in my head. "Oh my god. I think I get it. Using the pop-up stores as a front and having a friendly local bank who didn't ask questions when she brought in the cash."

I had to find Bronte, and I had to get help somehow. I pushed myself up. "One question, Roger, did the school shooting have anything to do with Roger and Charity's business?"

He emitted a sour laugh. "That Indian teacher? I heard he figured things out."

"What do you mean?"

"I ain't got details. Just heard from the other boys that they took him out. Scared the hell out of everyone. Maybe, if they said something, they'd be next—or their family."

Maybe Neil really did the shooting, but it wasn't a hate crime, it was to cover up a money-laundering operation. But why Neil?

Outside, the rain was letting up. I thought I heard a faint bark. "I've got to find my dog and get to the boat. You'll be dry here."

248

"Not going nowhere."

The clearing was filled with a haze of smoke and smelled of burned, soggy wood. Without my phone, I had no idea what time it was or how much time had passed since the canoe had left. The gray sky had cleared of the darkest clouds and the temperature was dropping. My feet and jeans were soaked. If I didn't get off this island, I'd probably die of hypothermia.

Putting those thoughts out of my head, I called, "Bronte! Here girl!"

From behind the burned down shack, I heard a woof. I ran toward it and was greeting by Bronte as she bounded out of the woods. It was the happiest thing that had happened to me all day. "Here girl! Let's find a boat." She jumped up on me, her paws leaving muddy prints on my windbreaker.

I picked up my bag which I'd dropped when I ran into the shack and offered Bronte a sodden granola bar. She nearly swallowed it whole. Before heading down the path that led to the other boat landing, I went back to the shed. Roger's head was down, chin resting on his chest.

"Here," I poured hand sanitizer on the bandana I kept in my bag. "Use this to keep pressure on the wound."

In the murky lighting of the shed, I caught a dullness to his gaze. Perhaps this wound was deeper than I thought. Bronte stood beside me, growling in a low rumble. Sometimes she could be a good judge of character.

"I'm going for the boat."

"Watch out for Bill." He mumbled.

Finding Bronte gave me an extra boost of energy. Maybe the boat had a first aid kit or some water. I realized as we hurried through the cold mist that had formed in the wake of the storm, how thirsty I was. At least if I was desperate, I could drink lake water and hope it wasn't filled with bacteria.

I closed my eyes and pictured the crude map from Tony's box. The path wound through the middle of the island. I guessed we were about a half-mile from the landing. As I traced the map in my head, I remembered the cryptic words printed on the lower right corner. *Mt me on Sat. I'll explain. C*

Charity? Had Tony gone to Charity with his suspicions? Maybe this was another puzzle piece, although I wasn't sure where it fit.

I was so involved with my inner thoughts that I didn't notice how the fur on Bronte's back rose until I heard her growl. Ahead, the path twisted. Bronte was reacting to something in front of us. Before I could act, she took off, barking like a crazed animal.

I ran after her and caught up, just as Bill's hand shook as he aimed a pistol at her.

No one was ever going to shoot my dog again!

"No!" I launched myself at Bill before he could squeeze the trigger. I hit him with a glancing blow but it was enough to knock the pistol out of his hand.

"Bitch!"

Bronte lunged at him, catching his ankle. She clamped her jaws around him shaking her head back and forth like she would if she'd caught a chipmunk. He slipped backwards and fell onto the path.

The gun skittered across the path and landed near my foot. I kicked it away into the underbrush. I found myself staring down at a man who outweighed me by over 100 pounds and who had a homicidal fire in his eyes.

"You," I said. "You ran Winnie off the road."

Distracted, he stopped trying to kick at Bronte, who still held tight to his ankle. An ugly grin crossed his face. "They just told me to scare him. He ran himself off the road. Dumb fucker."

I remembered the curve where I almost lost my life. I could have ended up like Winnie.

My head ached and my whole body felt like it was on the verge of collapse. "Did you shoot Tony and the kids?"

I heard confusion in his voice. "Hell no. I hate kids, but I didn't kill 'em."

Betsy and her friends were wrong. Neil must have been the lone shooter. "Oh god," I gasped. "I sent them off with a murderer."

Bill kicked out, trying to shake Bronte. It was strong enough and vicious enough that she let go and jumped back with a sharp yelp. I had no one between me and the bully. He read my fear and lunged at me.

Next thing I knew, I was on the ground and he was on top of me holding my arms down while I struggled. He panted, his hot stale breath on my face. Without thinking, without pondering what to do and coming up with a plan,

I turned into Vladess. Perhaps reading how she sucked the life out of men propelled me to jerk my head up and bite him in the face. Nausea rose inside me with the metallic taste of blood. He howled and let go as his hand came up to his cheek.

For just a second, he was stunned. Then his face suffused in rage. I think I would have been beaten to death by this man if two things hadn't happened at once. Bronte leapt at him sinking her teeth into his butt and voices came calling from down the path.

I screamed, "Help!" before Bill slapped his hand over my mouth pushing my head hard into the packed dirt of the trail. Bronte snarled and bit again. After that, it was a little blurry. Bill's body pressing on my chest was smothering me. With his hand over my mouth, I couldn't breathe. Gravediggers Island suffocated me.

Chapter Forty-Three

The Drill

As my world darkened, I heard yelling. Bill's weight was pulled from me. I gasped, fighting for air and like a miracle from one of Florice's books, Jim had his arms around me and was saying something. I couldn't hear him, my head muddled from being slammed into the ground.

"Jamie! Are you all right?"

Was I all right? I wasn't sure until I saw the look on his face. Blood dripped down my chin. "I am now." Letty DeVoss would have been so proud.

Wrapped in a blanket with Bronte at my feet, I rode across the lake in the same boat that held Roger and Bill. I didn't care because I had Jim next to me, holding me close.

He told me over the roar of the outboard that he was on his way to Nearbow Lake when he got the call from Tess. He alerted the state patrol and an avalanche of law enforcement came to the rescue. Or so I imagined. It might have only been a couple of state troopers and a sheriff's deputy or two.

George and Travis were sent by ambulance to the Killdeer Hospital ER. Jim didn't know how they were doing.

I leaned into him and whispered, "Did Neil tell you anything about the school shooting?" I shuddered, hoping he hadn't gotten away.

He stroked my cheek. "He's being questioned."

"And the motel? Was it filled with cash?"

"Shhh. Let us worry about that."

It was well after dark before we got home. Bronte and I slept for most of the trip in Jim's truck. After a long hot shower and a plate of scrambled eggs, I sat curled up next to Jim in front of a roaring fire. He told me what he'd gleaned from Tess and Neil as well as the Cascade deputy.

"*Charity's Americana* was a pretty convincing front for the money laundering scheme. It might have gone on for quite some time without notice except Marla Kavanaugh overheard Matt in his office one day talking with Stone about how to speed up the laundering. She took it literally and in trying to be helpful to her boss offered to do his laundry."

"Oh my god. She accidentally stepped into it."

"Matt told her she was snooping and people who snooped got hurt and lost their jobs. The way he talked scared her. She was so upset, she blurted it out to the only teacher who was nice to her—Tony."

Even in my exhaustion, I could put it together. "Tony must have gone to Charity. He'd worked for her in the summer, taking care of the horses." I wondered if they had more than horses in common that summer.

Jim's phone rang. He stood up and walked to the kitchen talking in a low tone. After the phone call, he pulled me close again and said, "George and Travis are being helicptered to St. Luke's in Duluth. Travis has a pretty severe concussion, and they want him evaluated by a neurologist. George needs heart surgery."

"This was all my doing."

Jim peered at me with a stern expression. "Nonsense. They'll be in good hands."

I pictured the canoe weighed down with the adults as Tess and Neil paddled for help. "The kids saved them."

By now I was beginning to fade. The exhaustion, the relief, the wine. "I can't wait to hear what's next, but I have to go to bed."

I slept poorly, drifting in and out of vivid dreams. In the last one, I was in the janitor's closet trying to put together a jigsaw puzzle in the dark. I had to get it done before someone found me. A masked man was slinking down the hallway. He yelled, "Get the mask." He wore a whistle around his neck, and I knew that when he blew it, they would catch me. He came closer and closer, his hand almost on the door, when I woke up with a start, shivering under the warmth of the covers. Jim slept next to me, his chest rising and falling in a gentle cadence.

Slipping out of bed, I pulled on my robe and padded barefoot to the kitchen. Something about the dream sparked a memory. Bronte joined me, settling at my feet with a long sigh.

"Put together the puzzle pieces," I whispered to her as I quietly found my notebook and paged through it. Who had the most to gain by killing Tony and the students? Two words stuck out in my pages of writing—mask and drill.

I thought back to my brief meeting with Winnie at the restaurant. He'd dropped the ski mask when he stood up to follow Charity. As for the drill, Tess had defended Neil saying, "It was supposed to be a drill." Betsy said she thought she heard Neil yell something about a drill.

The man with the whistle in my dream. The man who commanded. Suddenly, it was clear. Clear enough that I stood up and ran back into the bedroom.

I shook Jim. "Wake up! I've got it! Neil didn't do the shooting!"

It took me several minutes of excited and jumbled talking to finally explain clearly enough for Jim to sit up and grab his phone.

After a number of phone calls, we sat at the kitchen table drinking coffee and listening to the sounds of the night. Outside, the trees shimmered in the breeze and a lone owl hooted in the distance. I stared at Jim's phone waiting for it to ring again. Jim studied me with a bemused expression. "If you're right, you've cracked the case."

"We Eastern tree-hugging mafia types can be pretty clever. It's because of all the noise and pollution we grew up with."

When his phone rang, he talked for several minutes. I tried to make out the conversation from his end but mostly he said, "Uh huh. Good. Got it." He smiled broadly and said, "Thanks."

I tensed suddenly worried that I'd gotten it all wrong. "Well?"

"Believe it or not, Matt Whitacre didn't stick around to defend and support

254

his Charity. They found him at the Minneapolis/St. Paul airport, about to board an international flight. He'd abandoned his lovely wife and had a suitcase full of cash. We're guessing he also had a hard drive with all his offshore accounts. The man was headed for a new identity and a cushy retirement."

"He was the shooter, wasn't he? That's what got Winnie killed. His crew of kids had found the ski mask in his office and Winnie got suspicious. He went after Charity to tell her about it." I remembered what Roger had said. "Or to blackmail her."

"Neil told the deputies Matt convinced him to go into the cafeteria and wave the rifle as a live shooter drill. If he did that, Matt would let Marla keep her job. He heard someone behind him when he got to the cafeteria. When the shots were fired, he ran. His gun wasn't loaded. He figured he was also a target. Scared and not knowing who to turn to, he hid for a couple of days and then hitched to Minneapolis."

"To his credit, he came back." I remembered he said he wanted to "make it right" after Winnie was killed.

"Tess found out he was alive when she started searching Facebook and Instagram. He'd been couch surfing and living on the streets in Minneapolis trying to figure out what to do. One of his friends posted a photo of him on Instagram and Tess found it."

My eyes filled with tears as I thought about the lives lost and the lives ruined for money, and in Matt's case, power. "I don't get why he kept that ski mask?"

Jim stood up and came over to me. "Maybe it was his trophy, since he couldn't tell anyone he'd murdered his own teacher and students."

This time, when I settled under the covers, I fell sound asleep. No puzzles, no masks, no evil beings lurking in the background.

Chapter Forty-Four

Sunny Morne

I wish I could have been there when they raided Whitacre's Acres and the office of *Charity's Americana*. Instead, I had to hear it second and sometimes third hand. After the nightmare on Gravediggers Island, a number of law agencies descended upon Cascade. *Charity's Americana* turned out to be a very lucrative money-laundering operation fully supported by Stone and Charity. But the mastermind, the person who actually called the shots, was Matt. They paid the Red Caps well to courier money and keep control of the townspeople. Anyone raising suspicions about the amount of money thrown around town suddenly found their garages on fire or their kids threatened.

Charity, looking like Melania Trump in the news photos, claimed she had no knowledge of the scheme. "I am a good businesswoman who sells fine products."

I watched the news clip on my laptop with a scowl. "You sell junk and cook your books."

Jim and I had a couple days of bliss until he had to go back to Minneapolis. Once again, I stood in the yard and waved as his truck rumbled down the road. Two days later, a Ford Focus pulled up. Travis stepped out looking thinner and not quite as boyish. The bruising on his face had faded to a greenish-yellow, and he still had some swelling around his jaw.

"Hey," he said. "Just checking on you."

I invited him in. "You look better than the last time I saw you."

"It's pretty much a blank except for snatches, like you locking those guys in the cabin. Gutsy broad."

I laughed and invited him in. Before moving to Minnesota, I doubt anyone had ever called me a gutsy broad.

He drank a beer as he filled me in on the rest of the story.

"I had a long talk with Jay. He's resigning as sheriff, and they'll have a special election in January. I'm putting my hat in the ring."

I smiled. "Good for you. What happened with him?"

"He knew Stone was up to something and it involved Charity, but he chose to keep a blind eye. Partly, I think, he was lazy, and partly he was scared. When Tess disappeared, though, he knew he was in way over his head. Stone threatened to hurt her and told him to keep his mouth shut."

"He told everyone she was fine."

"He thought Stone would eventually let Tess go as soon as he figured out what to do with Neil. Stone claims he never meant to hurt either of them."

"And you believe him?"

Travis chuckled. "A convicted felon? Let the courts decide."

I drank my beer, enjoying the dark richness of the local stout. "Clarence is representing Neil. He thinks the courts will go easy on him because he didn't really shoot anybody, he simply fled the scene."

Bronte scratched at the door to be let out. I stood up. Travis drummed his fingers on the table and gazed at me. "I was wondering if you'd like to be my campaign manager?"

I thought about it for a second and grinned. "I guess you don't really want to win that election. An outsider, maybe even from the Mafia as your campaign manager? I don't think so. You need some youth. I know some smart high school kids who'd be excited to help you."

Travis had something else in his eyes. I could see it—a kind of longing that I wasn't able to help him with.

He cleared his throat. "You know I really enjoy hanging around with the Mafia."

"I'm committed right now, Travis. But thanks for the offer."

After he left, I felt a sadness for what might have been.

A little money trickled in when I spotted Sunny Morne after Bill was arrested. The *Star Tribune* published a photo from his arraignment. She stood in the back of the courtroom and was identified as his wife. Clarence, in his wily attorney way, managed to get some of Pete Peterson's money back in exchange for not pursuing fraud charges against Sunny aka Mrs. Billy Barre.

My article proposal to *The New Yorker* was accepted with an advance that assured I'd have enough propane to take me through at least Christmas. The article was called "How I Got that Story," and began *On an overgrown trail on Gravediggers Island, I nearly lost my life trying to find out who killed a teacher and two students.*

The check came as the first snow of the winter fell from the sky. I stood out in my yard, leaning against Jim enjoying the quiet rhythm of the lake. Absorbing his warmth, I hoped the moment would last forever. If Rose could have her love and Vladess her mortal happiness, maybe I could have mine, too.

Acknowledgements

Thanks to Level Best Books and Shawn Reilly Simmons for your faith in me. To Dawn Dowdle for your calm reassurance. To my readers, Jerry Mathiason, John Mathiason and Jan Clausen. To my writing group, Jan Kerman, Carol Williams and Randy Kasten. To all the book clubs who welcomed me in to talk about *Death of an Editor*. I hope you will have me back. As always, to Jerome who is my best editor and critic.

About the Author

Linda Norlander is the author of a Cabin by the Lake mystery series set in the woods of Northern Minnesota. *Death of a Starling* is a continuation of Jamie Forest's adventures. Norlander has written award-winning short fiction, nonfiction and humor. Before taking up the pen to write murder mysteries, she worked as a nurse in public health and end-of-life care. She lives with her husband in Tacoma, Washington.

CPSIA information can be obtained
at www.ICGtesting.com
Printed in the USA
LVHW090237100721
692210LV00001BA/15

9 781953 789730